# *The Earl's* DILEMMA

## EMILY LARKIN

Copyright © 2008 by Emily May

All rights reserved.

No part of this book may be reproduced in any form or by any
electronic or mechanical means, including information storage and
retrieval systems, without written permission from the author, except
for the use of brief quotations in a book review.

**www.emilylarkin.com**

Publisher's Note: This is a work of fiction. Names, characters, places,
and incidents are a product of the author's imagination. Locales and
public names are sometimes used for atmospheric purposes. Any
resemblance to actual people, living or dead, or to businesses, compa-
nies, events, institutions, or locales is completely coincidental.

**The Earl's Dilemma / Emily Larkin.** – 2nd ed.

ISBN 978-0-9951396-6-4

Cover Design: JD Smith Design

# THE EARL'S DILEMMA

# $C$HAPTER 1

$K$ate Honeycourt was sitting on the floor of the priest's hole when he arrived. The library door opened and she heard his voice, and her brother's. She started, spattering ink over the page of her diary. James was here!

Her gaze jerked down to the diary in her lap. *I shall, of course, treat James as if my feelings go no deeper than friendship. That goes without saying. But why does it grow no easier? One would think, after all these years, that*— The sentence ended in a splotch of ink.

The voices became louder. Her secret hiding place had become a trap.

Kate dropped the quill and hastily snuffed the candle. The hot wick stung her fingertips. She blinked and for a moment could see nothing. Then her eyes adjusted to the gloom. The darkness wasn't absolute. A tiny streak of light came from the peephole.

"—can't offer you any entertainment," her brother said.

Kate rose to her knees in the near-darkness. The diary slid off her lap with a quiet, rustling thump that made her catch her breath.

"I don't expect to be entertained!" James sounded affronted. "Honestly, Harry, what do you take me for? *You* didn't invite me. I invited myself!"

Kate leaned forward until her eyes were level with the peep-hole. She saw her brother, Harry, the Viscount Honeycourt.

"Don't cut up stiff," Harry said, grinning. "You're always welcome. You know that." He walked across the room to where the decanters stood. "Sherry? Scotch? Brandy?"

"Brandy," James said. He came into Kate's line of sight and her pulse gave a jerky little skip. His back was towards her, but his tallness and the strong lines of his body were unmistakable. He ran a hand through his black hair and turned. Kate's pulse jerked again at the sight of his face, with its wide, well-shaped mouth and slanting black eyebrows. His features were strong and balanced, handsome, but some quirk of their arrangement gave him an appearance of sternness. The planes of his cheek and angle of his jaw were austere. When lost in thought or frowning, his expression became quite intimidating. She'd seen footmen back away rather than disturb him. The sternness was misleading; anyone who knew James well knew that his face was made for laughter.

*Had been,* Kate corrected herself. James hadn't laughed during the past months and today his face was unsmiling. He looked tired, and as always when not smiling, stern.

Kate clasped her hands together and wished she knew how to make him laugh again. She watched as he walked over to one of the deep, leather armchairs beside the fire and sat. He stretched his long legs out and leaned his head back and closed his eyes, his weariness almost tangible.

"Your timing is excellent," Harry said, a brandy glass in each hand. Late afternoon sunlight fell into the room. The crystal gleamed and the brandy was a deep, glowing amber. "My cousin Augusta has gone to Bath for two months."

James opened his eyes. "I count myself very fortunate," he said, as he accepted a glass.

"So do we!" Harry sat so that Kate could only see the back of his head, his hair as bright red as her own. "Well? Your letter didn't explain a thing. What's this matter of urgency?"

Kate drew back slightly from the peephole. Should she cover her ears? Whatever Harry and James were about to discuss was none of her business. She raised her hands. To eavesdrop would be—

"Marriage," James said.

Kate flinched. Her heart seemed to shrink in her chest. She'd known this moment must come one day, but that didn't stop it hurting. *James is getting married.* She lowered her hands and leaned closer for a better view of the library.

"Ah." Harry settled back in his chair. "You've found a suitable wife?"

James's laugh was short and without humor. "No," he said, and swallowed some of his brandy.

"You want me to help you? Is that it?"

James frowned at his glass. "My birthday's soon," he said. "You know I must marry before then."

Kate wrinkled her brow. *What?*

"You could let Elvy Park and the fortune go," Harry said in an offhand tone. "I'm sure your cousin would appreciate them."

James transferred his frown from the brandy to Harry. "Would you?"

Her brother, possessor of an extensive estate and a comfortable fortune, shook his head. "No."

"Of course not. And neither will I. I'll marry before my thirtieth birthday, but . . ." James rubbed a hand over his face and sighed. "I wanted— Oh, God, I know it sounds stupid, Harry, but I wanted what my brother had."

He didn't need to explain what that was. Harry knew as well as she did: a love match.

Her brother didn't scoff. "It doesn't sound stupid," he said quietly. "It's what I want."

It was what Kate wanted, too, but she'd given up hope of it years ago.

James acknowledged Harry's reply with a brief, bitter

movement of his lips. He said nothing, but drank deeply from his glass.

"Are you certain the will is legal?" Harry asked.

"It's legal." James's smile was humorless. "Edward tried to find a way around it, but the lawyers said there wasn't one. And then he met Cordelia and it didn't matter." His face twisted. "Oh, God! If only he—"

For a moment Kate thought that James might cry. The notion shocked her. Even after the tragedy last year, when a carriage accident had taken the lives of his father and brother and sister-in-law, she'd not seen James lose control of his emotions. His face and manner had been composed, but his eyes . . . She'd wept in the privacy of her bedchamber for the silent grief in his eyes.

James shook his head, his expression bleak, and swallowed the last of the brandy. "I never expected to inherit Elvy Park and—and everything else. Never wanted to! But damn it, Harry, I'm not going to give it all away now that I've got it."

"No." Harry sighed and got to his feet. He walked over to the brandy decanter. "More?"

James nodded.

Kate's knees began to ache from kneeling on the hard floor. She shifted slightly and wished she'd brought a cushion in with her.

"You've got two months to find a bride," her brother said, as he refilled James's glass.

"Yes."

"So what the devil are you doing in Yorkshire?" Leather creaked as Harry sat down again. "The Season has started. You should be in London."

"Débutantes." An expression of distaste crossed James's face.

"What's wrong with débutantes?"

James swallowed a mouthful of brandy. "*You* don't get mobbed by them—and their mamas."

Harry laughed. "Of course not! I'm not half so well-favored as you."

Much as Kate loved her brother, she had to admit he was correct. Poor Harry had the Honeycourt red hair and freckles. James had no such flaws, unless the stern cast of his features could be called one. He'd always been handsome, but in his uniform, with his grin and his slanting black eyebrows, he'd been astonishingly so. She had heard—with no surprise—that he'd cut a swath through ballrooms in England and abroad, despite being a younger son with no title or fortune.

That status was a thing of the past, as was his military career. James no longer wore a hussar's colorful uniform. His riding-dress was somber-hued, the breeches dun-colored and the coat a dark brown. The clothes were elegant and expensive, as befitted an earl, but not dashing. Even so, he looked finer than any gentleman Kate had ever seen.

James's appearance wasn't the only reason débutantes and their mamas sought him out, but Harry didn't mention the earldom or the fortune. "What's wrong with débutantes?" he asked again.

"I could have my pick of a dozen of them," James said, frowning at his brandy.

"Only a dozen?"

James looked up. His mouth curved into a reluctant smile. "All right, I could have almost any débutante I wanted." The smile faded. "But I don't want one."

"Why not?"

"I don't want a chit straight out of the schoolroom."

"Why not?"

James shrugged. "They giggle too much."

"Nonsense!" Harry said. "A young and pretty miss would be just the thing."

"I can get young and pretty from an opera dancer," James said, exasperation in his voice. "We're talking about a *wife*."

"So?"

"So, I want a wife whose company I can tolerate. Damn it, Harry, I'll be spending the rest of my life with the woman. I want her to be someone I like!"

"And you can't like a débutante? Come on, James, that's a bit steep."

"Remember Maria Brougham?" James asked, swirling the brandy in his glass.

Kate had heard the name before, but she couldn't recall the context. Harry clearly did. He nodded. "Those eyes," he said. "That mouth. And her breasts!"

"Yes," James said. "Exactly. And look at her now. She's become a regular Devil's daughter. Poor Edgeton lives in terror of her tongue."

"She's still beautiful," Harry protested, while Kate realized who Maria Brougham was: the Duke of Edgeton's wife. A woman with the figure of a Venus and face of an angel—and the sharp tongue and uncertain temper of a shrew.

"Certainly," James agreed. "But would you want to be married to her?"

"No," Harry said. He tapped his fingers on his knee. "I offered for her, you know."

Kate's eyes widened. Her brother had offered for the waspish Duchess of Edgeton?

James grunted as he looked at his brandy. "So did I."

Kate blinked, astonished. She wasn't sure what surprised her most; that James had proposed, or that Maria Brougham had refused him. How could anyone refuse an offer of marriage from James?

"She held out for a duke," Harry said, his tone faintly resentful.

James glanced up. A hint of a smile touched his mouth. "For which we should both be thankful."

Harry made a brief sound of agreement.

James eyed him, and Kate watched as his smile widened. "I remember you fought a duel over her."

Harry cleared his throat. "Mmm."

"Some slur on her appearance. What was it? Her lips?"

"Her eyelashes," Harry said, shifting uncomfortably in his armchair. Kate stared at the back of his head. Her brother had fought a duel over the Duchess of Edgeton's eyelashes?

James grinned, and Kate's breath caught in her throat. She hadn't seen him look like that in a long time. "Her eyelashes."

"*You* fought a duel over a pair of *boots*."

James's grin faded to a reminiscent smile. "So I did. I'd forgotten. Lord, what a young fool I was."

"And you broke Camden's jaw over that opera dancer."

The amusement left James's face. His features became stern once more. "Bella," he said. "Yes, I did." He looked at his brandy and swirled it gently in the glass. "He hit her, you know."

Harry nodded.

"I liked Bella," James said. "She was . . ." His voice trailed off.

"Expensive."

James shrugged a shoulder. "Worth it."

"If you say so."

James looked up. His brown eyes seemed very dark and his mouth was almost smirking. "I do," he said, and something in his voice made Kate's cheeks flush hot.

The library was silent for a moment, apart from logs shifting in the fire. Harry cleared his throat again. "So, not a débutante?"

James's face became blank. "No," he said. "A woman whose character is formed. I want to know what I'm getting. I have no wish for a wife whose company will grow irksome."

"And you want my help. That's why you're here, isn't it?"

James looked at Harry. It seemed to Kate that he didn't wish to speak. "No," he said finally. "It's not."

"Not?" Harry sat up straighter, his tone baffled. "What then?"

James frowned past Harry at the wall. It was as if he stared directly at Kate. She shrank back in the priest's hole.

"I'm here because I want to marry your sister," James said.

Harry choked on his brandy.

Kate jerked back, knocking over the candlestick. She

reached for it desperately, blindly, and missed. The muted clang went unheard beneath Harry's coughing.

She knelt in the dark, unable to breathe, while the candlestick rolled across the floor of the priest's hole. James wanted to marry her?

"You want to marry Kate?" Harry said, when he'd regained his breath. "Why?"

*Yes, why?* Kate leaned closer to the peephole again and looked at James's face. There was a crease between his eyebrows. His lips were pressed tightly together.

"Because I think we should deal tolerably well together."

She closed her eyes. *No.*

"That's no reason to marry," Harry said.

"I have to marry." James's tone was flat. "And I like Kate better than any other lady of my acquaintance. I *know* her. She's not going to turn into a shrew on me."

"But you don't love her."

For a brief, foolish second there was hope. James's words extinguished it: "Of course I don't."

"James . . ." Harry sounded worried. "You're my best friend and I'd be pleased to have you for a brother, but—"

"You think it's a bad idea."

"I want you to be happy. Both of you. And I don't know whether this . . ." Kate opened her eyes to see Harry shaking his head.

"It's the only choice I have left. Damn it, Harry, if it must be a marriage of convenience, then I want a wife I can tolerate." James's voice was hard and his expression would have sent a dozen footmen scurrying for cover.

*Tolerate.* Something in Kate's chest clenched miserably.

"But would you be happy?"

"Happy?" The word sounded bitter in James's mouth. He shrugged. "Why not?"

"Would Kate?"

"She'd be mistress of Elvy Park. She'd have a title and a husband who respected her."

"Respect," Harry said. He shook his head. "Respect is all very well, but—"

"But?"

"But . . ." Harry shifted in the armchair. Leather creaked. When he spoke, he sounded uncomfortable, embarrassed even: "Shouldn't a happy marriage have an element of . . . of passion?"

James's mouth tightened. "Many women would prefer a passionless marriage."

*Not I.* Spinsterhood would be preferable to such a fate.

Harry stiffened in his chair. "You don't believe the marriage bed should be pleasurable for both parties?"

James clenched his jaw. "Damn it, Harry, don't lecture me!" His grip tightened on the brandy glass, becoming white-knuckled, and then his anger appeared to ebb. His face became devoid of expression. His voice, when he spoke, was flatly neutral: "You think I can't give a woman pleasure, even if I feel no desire for her?"

Harry put down his glass and leaned forward in his chair. "I've no doubt you can. But would you be happy doing so?"

James lowered his gaze to the brandy. A muscle worked in his jaw. "One woman is like another in the dark," he said.

"You really believe that?" Harry's voice was disappointed.

James looked up. His eyebrows drew together in a savage frown. "Damn it, Harry," he said fiercely. "What do you want me to say? I have to believe it!"

Harry was silent.

Weariness replaced the scowling anger on James's face. "If I could marry for love, I would," he said. "But my time's run out, Harry, don't you see? I have no other choice. I've thought about this seriously. I don't love Kate, or desire her, but I *like* her. If she married me I'd see that she was happy; you know I would."

Harry sighed. "Very well," he said. "Ask her. I don't know what her answer will be."

James looked momentarily startled. "You think she'll refuse me?"

Harry shrugged. "She's refused several offers."

"Really?" James's eyebrows rose. Kate was stung by his surprise. Resentment stirred in her breast. He needn't be so astonished. He wasn't the only man to see some use in her as a wife. "Such as?"

"Reginald Pruden proposed when she first came out."

"Pruden?" James laughed, but there was little amusement in the sound. "Dear God, no wonder she refused! The man's a pompous ass." He drank a mouthful of brandy and then shook his head. "Pruden." His upper lip curled with scorn.

"And . . . oh, there was Sir Thomas Granger, five years ago."

"Granger? Don't know the man."

"You haven't missed anything," Harry said. "He's a local baronet. Resembles a peahen."

The description should have made Kate smile—for Sir Thomas Granger *did* resemble a peahen—but instead she shuddered with memory of that proposal: Sir Thomas clasping her fingers with a plump, damp hand and leaning earnestly towards her, and then, when she refused him, flushing with rage and calling her a bran-faced dowd who set herself too high.

James laughed again, a humorless sound. His voice held pity: "Poor Kate." He looked at Harry and swirled the brandy in his glass. "Do you class me with Pruden and your baronet?"

Harry shook his head. "Of course not."

"So why should Kate refuse me?"

Why indeed? James Hargrave, Earl of Arden, was a prize on the marriage mart. His wealth and title made him one of the most eligible men in Britain. And he was handsome. He could have his pick of ladies. His offer was extraordinary.

*I should be flattered.* Why, then, did she feel so wretched?

Harry shrugged. "I don't know. I'm just saying, she might. Kate has a mind of her own. You know that. She's not some milk-and-water miss."

"She would have jumped at the offer eleven years ago," James said, raising his glass to his mouth.

Kate flinched at this comment. Hot humiliation rose in her cheeks. The memory of that girlish infatuation was hideous. It made her cringe to think of it.

"Do you think she's still partial to you?" Harry sounded surprised.

"No." James shook his head and swallowed a mouthful of brandy. "She treats me the same as she does you—thank God! Having Kate making sheep's eyes at me all the time would be dashed uncomfortable."

Harry grunted agreement. His tone, when he spoke, was unexpectedly glum: "When will you ask her?"

"Tomorrow," said James, looking as if the brandy had left an unpleasant taste in his mouth. "Unless you have an objection?"

"No." Harry was silent for a moment. "I suppose I should wish you luck."

"Thank you," said James. "But I doubt I'll need it. Kate's been on the shelf for years. Of course she'll accept my offer." His voice was even, toneless almost, and his face was without expression. He looked trapped, Kate thought. As trapped as she was in the dark priest's hole.

When the men had gone, Kate fumbled for the tinderbox and lit the candle again. In the flickering light she stood the goose feather quill in its holder and tried to blot the spattered ink. It had dried. The page was ruined. Not that it mattered; no one but herself would ever see it.

Kate gathered the diaries together. There were eleven of them, one for each year she'd been using the priest's hole. She picked up the earliest one and opened it at random. Her handwriting was young and unformed, the entry hastily written. *He's coming again. I am determined to treat him as if he is nothing more to me than an acquaintance. No one must know of my feelings for him.*

She closed the diary. She'd been seventeen when she'd written those words, seventeen and desperate not to make a fool of herself again. Her pretense had worked. James didn't know, and neither did Harry.

Kate made a pile of the diaries and sat looking at them. What was she to do? She was no longer in the throes of a foolish infatuation, stammering and stuttering whenever she spoke to James and blushing hotly if she met his eyes. That youthful passion had long since matured into something deep and lasting. She loved James, and would do so until the day she died. There was no other way it could be.

He was going to ask for her hand in marriage. What would she say? What *should* she say?

Kate touched her mouth lightly with a fingertip, imagining James kissing her. She wasn't a complete innocent. She knew something of what the marriage bed entailed: kissing, and much more intimate acts. To do those things with James would be marvelous beyond anything—except that he wouldn't really want to touch her. He'd do so because he had to, because it was his duty, not because he desired her.

And why should James desire her? She was too tall to be considered feminine, and quite plain. The natural curl in her hair might be the envy of other ladies, but the color was a garish red and was accompanied by that worst of disfigurements, freckles. Looking as she did, it was inconceivable that any man would feel passion for her.

Kate closed her eyes. She wanted nothing more than to marry James—only not like this, without his love. He'd said that one woman was like another in the dark, but he was wrong. He might be able to imagine away her hair and her freckles, but darkness couldn't give her a voluptuous figure. He would touch her and, even if he couldn't see her, he would know that she wasn't the woman he wanted in his bed.

She couldn't do that to him. Or to herself.

Kate opened her eyes. She reached out and picked up a diary. It was dated 1813. Three years ago. She flicked through the pages. *James has sailed to Spain again with his regiment. I am so afraid* . . .

She closed the diary. Eight years he'd served in the 10th Hussars. She touched the calfskin cover lightly with her fingertips, tracing the date and remembering the changes she'd seen in him. It had been more than the uniform. He'd become quieter, more serious, although he'd never stopped laughing. The loss of laughter had occurred in the past nine months. Perhaps it had something to do with the action he'd seen at Waterloo, which she'd heard had been bad, but she thought mostly it was because of his father and brother. Grief could stop a person laughing, and so could responsibility.

She wanted James to laugh again, and she wanted him to have a wife he loved. Not someone he could tolerate, such as herself, but someone he could love. Someone who would make him happy.

When he asked her tomorrow, she knew how she would answer.

# $C$HAPTER 2

$J$ames was resigned to his fate. He'd realized a month ago that there was no hope of making a love match before his thirtieth birthday. It had been a bitter moment. There was nothing he wanted less than a marriage of convenience, but, equally, he didn't want to lose Elvy Park. His world had seemed very bleak—until he'd thought of Kate. She wasn't a woman he could imagine loving, but she was one whom he liked. She would make an excellent wife and the emotion that he felt now, on the morning of his proposal, should be relief. It wasn't.

*Kate,* he thought, as he fastened his shirt. One of the buttons came off in his hand. He stared at it and swore, a crude oath, from the stables. It made him feel marginally better.

"Sorry, Griffin," he said. "I've done it again."

The valet glanced up from where he was laying out James's waistcoat. "I'm getting used to it, my lord."

James frowned at the button. It wasn't the first one he'd pulled off this week. Damn, who'd have thought he'd be so angry? It wasn't Kate's fault. It was his father's. He swore again.

Griffin paused. "Another one, my lord?" he asked, in a startled tone.

"No, no."

James stripped off the shirt and held it in his hand, the fine cambric clenched between his fingers. *How could you do this, Father?*

He tossed the shirt on the wide bed. His eyes caught the movement in the heavy mahogany mirror and he glanced at his reflection. His face was dark and unsmiling. He ran a hand roughly through his hair. Of course Kate would say yes. Why should she refuse?

He watched his jaw clench, and turned away from the mirror. Kate would be a fine wife. She had a clever mind and a good sense of humor. It was of no matter that he didn't love or desire her. They would deal well together. It would be a better marriage than his parents' had been.

James put his hands on his hips and frowned at the room. It was decorated in shades of brown and gold. The brown suited his mood; the gold did not. He transferred his gaze to the waistcoat he'd chosen for this morning and told himself that he *wanted* to marry Kate. But in his heart he knew it was a lie. He sighed.

"You'd prefer another waistcoat, my lord?" Griffin asked, as he brought a fresh shirt.

"No." James shook his head. "The waistcoat is fine." The silk was cream-colored, subtly embroidered, and elegant enough for a proposal. He took the shirt Griffin held out and shrugged into it and began to fasten the buttons. This time he managed not to pull any off.

He found Kate in the morning room. There had been a frost overnight, but the room was pleasantly warm. A fire burned in the grate and mild sunlight shone in through the windows. Kate sat at a rosewood writing table, her head bent and her expression solemn. The quill moved quickly over the paper. She was so intent on her task that she didn't hear him.

James paused in the doorway and thought, not for the first time, how like her brother Harry she was. She had the same freckled countenance and gray eyes, the same red hair. For some reason his mind wanted to compare her with Maria Brougham. It was a painful comparison, and not fair on Kate.

He reminded himself that Kate's looks weren't why he wanted to marry her. She didn't have the golden ringlets and pouting mouth of Maria Brougham, but what she did have was far more valuable. Her manner was calm and sensible and her conversation intelligent. And she liked to laugh. They would deal well together. There'd be no passion, but there would be respect.

Kate turned her head and saw him. She started slightly, and James thought that faint color rose in her cheeks. He was reminded, horribly, of her youthful infatuation for him. He'd not been able to be in the same room as Kate without her blushing an ugly, livid red, and any attempt at conversation had been tortuous. She'd been unable to put two coherent words together.

Kate glanced back at her letter and laid down the quill. James saw that ink had spattered across the closely written lines. "I apologize," he said. "I didn't mean to startle you."

Kate smiled and shook her head as she blotted the letter. "No matter." There was no sign of partiality in her expression or tone, nothing more than friendliness.

James decided that he'd imagined the faint wash of color in her cheeks. It had been a trick of the light, a reflected glow from the room's rose-colored walls.

"Did you wish to speak to me?" Kate finished blotting the letter. She turned in the chair and smoothed her gown over her lap. A delicate pattern was woven into the ivory-white muslin.

Now that the moment had come, James found himself reluctant to make his offer. He walked across the room and halted beside the fireplace, his shoulders tense. He unclenched his jaw and made himself smile at Kate. She would make him a fine wife. She was no termagant, no silly chit who'd giggle at him and be frightened by his frowns.

He cleared his throat. Kate's face was freckled and alert. For an instant, gazing at her, he had the impression that she braced herself. He dismissed the notion as absurd. Harry had given his word not to inform her; she could have no idea what he wished to say.

James realized that his smile had faded. His neckcloth felt too tight. He controlled the urge to loosen it and reminded himself that he'd faced worse moments than this. Briefly, the smell of cannon smoke and blood came to him. He pushed the memory aside. "Kate, will you marry me?"

As a proposal it was blunt and abrupt, and he was instantly ashamed of his lack of eloquence. He could have done better.

Kate's expression became completely blank. "I beg your pardon?"

James abandoned the fireplace. His gait was stiff as he crossed the room, his legs moving awkwardly. He sat opposite her on a silk-covered chair, tense. "Will you marry me, Kate? Please?"

He wanted her to say *Yes,* but instead she asked: "Why?"

"Because if I don't marry before my thirtieth birthday, I lose Elvy Park and the fortune and—oh, almost everything except the title." Anger and frustration bunched in his muscles. It took effort to keep his voice calm.

Kate frowned at him. "That's ridiculous."

James's jaw tightened. He didn't need to be told it was ridiculous. He knew.

"Why?" Kate asked. "How?"

"My father wanted grandchildren before he died."

Kate's brow creased in confusion. "So?"

"So he tried to force Edward to marry."

"How?" Kate asked again.

"He wrote a will, leaving everything on the condition that his heir marries before his thirtieth birthday." The words came out flat and without inflection. "If the heir . . . if *I'm* not married by then, I inherit the title and the old Grange, but little else. Not Elvy Park and the other estates, and not the fortune. Nothing that is unentailed."

"What?" Kate said. "That's absurd!"

"Isn't it just?" he said bitterly. And, absurd or not, it had failed to serve its purpose; his father had died before seeing any grandchildren.

Kate shook her head, staring at him.

"It wouldn't bother me to lose the title—I never expected it. But Elvy Park! I . . ." He paused and tried to find the words to make her understand. "I don't think I could bear to lose Elvy Park, Kate. It . . . I love it."

Kate nodded, her expression sober. She said nothing. That was one of the things he liked about her, he realized: that she didn't need to fill silence with chatter.

"So . . . you see that I have to marry?"

She nodded again.

"So, please, will you marry me?"

Kate clasped her fingers in her lap and shook her head. "No," she said. "I'm sorry, James."

His first emotion was astonishment. His second was relief. His third was panic. "What?" he said. "Why not?"

"Because I don't wish to," she said, looking past his shoulder at the fireplace.

He blinked. "Are . . . are your affections otherwise engaged, Kate?" It was the only reason he could think of for her extraordinary answer.

Her eyes came back to his face. "Otherwise engaged?" She shook her head. "No."

His astonishment and relief were replaced by pique. Kate was refusing for no other reason than that she preferred spinsterhood to marriage with him?

She smiled at him. "But I'll help you find a wife."

"What?" James said, in no mood to be humored.

"I'll help you find a wife. Tell me what you're looking for." She picked up the quill and drew a fresh sheet of paper towards her. Her head tilted at an enquiring angle.

"Kate." There was a bite of frustration in his voice. "I have less than two months left."

"I know," she said calmly.

James stared at her. He clenched his jaw. This morning was not progressing as he'd planned.

Kate shrugged at his silence, and dipped her quill in the inkwell. "What sort of wife would you like?"

Pique and panic combined to make him surly. He stood. "There's no point."

She looked up at him. "I'm perfectly serious," she said. "I know dozens of eligible young ladies. One of them is bound to suit you better than I."

He shook his head. "You would suit me," he said, and he knew in his bones that he was correct. They had compatibility, which was as important as passion.

Kate averted her head and put down the quill. "No."

James stared at her, and wondered how to make her reconsider her answer. Inspiration dawned. "We could go to Venice on our honeymoon."

Kate glanced back up at him, frowning.

"Rome," he said. "Florence, Naples, Capri."

Her frown deepened.

"Greece."

"Honestly, James!" Kate shook her head, the frown giving way to laughter. "You can't *bribe* me to marry you."

James sat down again. "What would make you marry me?" he asked. "Tell me, and I'll do it."

Kate looked down at her hands. "I am a foolish romantic," she said. "I shall only marry for love. I'm sorry, James."

James opened his mouth and then shut it again without speaking. There was nothing to be said. Neither of them loved the other and he couldn't alter that. It was quite beyond his power.

Kate smiled at him, an apologetic movement of her mouth. She picked up the quill. "So tell me, James, what is it you're looking for? Does she have to be of noble birth?"

His tone was heavy: "Kate, I really don't think there's any point."

"Two months is perfectly long enough to shop for a wife," she said calmly.

"Seven weeks," he said.

"Long enough."

"But—"

"Consider Mr. Collins."

"Mr. Collins?"

"*Pride and Prejudice.* Haven't you read it?"

James had. He narrowed his eyes. "Are you comparing me to Mr. Collins?" As he recalled it, that man's courtships had been hasty and ludicrous.

Laughter lit up Kate's face. "Of course not."

James eyed her. She met his gaze. The amusement faded from her face, leaving it serious. Silence grew in the room. "A sense of humor," he said.

Kate blinked. "I beg your pardon?"

"I should like my wife to have a sense of humor."

"Very well." Kate dipped the quill in ink and began to write. The nib scratched swiftly over the paper.

James watched her. His pique faded and some of his panic began to ease. He felt a glimmer of hope. Maybe Kate was correct. Maybe she could find him a bride who would suit him as well as she would—maybe even one he could feel passion for. Making love to one's wife should be a pleasure, not a duty.

Unexpectedly, the thought of making love to Kate slid into his mind. To his astonishment, James felt a faint stir of arousal. He frowned at Kate's bent head. In the sunlight her hair was as bright as flame, astonishingly vivid above the ivory-white gown. He didn't want to make love to Kate. Nothing was further from his mind. And yet the thought *was* in his mind and it brought a flush of heat to his body. How odd. He didn't desire Kate, didn't want her in his bed, didn't—

Kate turned her head and smiled at him. "What else?" she asked.

"I beg your pardon?"

"What else would you like in a wife?"

James looked at her red hair and freckles. A degree of beauty would be nice, but he couldn't say so without offending her. "She should be at least moderately intelligent," he said. "I couldn't bear a bird-witted wife."

Kate nodded.

James watched as she wrote. He didn't want Kate in his bed. Why, then, did the notion bring heat to his blood?

He deepened his frown and concentrated on the list that she wrote. It was unsettling to have such thoughts in his head, and it was vulgar and discourteous to Kate. He didn't understand it at all.

Kate looked at the list once James was gone. It contained only four items. She frowned as she read them.

*Sense of humor.*

*Moderately intelligent.*

*Not straight out of the schoolroom.*

*A gentleman's daughter.*

The requirements were certainly adequate for a wife he could tolerate, but not for one he could love. *Pretty,* she wrote firmly on the sheet of paper.

Kate stared at the list and sighed. Then she pushed it aside and began to think of names. With the London Season under way, the neighborhood was somewhat depleted, but quite a number of eligible young ladies were still in residence. She drew another piece of paper towards her. *Miss Marianne Charnwood,* she wrote. *Miss Caroline Charnwood. Miss Eudora Wilmot. Miss Cecily Mornington.* She chewed on her lower lip, frowning at the paper. *Miss Dorothea Ingham. The Hon. Isabella Orton. Miss Olivia Bellersby. Miss Fanny Bellersby. Miss Amelia Hart. Miss Sarah Durham.*

Kate tapped the quill against her chin. She'd forgotten to ask James about his views on widows. Would he only consider a virgin bride? She added *Mrs. Emmeline Hurst* to the list and then laid down the quill, satisfied. The ladies met James's criteria and all were prettier than she was. Any one of them would make James a suitable wife. She could begin showing him prospective brides this afternoon, starting with the Misses Bellersby. And tomorrow she could introduce him to Miss Ingham. And after that . . .

Kate rummaged through the papers on the little writing table until she found the letter she'd been writing. It was spattered with ink.

"Lizzie," she said, under her breath. "I think I've found you a husband." She picked up her quill and copied the letter onto a fresh sheet of paper. *Dearest Lizzie, I know we had decided on June, but please tell me that you can make your visit earlier . . .*

Kate wrote swiftly. The sooner Lizzie received the letter, the sooner she could be here. And once James met Lizzie, how could he not wish to marry her? She was everything he needed. She was clever and sweet-natured and pretty, and she had a gift for laughter. She would suit James well. And more than that, she'd make him happy.

Kate reread what she'd written and was satisfied that no hint of her intention was evident. She wanted James to be a surprise for Lizzie. "Fall in love with him, Lizzie," she whispered, as she sealed the letter with a wafer. "And make him fall in love with you. Please."

She sat at the writing table for a moment, looking at the letter in her hand. Foolishly, she felt like crying. It wasn't too late to change her mind. She could throw the letter and the lists into the fire and tell James she'd marry him after all. And they could go to Venice on their honeymoon, and Rome and Florence and Naples.

Her mouth turned up in a lopsided smile as she remembered James's attempt at bribery. He knew her well to make such an offer. London held little lure for her—after three tedious Seasons she had no great liking for the place—but Italy was another matter.

To think of going there with James!

Kate's smile crumpled. Tears stung beneath her eyelids and gathered chokingly in her throat. She wiped her eyes with the back of her hand and swallowed and took a deep, steadying breath. Then she rang for a footman and gave instructions that the letter be sent by express. That done, she folded the lists and went upstairs to her room. She should find James and tell him about the Misses Bellersby this afternoon, but she couldn't face him again so soon. Their interview had been harrowing. She'd learned not to wear her heart on her sleeve, but it was like walking on glass to be in the same room as James, to talk to him and pretend that she didn't love him. Her head ached. She needed fresh air and to be alone.

# CHAPTER 3

James watched from the library windows as Kate came out of the trees on the far side of the lawn. Her hair was bright, even at such a distance. He frowned as he looked at her. He understood her aversion to marriages of convenience. It was an aversion he shared, having been witness to his parents' miserable marriage. Not that Kate's parents had been unhappy together—quite the opposite, in fact. The late Viscount Honeycourt and his wife had been devoted to each other. But theirs had been a love match.

James watched Kate and frowned. He wanted a love match. He wanted passion. But . . .

Passion was all very well, but a marriage couldn't survive on passion alone. Respect and friendship were equally important, if not more so, and he had those with Kate. And despite her airy assertion, seven weeks was an alarmingly short time to find a suitable wife. Panic twisted beneath his breastbone. He should have bargained harder. Did Kate really think she was going to make a love match at her age?

He looked at Kate across the stretch of lawn and made up his mind. Damn it, he *was* going to bargain harder. He could easily seek his pleasure outside the marriage bed. Many husbands did. London abounded with pretty opera dancers, the majority of whom possessed skills other than performing on stage. Quite startling skills, on occasion.

James opened the French windows onto the terrace, smiling as he recalled Bella. Yes, an opera dancer would be just the thing. And there would be no disrespect to Kate. If he was discreet, she would never know.

He walked down the steps and cut a tangent across the lawn. The grass had been shaved short by scythemen and was faintly damp beneath his boots. He kept his eyes on Kate. Her hair glowed in the sunlight.

Kate's step faltered when she saw him coming towards her across the grass. Then she altered her direction and came to meet him.

"Isn't it a beautiful day?" Her smile was wide and her cheeks faintly flushed with exertion. She wore a fur-trimmed blue pelisse over her gown, but had removed her bonnet and held it upside-down by the silk ribbons. The crown was filled almost to overflowing with spring wildflowers. He saw snowdrops and primroses and sweet violets.

"Yes," he said. "Kate, about my offer—"

"I've made a list of suitable ladies." Her tone was brisk and businesslike. She began to walk again. "We can start with the Misses Bellersby."

"The Misses Bellersby?" he asked, strolling alongside her.

"Yes. They're stopping by this afternoon."

"I see."

"Olivia is the elder and Fanny the younger. They're very nice girls."

"I'm sure they are," James said. "But Kate, about this list of yours . . ."

"What about it?"

"What if I like none of them well enough to marry?"

"You will," she said, in a tone that he thought was overly confident.

"But what if I don't?"

"Well—"

"A deal," he said. "If I don't like any of them better than you, then you agree to marry me."

Kate halted on the grass. "No."

"Please," he said.

"No." Her tone was firm.

James looked at her. The color had gone from her cheeks. Her face was pale. The freckles stood out quite clearly.

"I know you want a love match," he said. "But Kate, what do you think the chance is of that happening?" He regretted the words as soon as they were uttered. Too blunt, too cruel.

He watched in shame as Kate flushed and her eyes dropped from his. "I know it's never going to happen," she said, her voice low and stiff.

James's sense of shame deepened. "I beg your pardon, Kate," he said. "I didn't mean to—"

"No." She shook her head, not meeting his eyes. "It's the truth."

James raised a hand to loosen his neckcloth. He thought that he was flushing, too. His face felt hot. "Is . . . is spinster-hood more appealing than becoming a countess?" he asked.

He was unsurprised when she answered: "Yes." He'd broached the subject remarkably ill. James cleared his throat and tried again. "But, Kate—"

"I'm happy," she said, her tone defensive.

"I know you are. But have you thought what will happen when Harry marries?" Kate would no longer be mistress of Merrell Hall. Harry's bride would have that role, and while James had no doubt that Kate would always be welcome in her brother's home, he thought she'd find her position awkward.

"Yes. I have thought about it," Kate said, raising her eyes and frowning at him. "I'll take a cottage in the village. I'm not destitute, James. I'll be perfectly comfortable."

"And who will you have for a companion? Your cousin Augusta?"

Distaste flickered across her face. "No. I'll hire someone."

"You could be mistress of Elvy Park," James said, watching

her closely. "The house is beautiful, Kate. And the park is one of the finest tracts of land in England."

Kate's mouth tightened.

"And there's an estate in Somerset, and one in Cornwall. And a house in Mayfair." He didn't mention the old Grange, which, although it was entailed to the Arden heir, was an uncomfortable pile and not somewhere he'd ever choose to live. "And we could travel, Kate. Wherever you wish to go. Rome, Florence . . ." He said the names again, persuasively. "Capri."

Kate turned her head away.

"Is that worse than spinsterhood, Kate?"

"Of course not," she said stiffly.

"Then say you'll marry me," he said, looking down at her bright hair. "If no one on your list suits me."

Kate said nothing.

"Please, Kate."

She met his eyes, still frowning. "Very well. But you have to give them a fair chance."

Relief made him almost light-headed. "You have my word," he said, ready to promise anything. "Thank you, Kate."

She didn't return his smile. She looked as if he'd backed her into a corner. Which he had.

"Tell me about the Misses Bell-whatever," James said, as guilt came on the heels of relief. He'd been no gentleman to force the agreement from her. He'd meant to coax, but instead he'd bludgeoned. It was nothing to be proud of.

Kate's face relaxed. "Bellersby. Olivia is twenty-one and Fanny twenty. They've never had a London Season although their father could easily afford it. He's a widower and quite dotes on them. I don't think he wants them to leave. Certainly, he's not made the slightest push to see them married . . ."

James listened to her description of the Misses Bellersby as they walked across the lawn towards the Hall. He was ashamed of his conduct, but his anxiety was gone. He'd view the ladies on Kate's list and perhaps he would like one, but if he didn't, then it was of no consequence, because Kate had promised to marry him. He glanced at her. It would be no love match, but they'd be comfortable together.

*Passion,* he thought, frowning, remembering the odd stir of arousal he'd experienced at the thought of Kate in his bed. He shook his head. It had been an aberration, born of panic.

Although . . . James looked at her more closely and was startled to realize that her profile was very fine indeed. He was so disconcerted by the discovery that he missed part of what Kate was saying.

"So, are congratulations in order?"

James looked up from the *Gazette.* Harry stood in the doorway to the library, his curly hair awry, as if he'd been dragging his hands through it.

"Not exactly."

"What do you mean, not exactly?" Harry came into the room and threw himself down on a couch. The wine-red damask should have clashed with his bright hair; somehow it didn't.

James folded the newspaper and put it aside. The armchair creaked slightly as he stretched. "Kate wishes to try her hand at matchmaking."

Harry's brow creased. "What?"

"She has a list of eligible candidates for me."

"She does?"

The expression on Harry's face almost made James laugh out loud, something he hadn't felt like doing in a long time. "Yes," he said. "Starting with the Misses Bellersby, this afternoon."

"So . . . you're not going to marry Kate?"

"If none of the ladies on her list are suitable, then she'll marry me."

"She will?"

James nodded. "We have an agreement." Which Kate wasn't pleased with. He shrugged off his guilt. Chances were that someone on her list would suit him.

"An agreement?" Harry's eyebrows rose.

"Yes."

Brass-headed studs trimmed the armchair's leather upholstery. James rubbed a finger over them. He didn't tell Harry that Kate's first response had been refusal. It had been arrogant of him to assume she'd jump at his offer of marriage, as she would have eleven years ago, but he was offended that she preferred spinsterhood to marriage with him. It stung his pride.

"Well," said Harry, looking bemused. "Uh . . . well." He blinked several times and then shook his head. "Would you like to go fishing this afternoon? I've nearly finished with Crake."

"Sorry," James said, with regret. "I have the Misses Bellersby."

"Oh," Harry said. "Right. Of course."

Harry took her aside after luncheon, before he returned to his study. His hair was standing on end, as it always did when he went over business with his steward, Crake. It gave him a deceptively frazzled air; Kate knew he enjoyed the sessions. Land management was Harry's passion.

"What's this about you and James?" he said, frowning. His voice told her that he spoke as the Viscount Honeycourt, not her brother, Harry. It was a tone he'd perfected in the six years since he'd succeeded to the viscountcy.

"I'm helping him find a wife."

"The Misses Bellersby?" Harry shook his head. "Kate, I don't think James is going to marry a Bellersby."

"They're perfectly amiable."

Harry didn't disclaim this truth. He continued to frown at her. "James told me about your agreement."

"Oh."

"Will you really marry him?"

"Only if I can't find him a more suitable bride." Kate made her voice cheerful. "And I shall!"

"A Bellersby?" Harry shook his head again. "Certainly they're amiable, but—"

"They're as suitable as I am, if not more so."

"Nonsense," Harry said staunchly. His frown deepened. "Kate, are you certain you want to marry James?"

"It won't come to that."

"It might."

Kate shook her head. "I doubt it. But if it does, then yes, I think we should deal tolerably well together." Too late, she realized she'd repeated James's words, overheard in the library. She turned the subject. "I thought we could have the Charnwoods to dinner."

"The Charnwoods?" Harry narrowed his eyes. "You're thinking of Marianne, aren't you? Trust me, Kate, James is *not* going to want to marry Marianne."

Kate shrugged lightly. "There's Caroline, too."

Harry observed her narrowly while the mahogany longcase clock in the hallway ticked the seconds away. His mouth twitched as if he struggled to hide a smile. "Very well," he said. "Let us have the Charnwoods to dinner."

"Thank you," Kate said.

Harry shook his head at her. "What else have you planned, Kate? Tell me the worst."

"Well . . . I've asked Lizzie to come a little earlier."

"Lizzie?"

"Miss Penrose."

"Miss Penrose?"

"My friend from Derbyshire. She was coming in June. Remember?"

"Oh," Harry said. He blinked. It was obvious he'd forgotten. "Of course. Whatever you wish."

"And I thought . . . could we have a ball?"

"A ball?" Harry frowned again.

"Yes," Kate said. "We haven't had one since . . . oh, I forget when."

"A ball." Harry's brow cleared. "Why not? When's the next full moon, Kate? Do you know?"

Kate did. She'd checked. "Three weeks."

"Perfect," said Harry.

Kate nodded. It *was* perfect. With a full moon to light the country roads, they'd receive few refusals. "I'll send the invitations out tomorrow."

"Good." Harry nodded, and turned towards his study.

"Only, there's one thing . . ."

He turned back. "What?"

"Cousin Augusta. Shouldn't we inform her that James is staying?"

There was a long moment of silence. "Do you think we should?" Harry asked finally, slowly.

"Well . . ." Kate twisted her hands together. "Are you certain that's it's quite . . . quite *convenable* for me to be your hostess? I know I'm as much an old maid as Cousin Augusta, only . . . I'm not so . . . so *old* as she is, and—" She bit her lip. "Do you think . . . will it occasion talk to have James staying?"

"If I thought that, I would have asked him to put up at The Minstrel," Harry said firmly. "None of our acquaintances could think there's any impropriety. A friend of such long-standing! It's perfectly unobjectionable. *I'm* here."

"But . . ."

"Only a—a *sapskull* could imagine that Merrell Hall is anything but respectable!" Harry's tone was hot. "And if they did, Yule would set them straight, or Mrs. Hedley!"

Kate chewed her lower lip. It was true, the butler and the housekeeper would put tattlemongers right. "But—"

"Dash it, Kate, you're old enough not to need a chaperone!"

"But . . . what about when Lizzie comes?"

Harry's reply was prompt: "You shall be *her* chaperone."

"Do you think it will serve?"

"Yes," Harry said firmly. "No one can take exception to it."

"But—"

"Kate . . ." Harry sighed, a deep sound. He stepped closer and took hold of her hands. "If you truly want her back, I'll send word to Bath."

"I don't *want* her back." Kate sighed, too. Merrell Hall, without Cousin Augusta and her spasms and vapors and incessant scolding, was a much nicer place. "It's just that—"

"Only think, Kate, we'll ruin her holiday . . ." Harry's tone was coaxing, his smile mischievous. He looked, for an instant, like a schoolboy and not a man who'd recently celebrated his thirtieth birthday. "She's only been gone a week. It would be *such* a pity to call her back."

His shameless wheedling made her smile. "All right," she said.

Harry bent his head and kissed her cheek lightly. "Thank you, Kate." He squeezed her hands before releasing them. "And if the old tabby cats say anything, ignore 'em. *I* shall!"

# $C$HAPTER 4

$\mathcal{I}$t was patently evident that the Misses Bellersby were
sisters. Their hair was a similar shade of light brown and they
both had dimples. The elder sister, Olivia, seemed the more
intelligent of the two, but the younger one, Fanny, was the
prettier. James smiled at them over his teacup and tried to
imagine what it would be like to be married to either lady.

The discussion was about novels. Not clever works such
as *Pride and Prejudice,* but novels of the more lurid kind,
gothic romances and tales of horror. The Misses Bellersby had
brought back several they'd borrowed from Kate. The books
lay on a table. James put down his cup and reached idly for
one slim calf-bound volume.

"And when the heroine was trapped in the dungeon, I vow
I was so terrified I could scarcely breathe!" Olivia Bellersby
exclaimed. "Fanny nearly fainted when I read it out to her."

Fanny Bellersby nodded, her blue eyes large with remembered fright. She shivered.

"Are you afraid of the dark, Miss Fanny?" James asked. He
thought he already knew the answer to his question.

She shuddered and nodded. "Oh, yes."

He wondered what else she was afraid of. Many things, he
suspected. There was an underlying timidity to her prettiness.

Her blue eyes were as mild as her manner—and as unappealing. He must remember to tell Kate that he wanted a wife who wasn't timid.

He opened the book to a page at random and read the first few lines. *The castle stood shrouded in mist on the headland, hunched against the elements. Wind howled like a thousand mournful phantoms, wailing their grief through the broken ruin, and cold fingers of terror clutched at Matilda's heart.* He snorted softly. Did Kate really read such rubbish?

He chose another page, nearer the end. *Matilda gazed upon the face of her beloved. Golden curls fell across Sebastian's noble brow and his eyes were blue, a color as pure as the cerulean seas of Ionia.* This time his snort was slightly louder. He closed the book firmly and placed it on the mahogany occasional table beside him and looked across at Olivia Bellersby. She wore a gown of pale yellow, trimmed with plaited ribbon. A locket nestled in the hollow of her throat.

James examined her thoughtfully. She had none of the timidity of her younger sister. "Tell me, Miss Bellersby," he said. "Do you like to travel?"

Olivia Bellersby turned her smile on him. "I'm a terrible traveler. I become unwell even in an open carriage. Don't I, Fanny?"

Her sister nodded.

"You have my sympathy," James said.

"Oh, no," Miss Bellersby said, with a merry laugh. "There are much worse afflictions. One of our cousins has the most dreadful squint and Mrs. Greeley in the village has *fits*! I count myself fortunate, I assure you."

"Well?" asked Kate, when the Misses Bellersby had departed. She turned to him expectantly. "Do you like them?"

"You may take them both off your list," James told her.

Kate frowned slightly. "Why?"

"Because I don't wish to marry either of them."

"Why not?" she asked. "They're perfectly nice. And they meet all your requirements."

"Fanny Bellersby is too timid," James said.

"Timid?" Kate's frown faded into an expression of confusion. "She's a little timid, but I don't see what's wrong with that."

"I don't want a wife who'll be afraid of me," James said.

Kate blinked. "But why should Fanny be afraid of you?"

He scowled at her.

"Oh. I hadn't thought of that. James, you have a truly ferocious frown!"

"I know." It was the way in which his eyebrows slanted, or perhaps their blackness. Whatever the reason, when he frowned, people had a tendency to cringe. It had been a joke among his regiment that he could drive the enemy back just by scowling.

He looked at Kate and realized that she'd never flinched from his frown.

"Very well," she said. "I can see that you'd prefer a wife who's not timid. But what about Olivia Bellersby?"

"She's a bad traveler."

"So?"

"So I want a wife who enjoys traveling."

"That's not on your list," Kate pointed out.

James shrugged. "I've just thought of it."

"But can't you travel alone?"

"It's more pleasurable to have company."

"Oh," said Kate. "But . . . does it have to be a requirement?"

James looked at her. She stared back at him, her brow creased. He imagined showing her Italy. She'd be delighted with the countryside, the cypresses and the vineyards, the towers thrusting up from hilltops, and delighted too with

35

the rocky coast and its clear, blue water. She'd laugh at the absurdity of Venice, and love its beauty. And she'd—

"Does it have to be a requirement?" Kate repeated.

"Yes," James said firmly. He'd seen enough of the battle-fields of Spain to last him a lifetime, but he'd love to rediscover Italy and venture into Greece. And he'd like to do it with his wife. A wife who'd enjoy it as much as he would.

"Very well." Kate's tone was resigned. "Are there any more requirements that I should know about?"

He shook his head.

Kate began to gather the books together. "Will you take me driving tomorrow?"

"Of course." He paused. It was a request she'd never made before. "Why?"

"We can call in on the Inghams."

"They have a daughter?"

"Yes. Dorothea. She's very sweet."

"But not timid."

"No." Kate glanced at him. "You can frown at her if you wish. To check for yourself." There was a glint of amusement in her eyes. She held out a hand. "Could you pass that book please?"

James picked up the volume he'd flicked through. It was an absurd piece of nonsense. One corner of his mouth turned up as he recalled the hero's noble brow and golden curls and cerulean eyes.

"What's so amusing?" Kate asked.

He handed the book to her. "The hero. Sebastian." He found himself grinning. "Is that what you like, Kate? Golden hair and sea-blue eyes?"

To his surprise, she flushed faintly. "No," she said, adding the book to her pile.

James leaned back in his chair and looked at her. Curiosity overcame good manners. "What do you like?"

"Something darker," Kate said, not meeting his eyes. She

busied herself with straightening the pile of books. "What about you?"

"I prefer something darker, too," he said, remembering the exotic beauty of the Spanish women, with their olive skin and flashing eyes and black hair. But then he recalled Maria Brougham, who had golden ringlets and blue eyes. Cerulean eyes. He'd thought her beautiful. And Bella, his pretty opera dancer, had been fair. James rubbed a thumb along his jaw, thinking of the women who'd shared his bed. There had been as many blondes as brunettes. Perhaps he didn't have a preference after all.

He wondered what color Miss Ingham's hair was.

Miss Ingham's hair was a pretty shade of brown, but she was too girlish. James told Kate so once they were back in his curricle.

"Nonsense," Kate said, as he tooled his team down the Inghams' curving drive. "She's twenty-one. She's been out of the schoolroom for years."

"She's too girlish," he repeated firmly. "And she giggles."

"You have an objection to giggling?"

"In excess," James said. "Yes."

"Another requirement?"

"Yes," he said, but he didn't apologize. He'd come to the conclusion—while observing Miss Ingham—that girlishness would be an irritating trait in a wife. Kate was correct; Dorothea Ingham wasn't timid. She wouldn't be afraid of his frowns. On the contrary, she'd probably giggle and attempt to cajole him out of the sullens—which would only serve to aggravate him. She was sweet and diminutive and childlike, and not at all what he wanted. "And I'd like my wife to be taller," he said.

"Taller!"

He nearly laughed at Kate's tone of affront. "Yes, taller."

They reached the road and he gave the horses their heads.

"You never said anything about height before," Kate said, a slight edge to her voice.

"No."

Mature oak trees lined the road. Sunlight shone through the boughs, casting rapid patterns of shade and light. James glanced sideways at Kate. She wore a blue pelisse trimmed with dark sable and a high-crowned bonnet. Bright ringlets escaped from beneath the bonnet's brim. He watched as her eyebrows drew together and her lips quirked, her expression somewhere between thoughtful and exasperated. "How tall do you wish your wife to be?" she asked, after a moment.

"Tall enough for me to dance easily with."

They came to a bend in the road and he slowed the horses' pace. He'd been used to driving with a speed that bordered on recklessness, neck or nothing, confident that his skill was equal to any surprise the Fates could throw at him. The deaths of his father and brother last year had taught him caution. He'd been aware of his mortality on the battlefields, but that accident had shown him that sabers and cannons weren't the only ways a man could die before his time.

"How tall is that?" asked Kate.

James thought about it for a moment. "Your height," he said. "Or a few inches either side."

Her tone was startled: "My height?"

"Or thereabouts. A little shorter would be fine. Just not as short as Miss Ingham."

Kate was silent. James wondered whether she disliked the extra inches that made her stand taller than most ladies and quite a few men, inches that brought the top of her head higher than his chin. Probably she did. Her height could be seen as a flaw, but being tall himself, he'd come to appreciate tallness in a woman. It made many things easier, not merely dancing.

They rounded the bend. James let the horses pick up their pace again. It wasn't just Miss Ingham's figure that was dainty, her mouth was too. It was small and pretty and girlish, and not at all the sort of mouth that he wished to kiss. And damn it, he wanted a wife he'd *want* to kiss. But he couldn't tell Kate that.

"Why has Miss Ingham not married?" he asked.

He saw Kate shrug out of the corner of his eye. "She's the youngest of six daughters. I think her mother ran out of energy."

They traveled in silence for a moment, apart from the jingle of the horses' harnesses and the clop of their hooves. Six daughters. James experienced faint horror at the thought of all those ribbons and ringlets and frills—and all that giggling. No wonder Mrs. Ingham had run out of energy.

"Are there any more requirements you've thought of?" Kate asked.

*A mouth that I want to kiss.* "No," James said.

"Taller." Her tone was thoughtful. "Miss Orton is taller and she's definitely not girlish."

"Very well," he said. "Show me Miss Orton." He glanced at Kate and found himself staring at her mouth. He'd never noticed it before, but she had a surprisingly lush mouth. Its shape was generous, full and soft and inviting. It was a mouth made for kissing. He wondered what it tasted like.

James wrenched his attention back to the horses. He frowned over their ears and wondered what had gone awry in his world that he could want, even for a second, to kiss Kate Honeycourt.

"Today? Or would tomorrow suit you better?"

He turned to look at her. She was the perfect height for kissing. He cleared his throat. "I don't mind."

Kate spent the afternoon writing invitations for the ball on gilt-edged cards and discussing the upcoming event with the housekeeper and the cook. She had relegated Miss Orton to the morrow, claiming that she needed to plan for the ball, but the truth was that it disturbed her equilibrium to sit so close to James in the curricle, just the two of them. It wasn't an outright lie; she did need to plan. Her life seemed suddenly to consist of lists. Sheets of paper were spread over the large desk in the library, covering its surface. The guest list, the list of comestibles to be ordered, the list of housekeeping tasks that needed to be completed prior to the ball, the growing list of James's requirements and the shrinking one of eligible ladies.

She'd compiled the guest list last night and Harry had glanced at it this morning and given his approval, suggesting only that they not ask Mrs. Forster, because she'd complain if they danced the waltz. Kate had paid no attention to the suggestion; courtesy demanded that Mrs. Forster receive an invitation, as Harry well knew. And anyway, it wouldn't be a ball if Mrs. Forster wasn't there to stare balefully at the dancing couples and utter remarks about disintegration of morals and the laxity of today's youth.

Kate looked at the list of tasks. The chandeliers needed to be cleaned and the ballroom floor polished and musicians hired, and she should go down into the cellars and see whether they had sufficient champagne. And how many card tables should be set up for those who didn't care to dance? And, for that matter, did they have enough clean packs of cards? *Playing cards,* she wrote on the list. Hmm . . . Kate chewed on her lower lip and wondered whether she ought to order a new ball gown. Yes, she decided. "I may be bran-faced," she said under her breath, as she wrote *New ball gown* on the list. "But I am not a dowd."

Sir Thomas Granger had offered for the local justice of the peace's fourth daughter, Priscilla, the day after Kate had refused him. Priscilla had a face like a horse, with a long nose and big teeth, but she had no freckles. And she'd accepted the offer. Kate looked at her lists and compared Sir Thomas to the ridiculous—and fictitious—Mr. Collins and tried to laugh, but she couldn't. *Bran-faced.* Would James find her more attractive if she didn't have freckles? "Of course he would," she said.

Kate laid down the quill and closed her eyes and covered her face with her hands and wished, for a moment, that she wasn't who she was. Then she managed a laugh and pushed the invitations aside and reached for James's lists. She was a Honeycourt, and Honeycourts had freckles. The paintings in the Long Gallery upstairs attested to that fact.

She put a line through Dorothea's name. That was three candidates crossed off. How soon could Lizzie be here? *Not short,* she wrote on the list of requirements. And, *Doesn't giggle too much.* She should have remembered that last requirement. James had mentioned it to Harry. It was one of the reasons he'd given for not liking débutantes. And Dorothea Ingham certainly giggled a lot. Kate chewed on her lower lip as she stared at the sheet of paper. Lizzie giggled sometimes, but not in excess. And she met all the other new requirements. She was only a few inches shorter than Kate, was neither girlish nor timid, and her coloring was dark. Not that the latter was a requirement, merely a preference.

And Lizzie would love Europe. They shared a desire to travel, she and Lizzie. They'd planned wonderful trips together to places they'd only heard about, poring over maps and atlases, reading aloud to each other from the published journals of travelers. The places that James had mentioned—Venice and Florence and Rome—would send Lizzie into paroxysms of delight. And Greece. He'd spoken of Greece. Which meant Athens and Delphi and Corfu. Greece would be a dream come true. "Not my dream," Kate whispered. "Lizzie's dream."

Envy came then, so bitter that she almost tasted it, like bile in her mouth. And on the heels of envy came shame. How could she be jealous of one of her dearest friends? She *wanted* James to marry Lizzie. Nothing could be more perfect. James would be happy. He'd laugh again—Lizzie would make certain of that. And if anyone deserved James's love and all that came with it, it was Lizzie. Poor Lizzie, who dreamed of exotic travels and had never been out of Derbyshire.

Kate swallowed hard and rubbed a hand over her face. She stood, abandoning the lists.

The library was a beautiful room, with tall windows framing views of undulating parkland. Shelves brimmed with books, hundreds of them, thousands. It was here that memory of her mother was strongest. Kate stood, her hand clenched on the back of the chair, and stared at the shelves and recalled how her mother used to walk around the room, her fingers tracing a path along the rows of spines, how she would pull out a volume and open it carefully. It hadn't mattered whether the binding was plain or colored or gilded, worn or new, her mother's touch was always reverent.

The winters of her childhood had been spent almost entirely in this room, curled up in a leather armchair beside the fire, listening to her mother's voice as she read aloud. Harry had always been there, his face rapt, and often their father too, watching his wife with a smile in his eyes. Together they'd listened, drinking in fairytales and histories, myths and legends, philosophies and travelers' tales.

Kate released her grip on the chair. The library and its contents, books and memories, were precious to her. Of all the rooms in the house, it was her favorite. Harry felt the same; she was forever finding him here.

She shook her head to clear the memories and crossed to the east wall. A wealth of carved fruit and flowers decorated the wainscoting, but her fingers easily located the rosebud that opened the priest's hole. There was no fear of finding herself trapped today. Harry and James had ridden over to the Home Farm and wouldn't be back for hours.

Kate ducked her head and crept inside, reaching for the tinderbox and lighting the candle before she closed the panel.

The priest's hole was dark and cramped and uncomfortable, with a low ceiling and hard floor, but equally it was secret. Her brother knew nothing of it. He'd never find her diaries, as he had when she was a girl. Poor Harry. He'd meant it as a joke, there had been no spite intended, but she'd only been thirteen and she'd cried to think that someone else had read her private thoughts and foolish, girlish confidences—and Harry had been whipped.

That was long ago, and Harry was a grown man and would never do such a thing now, but it had taught her that nothing in her bedchamber was private. If not Harry, then a housemaid or her own maid, Paton. And not with any thought to pry; by accident perhaps, discovering a diary and wondering what it was, and opening the pages and reading . . . and then her secret would be known.

Kate uncapped the little porcelain inkpot and reached for her diary. *I am not jealous,* she wrote. *I refuse to be. Nothing could be more perfect. If anyone can make James happy, it is Lizzie.*

She held the quill between her fingers and read what she had written. There was a knot of something that felt like grief at the back of her throat. "I am not jealous." Her whisper was loud in the cramped, dark space. "I am *not.*"

She just wished it could be different.

# CHAPTER 5

The Honorable Isabella Orton was a handsome woman, and she was also tall, as tall as Kate, and also flat-chested. James glanced surreptitiously at Miss Orton's chest again and wondered how he could tell Kate that he wanted a wife with a bosom. Not necessarily a lush bosom. All he required was something soft and warm that filled his hand and his mouth. Something like—

Resolutely he refused to look at Kate. He had never, until this moment, spared one thought for her breasts, and yet now he found himself desperately wanting to compare them to Miss Orton's. Well, he was *not* going to. Kate's breasts were larger than Miss Orton's, and that was all he needed to know. He was *not* going to look.

Miss Orton laughed at something Kate said. James hadn't been paying attention. He thought they were discussing the upcoming ball.

"She'll make dire pronouncements!" Kate said. Her laugh was almost a giggle.

James stared at her. He'd never associated the words *Kate* and *giggle* together before.

"And she'll glare daggers at anyone who dares to dance the waltz!" Miss Orton said.

Kate's answering smile was almost wicked. "I know."

"The waltz?" James asked.

Both ladies turned to look at him.

"Mrs. Forster thinks that waltzing is a sin," Kate explained. "A *dreadful* sin. And she tells absolutely everyone so. Quite loudly. She holds very strong views."

Miss Orton nodded.

"Have you invited this Mrs. Forster to your ball?" James asked.

"Of course," Kate said.

"And is the waltz to be danced?"

"Of course," Kate said again. Her gray eyes gleamed with laughter.

Her amusement was infectious. James found himself smiling. His gaze strayed down from her laughing eyes, past the disconcertingly delicious mouth, towards her breasts. His throat tightened. It took effort to turn his head away, but he did so. He'd given Kate's breasts no thought in the eleven years he'd known her, and he was *not* about to look at them now.

James clenched his back teeth together and smiled at his hostess. "I look forward to making the acquaintance of the formidable Mrs. Forster. How will I recognize her?"

Isabella Orton laughed. "Merely by listening."

"Well?" said Kate, as the curricle swept down the lane. "Do you like her?"

"Yes," said James. "I like her. But I don't wish to marry her."

Kate turned her head and stared at him, her eyebrows drawn slightly together. "Why not?" she asked. "She's everything you require. She's tall and clever. And she has a sense of humor. She's *nice*."

"Very nice," agreed James. "But I don't want to marry her."

"Why not?"

He shrugged, unable to say that he wished for a wife with a bosom. "I prefer you," he said, refraining from looking at Kate's breasts.

"Why?" she asked. It was clear from her tone that she wouldn't be fobbed off with a vague reply.

"Because . . . because she's too thin."

"Thin!" said Kate indignantly. "You never said anything about thinness."

He shrugged again, and gave the eager team their head. "It didn't occur to me sooner."

She frowned at him. "So you want a wife who's not thin?"

James nodded, completely incapable of telling her why.

One of his horses snorted, and Kate looked as if she'd like to do the same. "Very well," she said. "Miss Hart, tomorrow."

If there was one word to describe Miss Amelia Hart, it was plump. The lady had voluptuous curves. A multitude of voluptuous curves. James glanced at Kate. She met his look. There was a glint of amusement in her eyes and her smile was sharp. Miss Hart, he realized, was Kate's revenge for calling Isabella Orton too thin.

He knew men who'd love to lose themselves in Miss Hart's embrace, but he wasn't one of them. Compared to Kate she was . . . he searched for a word. Ripe. That was it. Too ripe. Delicious to some palates, but unfortunately not his own.

Her bosom was magnificent. Unwillingly, his eyes were drawn to it. If there was one thing Miss Hart wasn't, it was flat-chested.

He'd managed yesterday not to compare Kate with the Honorable Isabella Orton. Today he failed miserably not to compare her to Miss Hart. Despite his best intentions, despite his heartfelt wish not to, James found himself glancing at Kate's chest.

The bodice of her gown was close-fitting and high-waisted, and what he saw beneath the figured muslin made his heart beat faster. Kate didn't have breasts for a man who liked to bury himself in lush and ample flesh, but neither was her bosom as meager as Miss Orton's. Rather, she had breasts formed for someone like himself, a man who preferred to savor his delights in small, sweet, succulent helpings.

His breath caught in his throat and he coughed. Both ladies turned to look at him. James found himself momentarily unable to speak. He coughed again and reached for his teacup. "Excuse me," he managed, and then he drank the amber liquid and found himself in control of his voice again.

Miss Amelia Hart smiled at him, a sweet smile that lit up her pretty, plump face. She had charming dimples. "Would you like more tea, my lord? With lemon, not milk, isn't it?"

"Yes." He passed over his cup. "Thank you."

For the rest of the visit he refrained from looking in Kate's direction. In the curricle, though, it was impossible not to glance at her without being rude.

"Well?" she asked, in what was becoming a familiar interrogation. "What do you think?"

"Not thin," James said.

"No." Kate met his gaze and he clearly saw her amusement. It gleamed in her eyes and hovered on the curve of her mouth.

He turned his attention back to the horses. "Very pleasant, but . . . her charms are too abundant for my liking."

There was silence for at least half a mile. When he glanced sideways at Kate he thought that she was struggling between laughter and annoyance.

"Another requirement?" she asked finally.

"Yes."

"Very well," Kate said. "I'll add it to the list."

"Thank you," James said, relieved that he didn't have to explain himself further.

"*But*," said Kate, in the tone of someone determined to argue, "I think you're being a great deal too particular! Isabella and Amelia are two of my closest friends, and they're *very nice*. You could do much worse than to marry either of them."

"Yes," James said. "The fault is clearly mine."

Kate's eyes narrowed. She didn't look mollified.

"Why are they unmarried?" he asked.

"Isabella . . ." Sadness touched Kate's face, chasing away the annoyance. "Isabella was to be married, but her fiancé . . . he died of the fever, two years ago. It was very hard for her. She hasn't had a Season since. She doesn't wish it."

James thought of handsome Miss Orton and her laughter yesterday with Kate. "I trust she has recovered?"

"I don't know," Kate said. She frowned slightly. "I think so. I *hope* so, because I believe that Mr. Renwick is interested in her."

"Then why did you show her to me?" James asked, with asperity.

His tone appeared to amuse Kate. He thought she suppressed a smile. "Oh, there's no attachment between them," she said. "In fact, I doubt Isabella's even aware of his interest. But . . ."

"But?"

Kate shrugged. "I've seen him watching her at the assemblies."

"Watching? Is that all?"

"So far. I've invited him to the ball. I'm hoping he'll dance with Isabella."

"Matchmaking, Kate?"

Color rose in her cheeks. She didn't deny it. "They would suit each other."

James was tempted to tease her further, but a goat was tethered beside the lane and one of the leaders took exception to the lowly creature. When they were safely past he turned to Kate again. "And Miss Hart? Why isn't she married?"

"Amelia?" A crease formed between Kate's eyebrows. "Too

many men share your opinion, it would seem." There was censure in her voice. "She had a Season, but there were no offers, except for one that was *quite* unacceptable, and since then—" Her mouth tightened. "It's not fair. She's a very nice girl."

The weight of those frowning gray eyes made James uncomfortable. He felt a flicker of guilt for his hasty rejection of Miss Hart. "Why was the offer unacceptable?"

"Mr. Farley," Kate said, grimacing with distaste.

James had an instant image of the elderly dandy as he'd last seen him, strutting around the perimeter of Almack's, his thin face encrusted with cosmetics and his black eyes glittering as he observed the dancing ladies. He could almost smell the man's overpowering scent, heavy and cloying. "He offered marriage?" James was astonished. "I hadn't thought—" Abruptly he recalled himself. "I beg your pardon." Mr. Farley's penchant for ample women was well known, but his offers were generally of a less formal nature and made to ladies of a different class than Miss Hart—and it was *not* a subject he could discuss with Kate.

"He was very taken with Amelia," Kate said. "As I understand it, his attentions were extremely particular. Amelia says she didn't like it at all."

James could well imagine that Miss Hart hadn't liked it. Farnham was a randy old goat. A well-heeled, randy old goat. "Her parents didn't, ah, encourage her to accept the offer?"

"For his money? No. They were as appalled as Amelia." Kate was silent for a short moment, her eyes considering him. The glint of amusement was back. "I'm sure they would find no fault with you, though. Are you quite certain . . . ?"

"Yes," he said firmly. "Quite certain."

Kate's mouth quirked in a manner that was eloquent of her exasperation. James chose to ignore it. "Do you have anyone in mind for Miss Hart?" he asked. "Other than myself?"

"No." There was a sigh in her voice. "I did think, for a while, that Mr. Wood was going to offer for her, but he's not made the *slightest* push . . ."

"Mr. Wood?"

"He purchased Brede Hall a year ago. He's a widower. Not at all handsome, but very personable. Amelia liked him, and I thought that he liked her and that perhaps he'd offer for her, but . . ."

"What happened?"

"Nothing. I must have been mistaken. Although I could have *sworn* . . ." Her lips twisted ruefully, drawing his eyes to them. "My imagination was clearly too active." She shrugged lightly and he almost—almost—looked at her breasts.

James turned his head away abruptly. Kate wasn't the only one with an overly active imagination. His own was telling him that her mouth would be warm and soft and sweet, and that her breasts would be like small, ripe fruit in his hands, smooth and formed perfectly for his taste.

The moment of lust was fleeting and intense—and deeply unsettling. James felt as if, in that second, his world had shifted—and he'd lost his balance. He clenched the reins between his fingers and frowned at the horses. What was wrong with him? Kate was . . . Kate was Kate. He didn't desire her.

"Who do you have for me next?" he asked, slight roughness in his voice.

"Two of the Reverend Charnwood's daughters," Kate said. "The family will be dining with us tomorrow. And then Miss Wilmot is paying a visit."

James risked a sideways glance at her and waited for a repeat of the unwelcome sensation. It didn't come. His relief was profound.

The next morning brought Lizzie's letter, fetched early from the receiving office by a groom. Kate read it sitting up in bed with a rosewood breakfast-tray across her knees. The blue chintz curtains were drawn back from the windows, showing a high, pale, spring sky. Sunlight fell in bright bands across the embroidered counterpane, making the blue and gold silk threads gleam. Kate sipped her cocoa while she deciphered the letter. Lizzie's normally neat hand was an eager scrawl that tumbled across the page, crossed and recrossed, making it a challenge to read.

*I shall depart on the twenty-seventh,* wrote Lizzie, *quite early, and anticipate arriving in the middle of the afternoon. I have been studying my maps until I know the route by heart. By my reckoning it is 68 miles. I look forward to the journey tremendously—and even more to seeing you again, dearest Kate. What fun we shall have together!*

"More than fun, Lizzie," she whispered beneath her breath. "More than fun."

Kate read the letter to the end and then refolded it. She turned her head and stared out of the window, the letter clasped loosely in her hand. Wisps of cloud trailed across a sky the color of duck eggs. How long would it take James to see that Lizzie was the perfect bride for him? How long would it take for him to fall in love with her? Not long, surely. Not long at all.

Kate looked away from the bright, pale sky and discovered that she'd crumpled the letter in her hand. She unclenched her fist and smoothed the creases with her fingers and laid the letter on the breakfast-tray. She had no appetite this morning. The day was fine and she would start it as she always did when she was able, with a ride. A good gallop was what she needed.

They sat down to dine at seven, a late hour by country standards. The Charnwoods were an ever-expanding family and those offspring not in the schoolroom—two sons and three daughters—had accompanied their parents. A white linen cloth covered the mahogany table, laid with a Wedgwood dinner service in green, finger bowls, ivory-handled cutlery, and long-stemmed wineglasses. Beeswax candles burned in the candelabra, their glow reflected in the gilt-framed mirror above the fireplace and in the gleaming silver of the ashets and cover dishes.

Protocol required that James sit on Kate's right, but she had been able to seat the eldest of the Charnwood sisters alongside him. Marianne was a lively young woman of twenty-three years, with rosy cheeks and brown ringlets, who met every one of James's requirements, even the new ones pertaining to figure. She also had the ability to talk, quite cheerfully, for hours.

Kate listened with one ear while Marianne began her conversation with James by mentioning the recent, clement weather. This was followed by an account of a rather muddy picnic she had attended the previous week, a balloon ascension she'd witnessed the summer before last, and a visit to York when she was ten. She then described the most recent book she'd read and launched into a discussion of Greek tragedies that became tangled with an exposition on Shakespeare's works. James followed the erratic track of her conversation, his expression that of a man diverted by a new entertainment.

"Have you come up from London?" Kate heard Marianne ask him.

James opened his mouth to reply.

"Such an *interesting* place. I've never been there, but I have visited York. Several times!"

James closed his mouth and nodded. Kate thought, from his profile, that he was trying not to laugh.

"Did you see the Cossack when he was in Town?" This time Marianne waited for a response.

"Er, who?"

"The Cossack! It was several years ago, to be sure, but . . . you did not see him?"

"No. I believe I missed that pleasure."

"So did I," Marianne said cheerfully. "I hear he was *such* a noble figure. His whiskers! And his *clothes.* And—would you believe it, my lord?—he had a spear quite ten feet long!"

"Oh." James glanced away from Marianne, and Kate clearly saw laughter on his face. He touched two fingers briefly to his lips, as if to remove the amusement from them, but it still gleamed in his eyes. Kate sat slightly back in her chair and studied him obliquely and wondered whether perhaps Marianne Charnwood would suit him as a wife. She hadn't thought of Marianne as a serious contender, but James appeared not to mind her voluble tongue. She was making him laugh . . .

The chicken à la tarragon, which had been so delicious, suddenly tasted like dust in Kate's mouth. She chewed and swallowed and reached for her wineglass, and realized to her shame that she was jealous of Marianne Charnwood. She scolded herself as she sipped the wine. She would be happy for James and Marianne both, if they were to marry—James, because he'd have a wife who would make him laugh, and Marianne because she was nearly on the shelf, poor girl, through no fault of her own.

"My cousin wrote me *all* about it," Marianne said.

James nodded.

"Sophy—my cousin, that is—she was in Town at the time—do you know, she saw the Tower and Madame Tussaud's *and* Weeks' Mechanical Museum—she said there was a mechanical *spider* there—can you imagine such a thing, my lord? A mechanical spider!" Her eyes widened. She asked breathlessly: "Have you seen it?"

James nodded. Kate thought that his mouth quivered slightly.

"Were you frightened?" Marianne didn't wait for an answer. "Sophy said she was! She said she *screamed* when it moved. I shouldn't scream. At least, I don't think I would." Her brow creased as she considered the issue. Then she shook her head. "Anyway, the Cossack! Sophy said she saw him. She said that it was simply marvelous how everyone adored him. She said he wore the *oddest* trousers, and he had the *longest* whiskers, and as for his spear . . ."

Marianne didn't draw breath until the first course was removed. Conversation was interrupted while the servants relaid the table. Kate rinsed her fingers in her finger bowl and watched as James turned to the youngest Miss Charnwood, a shy girl not long out of the schoolroom. "Your sister has been telling me about the picnic last week," he said. "Did you attend too?"

Horatia Charnwood colored and stammered and managed to nod her head.

James smiled kindly at her. "And did you enjoy it?"

Horatia flushed an even brighter red. She didn't attempt to speak, but merely nodded her head again. The girl's embarrassment reminded Kate of herself eleven years ago, when scarlet blushes and stammerings had been all she'd been able to produce in James's company. She could recall, quite vividly, how hideous it had been, and she opened her mouth to divert attention from Horatia.

The Reverend Charnwood beat her to it, leaning forward and asking James a question about his stables. Kate blessed the man and Horatia looked unutterably relieved.

Marianne Charnwood played the pianoforte in a fashion as lively as her conversation. Her singing voice was pretty. James enjoyed the music—and the respite from her company. She'd recaptured his ear when he'd entered the drawing room, and perhaps he'd drunk too much brandy, but he'd found her less diverting than he had at dinner. It wasn't that her conversation was tedious—on the contrary, it was entertaining—but it was also *endless.*

There was a pause, during which Marianne conferred with Kate about the next choice of song. James wanted to lean back in his chair and close his eyes; instead he turned to the younger Misses Charnwood. They sat alongside him on a handsome couch that was in the Grecian style, upholstered in green-and-gold striped silk and with scroll ends. "Do you also play the pianoforte?" He directed his question to Caroline Charnwood and hoped that she wouldn't blush as violently as her younger sister.

"Yes," she said.

"And do you, Miss Horatia?" He smiled politely at the youngest Miss Charnwood.

High color flamed in Horatia Charnwood's cheeks. She sent an agonized glance at her sister, Caroline, who spoke for her: "Yes. We all play the pianoforte. And the harp. I do love the harp, my lord! Don't you?"

"Ah, no. I must confess that the harp is an instrument I'm not fond of."

Caroline Charnwood immediately agreed with him: "Yes, of course. I find that I often dislike it, too."

James blinked and barely managed not to stare at her. "And . . . do you sing?"

Caroline Charnwood shook her head. She was a paler version of her elder sister, her coloring fairer and her manner lacking in liveliness. "I haven't the voice for it. But I do enjoy listening to others sing. The sung word is more eloquent than the spoken, don't you think, my lord? I quite prefer the opera to the theater!"

"My preference is for the theater," James confessed.

"Oh, but of course," she said instantly. "The theater is superior to the opera. I can't think why I said it wasn't."

There was a short pause. James endeavored not to display his bemusement.

"Have you seen Kean perform?" Caroline Charnwood asked.

"Yes. He has a remarkable talent."

"Yes!" She rushed eagerly to agree with him. "I hear his Shylock is quite extraordinary."

Her elder sister began to play another piece. James returned his attention to the pianoforte. He drummed the fingers of one hand on his knee. If he was not mistaken, Caroline Charnwood had twice changed her opinions to coincide with his. He took in the drawing room with a frowning glance, the walls a soft yellow and the carpet a particularly fine Savonnerie with curling green fern fronds against a pale yellow background. Did Caroline agree with everyone, or was it merely him?

During the next pause in the music, he politely turned to the Misses Charnwood again. Horatia avoided meeting his eyes, but Caroline smiled prettily at him. James found himself unable to think of anything original to say. He resorted to the weather: "A mild spring, we're having, isn't it? Very pleasant."

"Oh, yes," replied Caroline, since speech was clearly beyond Horatia's abilities. "Most pleasant. I do love the sunshine. It's so welcome after winter! It quite lifts my spirits."

A devil prompted him, spurred on perhaps by the quantity of brandy he'd consumed after dinner. "But the sunshine grows monotonous, don't you think?" he said. "Some rain would be agreeable."

Caroline Charnwood blinked and then nodded her head. "You're quite correct, my lord. The sunshine does become tedious. Some rain would be pleasant."

"Or even sleet," he said blandly.

"Yes, of course." She agreed with him without faltering. "Sleet would make a refreshing change." Beside her, her sister's eyes widened in astonishment.

James choked back laughter, and coughed into his hand. "Excuse me."

Horatia Charnwood glanced at him. There was no suspicion in those hazel eyes, merely confusion, but James lost the urge to laugh. His conduct was ungentlemanly. Caroline Charnwood might have more hair than wit, but it wasn't for him to make fun of her.

Horatia Charnwood averted her gaze, seemingly over-whelmed by the act of meeting his eyes. Color stained her cheeks. James suppressed a sigh and wished that he was back in the dining room, discussing horseflesh with the Reverend Charnwood and drinking Harry's brandy. Horatia Charnwood reminded him strongly of Kate at the same age. Kate, too, had been embarrassed beyond speech whenever he'd tried to talk to her, and yet she'd watched him as Horatia did, sending shy, sideways glances in his direction and blushing hotly if he intercepted them. It had been painful for everyone, and he'd been exceedingly thankful when Kate had outgrown her calf love. Not that he thought Miss Horatia was smitten with him. Her glances were scared rather than lovelorn, as if he was a terrifying ogre and she watched to make sure he didn't pounce. He guessed that she was very newly liberated from the schoolroom.

James looked across at Kate, laughing over the selection of music with Harry and Marianne and the eldest Charnwood boy, a youth of nineteen years whose name he'd forgotten. There was some argument, it appeared, about which piece should be played next. The group at the pianoforte beckoned to Caroline Charnwood. "Excuse me," she said, rising.

Abandoned by her sister, Horatia shrank back on the couch. She was clearly terrified that she would be called upon to converse with him.

James suppressed another sigh.

Kate crossed the room, elegant in a gown of smoke-blue silk with small puffed sleeves and *appliqué* above the scalloped hem. She took the vacated seat and bent her head and spoke to Horatia Charnwood. James failed to hear the words, for her tone was low, but he saw the grateful smile that lit the girl's face. Horatia rose and went to sit beside her mother, near the fireplace.

"Thank you," said James, as Kate turned to him.

"For what?"

"Rescuing me from Horatia Charnwood."

Kate laughed. "Why would you need rescuing?"

"She makes me feel like an ogre," he said, his tone slightly sour. He disliked being an object of terror. It wasn't as if he'd frowned at the chit. All he'd done was smile.

"Not an ogre," said Kate, clearly amused. "Merely the finest gentleman she's ever seen." She appraised him with a quick and indifferent glance. "You're extremely handsome tonight, James, *and* you're an earl. Naturally she's nervous." Having uttered these astonishing words, Kate turned her attention towards the pianoforte.

James glanced involuntarily down at his dark blue coat and cream satin waistcoat and tight-fitting knee breeches. Handsome? His eyebrows drew together in annoyance. It wasn't the compliment that displeased him; rather it was the complete disinterest in Kate's voice as she had uttered it. She might as well have been discussing the weather as his appearance.

And when had he become so conceited that he wished for compliments that were delivered with a degree of enthusiasm?

James frowned at Kate. Her hair was dressed in an elaborate topknot of braids, with long curls framing her face. Unwillingly, he noticed again how lovely her profile was. Her features were neatly balanced, almost classical in their purity. It unsettled him that it had taken him eleven years to notice this fact about her. And it wasn't just her profile that he'd failed to see. It was the curve of her eyebrows, the high cheekbones, the angle of her jaw and the line of her throat. And it was her mouth, the one that was so unexpectedly kissable.

James realized, to his astonishment, that beneath the freckles Kate was beautiful. Either that, or he was drunk.

Kate turned her head. Her expression became amused. "Stop scowling at me," she whispered.

James discovered that he couldn't.

# CHAPTER 6

"Well?" Kate asked the following morning. Her expression was expectant as she turned towards him. He'd found her in the library, seated at a large desk and surrounded by lists. The elegant silk gown had been replaced by a simple one of muslin with a delicate stripe woven into it.

"Not Marianne Charnwood." Obliquely, he surveyed her face. The loveliness of feature that he'd seen last night was no longer evident. Kate's face was put together nicely enough, but she wasn't beautiful. The wine and brandy must have clouded his mind to make him think so. "And not her sister."

"Not Caroline? Why not?"

"She agreed with everything I said. Tell me, Kate, does she do that to everyone, or is it just me?"

Kate's brow furrowed as she thought. "Caroline does have a tendency to agree with people. She is easily persuaded to change her mind. Her disposition is very . . . compliant."

"Hmph," said James. He lowered himself into a leather armchair and stretched out his legs.

"You don't like being agreed with?"

"Not to that extent."

"But think, James. A wife who never argues, who never contradicts—"

"Would be exceedingly boring!"

"You want arguments?" Her eyebrows rose.

"Not necessarily. But what I *don't* want is a wife who only says what she thinks I want to hear. Think how uncomfortable it would be, Kate."

"Oh," Kate said. "I hadn't thought— Yes, I quite see it would be uncomfortable. Very well, I'll remove Caroline from the list. And . . . I gather Marianne talked too much for your taste?"

"Definitely."

"But she made you laugh."

"Several times. Her conversation is very entertaining."

"But . . . ?"

James leaned back in the armchair and steepled his fingers and frowned as he recalled Marianne Charnwood's endless chatter. She'd skipped from one subject to another, barely stopping to draw breath, her comments and observations sometimes naïve, sometimes shrewd, and frequently amusing. She clearly had a lively and inquiring mind, but . . . "Is she ever quiet, Kate?"

"Very rarely."

"Then she's definitely off the list."

Kate rifled through the papers on the desk and drew one towards her. She dipped her quill in ink and crossed out one item, and then a second, on what James guessed was the list of names. He wondered how many candidates remained.

"So that makes two new requirements," Kate said, pulling another sheet of paper towards her. "Not too talkative, and not too compliant."

He nodded. "Yes."

The quill moved briskly as she wrote. "Honestly, James," she said, faint amusement in her voice. "Your list of requirements grows longer every day. You are a great deal too *fastidious*. You really should consider modeling yourself on Mr. Collins!" She paused in her writing and looked up. Her gray eyes seemed to be focused on something behind him. "There is Miss Shield," she said slowly. "I didn't put her on the list, but . . ." She tapped the quill against her chin, thoughtfully.

"Miss Shield?" he asked, watching as the feather brushed below her lower lip. *Tap tap.* Kate still had a surprisingly kissable mouth. He'd not imagined that last night, however much else he'd imagined.

Her attention snapped back to him and she stilled the movement of the quill. "She's a trifle . . . forceful. Definitely not compliant, and definitely not timid. Your frowns won't scare her and she won't agree with you just for the sake of it."

"Why isn't she on the list?"

Kate tapped the feather against her chin again, drawing his eyes to her mouth. "She'd manage Elvy Park admirably," she said, and he watched her lips shape the words. "But . . . her manner is somewhat domineering. I should warn you that she'd probably tell not only your servants what to do, but you as well, and most likely your neighbors too!" Kate paused, watching him. The quill went *tap tap* against her chin. "Would you like to meet her?"

"No," James said, wrenching his gaze from her mouth. "Definitely not. I have no wish to live under the cat's paw."

"She's a very handsome woman."

He narrowed his eyes at her. "No."

"I didn't think so." Kate shrugged. "She'll be at the ball, if you should change your mind. I'll introduce you."

"I don't think that will be necessary," James said.

Kate's eyes gleamed. "Faint-hearted, James?" There was laughter in her voice, and for a moment she was lovely. It was more than her mouth. It was the golden eyebrows, arched now in amusement, and the small, straight nose. It was the curve of her cheek and the line of her throat and the shining gray eyes. It was everything.

James looked away from Kate and managed, barely, not to frown. *I'm going mad,* he thought as he inspected the sleeves of his olive-green riding coat, straightening them at the wrist although it wasn't necessary. What were they talking about? Oh, the ball. "Who else will be there?"

"The Bellersbys are coming. The Ortons and the Inghams. The Charnwoods, of course—"

He looked back at Kate. To his relief, her face was ordinary again. "Horatia Charnwood?" he asked, remembering the girl's fiery blushes and inability to speak to him. "I shall take care to avoid her."

"Stop being so craven!" Kate said. "If you survived me at that age, then you can easily survive Horatia. I was *much* worse."

The comment was so unexpected that he almost gaped at her. "I beg your pardon?"

"Did I ever apologize for being such a goose?" Kate's voice was amused and self-deprecating, lightly flippant.

He shook his head.

Kate smiled at him, wryly, and again he caught the flash of beauty he'd seen earlier. "Then I apologize now."

James shook his head a second time. "Not necessary," he managed to say.

"Horatia would benefit from a Season," Kate said, turning back to her lists. "It would help cure her of her shyness."

"Won't she have one?"

Kate shook her head. "The Charnwoods haven't a feather to fly with. They can barely afford a good education for their sons. A Season for Marianne, let alone Horatia, is quite out of the question." She shuffled her lists together. "What they need is a wealthy husband for one of their daughters. Someone who won't mind a dowerless bride." She glanced at him. "Are you quite certain . . . ?"

"Quite," he said firmly.

"Do you perhaps know someone who would suit Marianne?" Her tone was hopeful.

"Matchmaking again, Kate?"

"No, it's just . . . Marianne's twenty-three. Practically on the shelf, poor girl. I should like to see her married. I know she wishes it." She turned the quill over in her fingers, frowning thoughtfully. "It would have to be someone who doesn't

mind her chatter. Someone who *likes* it, even. I wonder . . ."
She tapped the feather against her chin again. James's eyes
followed the movement. Kate really had a mouth that begged
to be kissed.

But not by him.

Voices sounded in the hall. To James's relief, Kate put
down her quill. "That sounds like Eudora," she said.

"Tell me about her."

"She's twenty," Kate said, as she stood. "Her mother died
some years ago. Her father's an absent-minded scholar."

Kate had heard Eudora Wilmot called a bluestocking, but
only by those who were intimidated by her intellectual attain-
ments. The term was inaccurate; although Eudora was highly
educated, she was neither poorly dressed nor lacking in social
graces, quite unlike her father who—when he ventured out in
public—was clearly both. Kate was of the opinion that if Mr.
Wilmot had cared to give his daughter a Season, she would
be married by now. Eudora's face, if not pretty, came very close
to it, and her manners were charming. She met every one of
James's requirements, including the latest two, and, despite
having flaxen hair when James had said he preferred darker
coloring, Kate thought that Eudora had a fair chance of fixing
his attention.

They took refreshments in one of the smaller saloons, a
room decorated in green and with a fine view of the pleasure
gardens. Eudora soon discovered that James had fought on
the Peninsula. Kate frowned and tried to introduce a new
topic of conversation. For a man who'd been mentioned in
the dispatches (for his part in the action at Benavente), James
was remarkably reticent about his war experiences. Perhaps
he discussed them with Harry, but he'd never said more than

a word or two in her hearing, and then only in passing. She had a feeling he wouldn't enjoy talking about such things over cake and tea.

But Eudora refused to be diverted. "A hussar?" she exclaimed. "The Prince of Wales's Own? How splendid! I wish I were a man and could go to war!"

"You do?" James's eyebrows slanted together.

"Oh, yes," Eudora said. "The *excitement* of it. The glory!"

James frowned formidably. "Glory?"

"Miss Wilmot has been working on her own translation of the *Iliad*." Kate hurriedly changed the subject. "Haven't you, Eudora?"

"Yes," Eudora said. "Such a thrilling piece of work!"

Kate recalled—belatedly—that the *Iliad* contained a great many graphic and bloody battle scenes. "Eudora has also translated the writings of Pliny," she said, turning to James. "His account of the eruption of Vesuvius is fascinating, I always think. Don't you, James?"

"Yes," he said, eyeing Eudora. "Quite fascinating." The frown was gone from his face, but he was unsmiling.

"Pliny is all very well," Eudora said. "But Homer is something else entirely. Such language! Such vivid imagery!" She put down her teacup and began to quote:

*Wedged in the trench, in one vast carnage bruised:*
*Chariots on chariots roll; the clashing spokes*
*Shake, while the madding steeds break short their yokes . . .*

She turned to Kate, her cheeks flushed. "Can't you *feel* it, Kate? Doesn't it make your blood stir? Is it not exciting!"

"Well . . ." said Kate. She cast a glance at James. He was looking at Eudora as if she had suddenly grown another head.

Eudora didn't wait for her answer. "Or this!" she cried, clasping her hands together.

*Tumultuous clamor fills the fields and skies;*
*Thick drifts of dust involve their rapid flight;*
*Clouds rise on clouds, and heaven is snatched from sight . . .*

Eudora drew a deep, quivering breath. Her blue eyes shone.

"Can't you *taste* the dust, Kate? Can't you *see* it?" She turned in her chair to face James. "Oh, how I envy you, my lord!"

"Why?" James asked bluntly.

Eudora widened her eyes at him. "You've been in battle. How glorious it must have been. How romantic!"

"There's nothing romantic about the battlefield, Miss Wilmot, unless you find blood and mud and death romantic." James's voice held a bite.

Eudora blinked.

"We have several pineapples growing in the succession houses," Kate said, desperately. "They're our first ones. Do come and see them, Eudora." She stood.

Eudora looked from her to James and back again. Her expression was confused.

Kate risked a glance at James. The angle of his jaw was particularly grim and there was anger in his eyes. "Come, Eudora," she said. "They're such comical things. You really must see them."

Eudora stood and allowed herself to be led from the saloon. Kate shut the door on James's rigid countenance.

"Romantic?" she said in the corridor, turning to Eudora. "You think that war is romantic?"

"Of course," Eudora said. "Don't you?"

Kate shook her head.

"But . . . how can you not?" Eudora seemed baffled. She laid a hand on her breast and recited in a low, breathless voice:

*"Loud over the rout was heard the victor's cry*
*Where the war bleeds, and where the thickest die,*
*Where horse, and arms, and chariots lie overthrown,*
*And bleeding heroes under axles groan . . ."*

She paused, her lips parted and her cheeks flushed with color. "Now, tell me Kate—is that not exciting? Is it not romantic?"

Kate stared at her. No. It was *not* romantic. She opened her mouth to argue this point, and looked at Eudora's wide and uncomprehending blue eyes and gave up the notion. "Come and see the pineapples," she said.

"I apologize," she said to James, once Eudora had departed. He stood at one of the windows in the saloon and stared out over the pleasure gardens. She couldn't see his face, but from the set of his shoulders she thought he was still angry.

James turned and watched as she closed the door. His expression was unsmiling. "*Romantic?*" He almost spat out the word. "How can war be romantic? It's blood and filth. It's men screaming. It's—" His jaw clenched. When he spoke again his voice was flat, although no less angry: "It's not romantic."

"I know," Kate said, her fingers resting on the door handle. "I'm very sorry, James. I had no idea Eudora held such views. It's not a subject I've ever discussed with her."

James frowned at her. "Do you think war is romantic?"

"Of course not."

His mouth twisted, his lips thinning. "It's an ugly business," he said, turning back to the window. "Ugly."

Stupidly, Kate felt like crying. Not because of James's anger, but because of the pain that so clearly lay beneath it. Her fingers tightened on the door handle.

"Miss Wilmot is off the list," he said, his voice harsh. "She may be able to read Greek and Latin, but she has no *sense.*"

Kate said nothing.

There was silence, while the clock on the mantelpiece ticked. Long seconds passed. James turned to face her again. The anger seemed to drain from him as he stared at her. Silhouetted against the window he no longer looked furious, merely bleak and weary. "War is butchery," he said quietly. "It's panic and terror and . . ." He halted. She thought a flicker of nausea crossed his face. He inhaled shallowly. "I've seen things, Kate. I've done things . . ." He swallowed. "I've killed men. You know that, don't you?"

She nodded.

"I can still remember some of their faces." He turned away from her abruptly and looked out at the gardens again. His figure was as strong and tall as ever, but there was something in the way he held himself, in the line of his neck and tilt of his head, the tension in his shoulders, that made Kate want to put her arms around him and hold him tightly. Grief choked in her throat.

She had no illusions about war. She knew it was ugly, but until this moment, listening to James, she'd not realized quite *how* ugly. Three times his regiment had sailed to fight Napoleon's army. She'd feared, each time, that he wouldn't return. He had, but never as quite the same man. The reckless, merry, dashing young officer had become someone older and quieter, more serious—and until this moment she'd not realized how hard won that maturity had been.

Kate released the door handle. More than anything, she wanted to go to James and hold him. Instead she walked across the room to stand beside him. She placed her hand lightly on the sleeve of his coat. The olive-green superfine was smooth beneath her fingers and warm from the heat of his body. "I'm sorry," she said. The words were terribly inadequate.

James shook his head, staring out of the window. For a moment they stood side by side in silence, her hand on his arm, then he spoke: "I thought as Miss Wilmot did once." He turned his head to look at her. His brown eyes were harder than she'd ever seen them. "I was as foolish as she is."

Kate shook her head, aware of the heat of James's arm beneath her fingers. She wanted, quite desperately, to tell him that she loved him. She bit the inside of her lip.

"The first time I rode to battle I was as eager as a child waiting for Christmas." He returned his gaze to the gardens. His jaw clenched briefly. "I never was again. I was always afraid. Always."

Her mind supplied a place and date for that event: Sahagún, Spain. December 1808. More than seven years ago. "Then you have great courage," she said.

His head swung around. His eyes were narrow beneath frowning eyebrows. "Don't paint me as a hero, Kate, for I'm not!"

Kate studied his face. She saw anger and bitterness, and great strength. "What is heroism, James?"

He stared at her for a long and silent moment. The fierceness of his scowl faded. She thought that uncertainty came into his eyes. "I don't know," he said, finally.

Kate knew. And she knew that James possessed it. It wasn't the swaggering heroism of Homer's heroes and it had nothing to do with the feat of valor that had earned him a mention in the dispatches. It was something quieter, something that required deep levels of courage. If he had been afraid and yet still fought, then he was very much a hero.

James turned away from the window, a movement that caused her hand to slide from his sleeve. "Excuse me, Kate. I'm going for a ride."

James rode hard, pushing Saladin, taking risks he normally wouldn't. He was angry at himself, furious, and that black emotion rode him as mercilessly as he rode the stallion. The anger wasn't directed at Miss Wilmot, although he'd been furious with her in the saloon. How could he condemn her foolishness when he'd started his military career with dreams of excitement and glory? He'd been older than she was when his father had purchased him his colors. Twenty-one—and a fool.

James rode until there was a glaze of sweat over his skin and Saladin showed signs of tiring. He let the stallion slacken his thundering pace. They slowed to a canter and then a walk and then finally halted, both breathing hard. James leaned forward in the saddle and laid one hand on the horse's damp neck. He shut his eyes for a moment and felt Saladin's strength and heat and life through his riding glove. He'd lost several horses in the fighting, two alone at Waterloo, one of them killed outright and the other not so lucky.

And he'd lost more than horses. He'd lost men. Friends. Rupert.

The scent of death came to him for a moment, nauseating. The muscles in his throat became rigid.

James opened his eyes and saw gentle hills green with the beginnings of spring growth, and woodland and a church tower behind the trees and a high, pale blue sky. This was no smoking, muddy battlefield, heaving with figures and rent with screams and gunfire. He straightened in the saddle and inhaled, filling his lungs with air that was untainted by cannon smoke and the reek of death. Artillery didn't roar here; instead there was birdsong and the lowing of cattle and a dog barking in the distance.

The memory of carnage retreated before the peaceful sights and sounds and scents of the English countryside. His tension eased and the nausea retreated. "England," he said, beneath his breath, while the sweat of his hard ride cooled on his skin. "Soft, green England."

# $C$HAPTER 7

$L$izzie arrived in a bright yellow post-chaise drawn by four horses. "Oh, Kate!" she cried, as they embraced. "I had the most fabulous journey! I wish you could have been with me. There was so much to see!"

Kate laughed.

Lizzie laughed back at her, her eyes bright and excited. "Thank you for inviting me," she said.

Kate clasped her friend's hands. "Thank you for coming." She wished that James was here. Lizzie's gown became her beautifully, even though it was old and made over. The muslin was rose-colored, the perfect complement to her dark eyes and ringlets, and if James saw her now, with her flushed cheeks and laughing mouth and shining eyes, how could he fail to fall in love with her? But unfortunately James had ridden over to the Home Farm with Harry to view some improvements. The only admirers of Lizzie's prettiness were the servants: two post-boys, the butler, the footmen, and the little maidservant whom Mr. Penrose had sent to accompany his daughter in the chaise and who was to return to Derbyshire on the stage tomorrow.

"Come inside," Kate said. "Are you tired, Lizzie? Would you like to lie down, perhaps?"

"Oh, no," Lizzie said. "Not tired!"

Kate laughed again. "Refreshments and a tour of the Hall, then. Or perhaps a walk in the gardens?"

"The gardens," Lizzie said. Her gaze flicked up to the façade of the house, built of red brick and with ivy staking its claim on the walls. She lowered her voice to a whisper that the servants couldn't hear: "I hadn't realized that Merrell Hall was quite so large. And the park!"

"Six miles around," Kate said. "Beautiful, isn't it? I shall show you all the walks."

Assured that the little maid would be safely delivered into the housekeeper's care, Lizzie climbed the steps and set foot over the threshold. Her eyes widened as she glanced around the entrance hall with its limestone-flagged floor and handsome plasterwork, and she hesitated for a second. Kate realized that to someone who came from a cottage in Derbyshire, gentleman's daughter or no, Merrell Hall must seem terribly grand. She slipped her arm through Lizzie's. "I can't tell you how glad I am that you've come," she said. "We shall have such fun!"

She led Lizzie up the sweeping staircase, and through the Long Gallery to the bedrooms. "Do you like it, Lizzie?" she asked, showing her the bedchamber that had been prepared. "There's a green one, if you'd prefer."

"No. This is lovely." Lizzie looked around. The chamber was a comfortable size, with a dressing table and washstand and chest of drawers, and a wardrobe in one corner and a tall mirror in another. Stripes of apricot and cream decorated the wallpaper, and the colors were repeated in the chintz curtains at the windows. Hangings of apricot damask framed the bed, and the counterpane was embroidered in a similar shade of silk thread.

Lizzie walked over to one of the windows and stood a moment, gazing out at the park, before turning back to face the room. "This is much finer than I'd thought." Her voice was hesitant. "I didn't realize. Kate—"

"Don't feel out of place, Lizzie," Kate begged. "Please don't! It's only a house."

Lizzie smoothed her gown. She had quite lost her sparkle.

Kate crossed the room. She took hold of her friend's hands. "Please, Lizzie."

"But my gowns are all made over," Lizzie said in a shamed whisper.

Kate drew her over to stand in front of the mirror. "Look," she said. "You suit this room much better than I."

Lizzie looked doubtfully at her image in the giltwood frame.

Kate watched, thinking that Lizzie would look beautiful even if she was dressed in a sack. Beneath the dark, glossy ringlets, Lizzie's face was lovely. Her brown eyes were large and expressive—lashes long and brows delicately arched—her nose was small and pretty, and her mouth sweetly curved. No freckles marred her smooth, creamy skin.

Kate glanced at her own image, and then away again. The contrast between Lizzie's beauty and her own plainness was painful. "Don't worry about your gowns, please, Lizzie. It doesn't matter whether they're made over or not. You look so lovely that no one will notice."

Harry certainly wouldn't notice, and she doubted James would either. In fact, she was certain that neither man would see anything beyond Lizzie's face and her fine figure. The vintage of her gowns would be of no interest to them.

"Paton will love you," Kate said, smiling at Lizzie in the mirror. "My maid. I'll share her with you while you're here."

"Oh, no! I'm used to dressing myself. I couldn't possibly—"

"Nonsense. Paton will be delighted. You are a much finer canvas for her to work on than I!"

Lizzie wore a white gown trimmed with a double pleating of pink ribbon to dinner. The gown was made over, but still she was extraordinarily lovely. A vision, no less. Kate smiled secretly to herself as they made their way down the staircase. She couldn't wait to see the men's faces when they set eyes on Lizzie for the first time. She was *much* prettier than the Duchess of Edgeton.

It was the custom of the house to gather in one of the smaller saloons prior to dinner. James and Harry were already there, talking in low voices. Kate thought she caught the words *crop* and *rotation*. Both men turned their heads and she watched in delight as their eyes found Lizzie. It was everything she'd hoped for. Harry, who'd been speaking, stopped abruptly, his mouth hanging open. He shut it again quickly and stood. James, leaning against the carved marble mantelpiece, blinked. He straightened and glanced at Kate.

Kate made the introductions and then moved to stand beside James while her brother welcomed Lizzie to his country seat.

"Well?" she asked, under her breath. "Do you like my surprise?"

"Yes," he said, his eyes on Lizzie. "I believe I do."

Kate thought that Lizzie was a little shy to find herself dining with a viscount *and* an earl, but Harry soon had her smiling, and by the end of the first course she was laughing at his jokes, looking flushed and pretty in the candlelight. Kate watched James watch Lizzie. There was a thoughtful half smile on his mouth.

"Well?" she asked in a whisper, under cover of the dishes being removed.

James's expression became amused. "Impatient, Kate?"

Kate had to be content with that, and with the fact that James's eyes rested often on Lizzie. She mentally reviewed the list of his requirements while she ate, and turned the conversation to travel, a subject that set Lizzie talking enthusiastically.

Kate met James's eyes for a moment and tried not to look smug.

After the meal, Lizzie and Kate left the men to their brandy. A fire burned in the hearth in the drawing room and the pale yellow walls glowed warmly in the candlelight. Lizzie sat on one of the striped green-and-yellow silk couches and smoothed her gown over her lap. Her eyes were bright and her cheeks rosy. The age of her gown no longer appeared to distress her.

"Your brother looks just like you," Lizzie said. "The resemblance is extraordinary."

"Freckles and red hair." Kate managed not to grimace.

"No," Lizzie shook her head. "I mean, yes, that too, but I was thinking more about your faces. They're the same shape, and you have identical smiles."

"Oh," Kate said. She sat alongside Lizzie. "Really?"

Lizzie nodded. "Yes. Very nice."

"What?" Kate said, taken aback. "Nice?"

Lizzie went into a peal of laughter, and Kate wished that James could hear it. Or maybe not. Perhaps Lizzie had consumed too many glasses of wine.

Lizzie repeated her astonishing remark once she'd stopped laughing. "You have nice faces, you and your brother."

"Nonsense," Kate said. "We have freckles." Harry even more so than herself. His face was covered in them.

"No." Lizzie stood, dragging Kate up with her. She turned towards the mirror that hung above the marble fireplace. "Look."

Kate glanced at her reflection within the gilded frame. She shook her head. "I don't see it." All she saw were freckles. To use Sir Thomas Granger's words, she was bran-faced, and no amount of Roman balsam or Gowland's lotion would remove the blemishes. She'd tried. Lord knew she'd tried.

Lizzie's mouth tucked in at the corners in exasperation. Even frowning, she was pretty. "Ignore the freckles," she said. "Look at the *shape,* Kate."

Kate looked, and shook her head again. The freckles were impossible to ignore. They disfigured her face. She turned away from the mirror.

"Well, *I* think you have a very nice face," Lizzie said, in the tone of someone stating an incontrovertible fact.

"Thank you." Kate sat. "And what about Lord Arden's face? Do you like it, too?"

"He's very handsome," Lizzie admitted, as she sat again. "Isn't he?"

"Yes," Kate said. "Very."

Harry and James made an early entrance into the drawing room, proposing a game of Speculation or Commerce, or even jackstraws.

"Jackstraws!" Kate laughed.

Harry grinned and shrugged, his eyes on Lizzie. "Which would you prefer, Miss Penrose?"

"Speculation, please."

"Speculation it is, then. I'll set out the table."

Kate followed her brother across the room, to where the round card table stood. "Did James say anything about Lizzie?" she asked under her breath. "Does he like her?"

Harry rummaged in a drawer and pulled out a pack of cards. "How could he not?" he said, in an equally low voice. He glanced across the room. "Well done, Kate."

Kate followed the direction of his gaze. James stood by the fire, talking to Lizzie. He was smiling down at her, his eyes on her face. They made an extremely handsome pair.

Kate felt a pain in her chest. She told herself it was indigestion and looked away.

Harry placed the cards on the baize surface of the table. "Why have you never invited her before?"

"I have," said Kate. "Many times. But her mother was an invalid and Lizzie would never leave her."

"Was an invalid? Has she recovered, or . . . ?"

Kate shook her head. "She passed away last year. Lizzie's only just out of black gloves."

"Ah," Harry said. His eyes turned again to Lizzie. "I see."

"We had settled on summer for her visit, but I thought, what with James needing a wife—"

"Yes," said Harry. "Too good an opportunity to miss. Does she know?"

Kate shook her head. "I'm hoping for a love match between them."

"You may well get one," Harry said, watching as James said something that made Lizzie blush prettily. "James has a great deal of address. And Miss Penrose is . . ." His voice trailed off.

Kate said nothing. She began to lay out the card table.

Miss Penrose was a very pleasant surprise. James observed her across the breakfast table. She was quite the best of Kate's candidates. She met all his requirements, and she was extremely pretty into the bargain.

He glanced at Kate and found her watching him. Her gaze was questioning. She was eager, he knew, to hear his opinion of her friend.

James smiled blandly at her, and resumed buttering his warm roll.

The breakfast parlor was a cheerful room, with white plasterwork and walls of Pompeian red. French windows with long, fringed curtains opened onto the terrace. Harry invited his guests outside for a stroll in the morning air when they'd eaten their fill. He offered his arm to Miss Penrose, who accepted with a pretty smile. James turned to Kate. "Well?"

"Exactly," said Kate. "*Well?*"

He laughed, and gave her his arm. "She is the best yet," he admitted, in a low voice.

"Yes," said Kate. "Isn't she? I knew you'd like her. She's perfect!"

James looked to where Miss Penrose stood with Harry, looking out over the park. Yes, she was perfect. Or, if not perfect, then very close to it. He glanced back at Kate. "I don't know . . ." he said in a doubtful tone, teasing her.

Kate didn't rise to his bait. "Lizzie meets all your criteria," she said, with calm confidence. "She's neither too young nor too girlish. She's not timid and she doesn't giggle in excess. She has sense, *and* a sense of humor—and she likes to travel."

"True," he conceded.

"She's not too short. And her figure is neither too ample nor too thin."

James turned his eyes back to Miss Penrose. She reminded him of his pretty opera dancer, Bella. "No," he said. "Neither too ample nor too thin."

"And she's a gentleman's daughter," Kate pointed out. "*And* she's pretty!"

James studied Miss Penrose. Yes, she was undeniably pretty, and she had refreshing lack of vanity for one so well-favored. She was a young lady of manifold charms and virtues.

"What more could you want?"

"Nothing," James said, his eyes on Miss Penrose. He said it again firmly, to convince himself: "Nothing. You're correct. She's perfect."

"I knew it!" Kate's voice was delighted. When he turned his head he saw that she was grinning. He stared at her mouth, watching while the grin faded to a smile. Such a beautiful mouth.

James wrenched his eyes away, back to Miss Penrose. "How do you know her?"

"Lizzie? She's a neighbor of one of my oldest friends, Charlotte. They live within sight of one another."

"Charlotte?" Dimly he recalled a Charlotte, a plump girl with quantities of fair curls who'd run tame at Merrell Hall many years ago. "Miss . . ." He racked his brain. "Miss Lacey?"

"Yes," said Kate. "She married a gentleman who lives in Derbyshire. I visit every year."

James nodded, his eyes still on Miss Penrose. She was a prime article, to use vulgar parlance. He wondered why she was unmarried. She looked to be at least three-and-twenty. "Why is Miss Penrose unwed?"

"In part because she didn't wish to leave her mother. Mrs. Penrose was an invalid. She passed away last year."

"An invalid?" James raised his eyebrows, surprised that someone who possessed such glowing health and vitality could have had an invalid for a parent.

"Yes," Kate said. "And also, I think, because none of the offers were . . ." He glanced at her in time to see her nose wrinkle. "The neighborhood is rather restricted."

"Has she not had a London Season?"

"No," said Kate. "Her family's circumstances are somewhat straitened."

"Hmm." James examined Miss Penrose again. Her gown, now that he noted it, wasn't in the latest fashion.

"But that wouldn't weigh with you, would it, James?"

He shook his head, his eyes still on Miss Penrose. His fortune was large enough for a dowerless wife and any number of indigent relatives. There were far more important things to be sought in a bride than fortune. Or rank, for that matter. His parents' marriage had taught him that.

"If . . ." Kate's voice was tentative. "If you could exert yourself only a *little,* James, I believe you could easily capture Lizzie's affections."

James turned his head to stare at her.

"If you want to, that is." Kate flushed. "I don't mean to . . . to dictate what you should do."

"Are you suggesting that I pay court to Miss Penrose?" he asked, in a disbelieving tone.

Kate's flush deepened. "Would it be so difficult?"

James said nothing. He stared at her, unable to make up his mind whether to be annoyed or amused.

"Well, would it?"

James looked back at Miss Penrose. No, it wouldn't be

difficult. Quite easy, in fact. Miss Penrose was a delightful young lady, in her manner equally as well as her person. He could find no fault with her. To have her as his wife would be most pleasant. He imagined her holding onto his arm, laughing up at him, standing on tiptoe for his kisses. "I shall think about it," he said.

"Thank you," Kate said. She moved away from him, walking along the terrace until she stood beside her brother and her friend. James stayed where he was, his eyebrows drawn thoughtfully together. Could he have a love match with Miss Penrose? He thought it was possible. His frown lightened. Pay court to Miss Penrose? Why not?

Miss Penrose and Kate began to walk further along the terrace, arm in arm. Harry accompanied them. James followed slowly, watching Miss Penrose. She had a very pretty figure, but—

His eyes moved to Kate, noting the differences between her and her friend. Miss Penrose was plumper than Kate, although not even the harshest of critics could call her heavy. Her figure was pleasing, but to his eye Kate's was even more pleasing. She was several inches taller than Miss Penrose, and he liked that extra height. Strange, he'd always thought of Kate as gawky, but she most definitely wasn't. Somehow, without him noticing, she'd grown comfortable with her height. Where she'd been awkward as an adolescent, he saw now that her posture was elegant and her movements graceful. More graceful than Miss Penrose's.

His eyes slid from one lady to the other, preferring the lines and curves of Kate to those of her friend. He frowned, noting that Kate's silk-clad ankles, glimpsed beneath the flounced hem of her gown, were slim and shapely, and superior to Miss Penrose's. And the line of her throat was slender and quite lovely. And her profile, when she turned her head—

James stopped on the terrace and closed his eyes for a moment. It was wrong of him to look at Kate like this. She had made it quite clear that she didn't wish to marry him. Miss Penrose would be his bride, not Kate.

When Kate told Lizzie about the ball, later that morning, she became quite pale. "But I don't have anything I can wear."

"Don't worry, Lizzie." Kate smiled. "I have a solution."

"One of your old gowns!" Lizzie said, her tone relieved and some color returning to her cheeks. "I can make it over."

"No." Kate shook her head. "*Not* one of my old gowns. Think how poorly blue becomes you—and that is mostly what I have!"

"I shouldn't mind," Lizzie said.

"I should. No, Lizzie, you shall have a *new* gown for this ball."

Lizzie became pale again. "I can't."

"A gift."

"But the post-chaise—"

"Lizzie . . ." Kate reached out and took hold of her friend's hand. "My father left me a respectable portion. I have ample money to pay for the post-chaise *and* a new ball gown. *Two* new gowns, in fact, for I shall have one, too."

"But, Kate, it's too much. I can't accept—"

"Yes," Kate said firmly. "You can. I insist. I won't enjoy the ball if you're there in one of my old gowns."

There was a crease between Lizzie's eyebrows. "But—"

"It's shockingly selfish of me, I know! But please, Lizzie, say you'll accept a new gown. We shall both enjoy the ball so much more."

Lizzie bit her lip.

"Rose-colored satin, with a gauze overdress . . ."

Lizzie sighed, but there was laughter in the sound. "All right," she said. "A new gown."

"Thank you!"

They took the afternoon to visit the dressmaker whom Kate usually patronized in Harrogate, a Frenchwoman possessing considerable skill with a needle. Lizzie settled on a rose-pink satin that was the perfect foil for her coloring, while Kate chose a length of silk in her favorite teal blue. Harrogate boasted a number of shops and, with the ball in mind, Kate made further purchases for Lizzie. She bought long gloves and silk stockings and dainty evening slippers and a scarf of spangled gauze.

"I can't accept . . ." Lizzie said, fingering the scarf wistfully.

"Yes, you can." Kate examined a pretty little fan with ivory sticks. It would match Lizzie's ball gown perfectly. She smiled at her friend and held out the fan. "Do you like it, Lizzie?"

Lizzie touched the fan with a fingertip. "Oh, yes. But . . . but I *can't,* Kate. I can never repay you."

Kate smiled at her. "You are repaying me ten times over by your company. Truly."

Lizzie must have heard the sincerity in her voice, for she accepted the gifts. Kate was relieved. She knew Lizzie would enjoy the ball a hundred times more if she had the confidence of being beautifully dressed.

Kate made another purchase, too. She bought herself a lace cap.

"But why?" demanded Lizzie. "Why?"

"An old maid such as I must have a cap," Kate said, laughing. "Surely you know that?"

Lizzie didn't laugh. Instead she frowned. "But you're not old."

"I am," Kate said, turning the lace cap over in her fingers. "I'm eight-and-twenty this year. Quite in my dotage." She smiled at Lizzie, making a joke of it. "At my last prayer, almost."

"No!"

"Yes," Kate said. "I'm an old maid, and I need a cap!" And she laughed and bought it. But when she unwrapped the purchase later, in the privacy of her bedchamber, she didn't feel like laughing. She smoothed the lace with a finger. An old maid. A spinster. An ape leader. She put on the cap and looked at herself in the mirror, not liking what she saw.

"Well, I shall just have to get used to it," she told her reflection. She removed the cap and held it in her hand. She should wear it now, to lend extra credibility to her role as chaperone for Lizzie, but somehow she couldn't bring herself to do so. It was too . . . too *final*.

Kate put the purchase away in the back of a drawer. She would join Cousin Augusta in wearing a lace cap once James had married Lizzie.

Kate watched James watch Lizzie that evening, while they dined, and later when they played cards in the drawing room. He didn't merely watch Lizzie; he exerted himself to please her. It was what she wanted, Kate told herself as she pushed her food around her plate, what she'd asked of him on the terrace, and yet she was horribly afraid that she was jealous of Lizzie. How could she be? It would be terrible of her to be jealous, quite terrible—but there was a constriction in her throat and something painful in her chest and her appetite had deserted her, and when Lizzie made James laugh out loud, Kate came close to crying.

She rallied over cards, a light-hearted game of Speculation, noting with pleasure how lovely Lizzie looked. She was—as the saying went—as perfect as a picture. A hackneyed expression perhaps, but true in this instance. And it wasn't merely Lizzie's appearance that excited James and Harry's admiration; it was her ready laugh and sweet nature. That, and the prettiness.

Kate had never felt so drab in her life. When James turned his eyes to Lizzie and watched her with a smile, Kate was more aware of her plainness than she'd ever been before. The freckles were heavy and ugly on her face and the red hair garish and hideous, prickling her scalp. She lowered her gaze to her cards and blinked back tears.

"Are you feeling quite well, Kate?" Lizzie asked quietly, as they climbed the stairs to bed. "You scarcely spoke this evening. Is everything all right?"

Kate looked at her friend's anxious face and smiled. "Everything's fine."

"Are you certain?"

"Yes," said Kate. "Everything is perfect." And it was. Quite, quite perfect. There would be a love match at Merrell Hall before long. Of that she was certain.

It was Kate's habit to have breakfast on a tray in her bedchamber, followed by a ride, and to take a walk in the park in the afternoon. This routine was altered by Lizzie's presence. Breakfast was eaten in the breakfast parlor, a sunny room that was used, in the general way of things, only by Cousin Augusta—and for that very reason, not by Harry and herself—and the morning ride became a walk, for Lizzie was no horsewoman.

If Cousin Augusta had been resident at Merrell Hall, there would have been no merriment over breakfast, but Cousin Augusta was in Bath and couldn't hear Harry's outrageous jokes, nor see Lizzie dimple so prettily and notice how James laughed silently with his eyes.

Breakfast was followed by a walk of several miles, just Lizzie and herself, while Harry and James rode out together on horseback. There was great enjoyment to be had in the countryside around Merrell Hall, not merely in the park and estate, but in the surrounding neighborhood. Kate showed Lizzie all her favorite paths, and together they took as much pleasure in the exercise as that ardent walker Marianne

Dashwood, heroine of one of Kate's favorite novels, *Sense and Sensibility,* could have done. They went further afield, too, in Kate's gig, and she had the pleasure of introducing Lizzie to Miss Orton and Miss Hart, and seeing them become friends.

The afternoons were for courting. Kate planned, with care, excursions to such places of interest as an abbey, a ruined castle, a celebrated viewpoint, and a waterfall. She watched, with rising hope and an oddly heavy heart, as James smiled at Lizzie, as Lizzie blushingly accepted his arm, as he teased her gently and she dimpled back at him.

When Kate observed Lizzie, she could see no sign that she favored James over Harry. Each man received an equal share of her smiles and laughter, but it seemed to Kate that although Lizzie's eyes were turned as frequently to Harry as to James, there was more warmth in them when she looked at James.

With that observation, Kate had to be content. Lizzie confided several things to her, but not the status of her heart.

"I haven't enjoyed myself so much in *years,*" she said on one of their morning walks. "Thank you for inviting me, Kate!"

And once, as they climbed the stairs to bed after a riotous game of jackstraws, so full of giggling and laughter that Cousin Augusta would have read them a thunderous scold for unbecoming levity, Lizzie said: "Your brother makes me laugh so!"

"And Arden does not?" Kate asked, glancing sideways at her. "I quite thought he made you laugh, too."

Lizzie's blush was dimly discernible in the candlelight. "He . . . yes, he makes me laugh, too."

That conversation was as close as they came to discussing James. It was certainly far from a declaration of partiality, but, watching Lizzie, Kate thought that her friend had a certain glow about her. If she wasn't mistaken, Lizzie's heart was in danger of being lost.

# $C$HAPTER 8

$\mathcal{J}$ames leaned back on his elbow and took a slow sip of wine. He couldn't remember the last time he'd taken part in an *al fresco* meal like this, in the company of friends. He contemplated stretching out on the rug and closing his eyes. The sunshine, the food and the wine, the laughter, combined to make him feel more relaxed than he'd been since his brother Edward had died.

He narrowed his eyes against the sun and looked towards the reed-edged lake, where Kate and Miss Penrose stood casting bread to the ducks. Harry, he saw when he glanced sideways, lay sprawled with closed eyes. James nudged him with a booted toe. "A fine host you are, Honeycourt."

Harry rolled over onto one elbow and opened his eyes, shading them with a hand. He grinned, unoffended. His gaze slid past James, to the lakeshore, and the grin faded. "You're a lucky beggar."

James followed the direction of his eyes. Miss Penrose still stood by the water's edge, but Kate was walking towards them across the grass. Her blue gown had a ruched bodice and an embroidered band at the hem. James watched her approach, unwillingly admiring the grace of her movements and the way the gown clung to her breasts and outlined the shape of her legs. He glanced away, discomfited, and was relieved to find that Harry hadn't noticed him ogling his sister.

Harry was watching Miss Penrose. His expression was regretful. James's sense of pleasure in the day vanished. He eyed his friend. *No,* he thought. *It can't be.*

Harry stirred and shook his head, and grinned again. "Well?" he asked Kate. "Have you succeeded in giving the ducks indigestion?"

"We've certainly tried." Kate reached for the covered basket of food. "Lizzie wants more bread for the ducklings. You should see them, Harry. So sweet!" She found the end of a loaf of bread, wrapped in cloth.

"I'll take it to her," Harry said, rising to his feet.

Kate handed him the bread.

James watched Harry. He walked across to where Miss Penrose stood and said something, smiling at her, that made her laugh. James frowned. Something in Harry's expression, a warmth, a tenderness, made him fear that his friend had lost his heart to Miss Penrose.

He glanced at Kate. Had she noticed? No, she wouldn't be smiling at him so cheerfully if she had. "Have you found fault with Lizzie yet?" she asked, her tone confident that he hadn't.

James shook his head.

"What?" Kate asked, in mock surprise. "Nothing?"

He shook his head again, unable to raise more than a faint smile.

Kate abandoned her teasing. She covered the basket again. "So . . ." Her tone was diffident. "Will you ask her soon?"

James looked at the pair by the lake. Until he'd seen that expression on Harry's face, he would have answered *Yes.* Now, though . . . He wasn't in love with Miss Penrose. He'd tried, but although he liked her, although he thought her pretty, his affections weren't engaged. He had no idea whether hers were, either. There was nothing of the flirt about Miss Penrose. She threw out no lures, either to himself or Harry. She treated them both with impartial friendliness. If she had a preference, a *tendre,* she was keeping it hidden.

He'd intended to offer for her tomorrow, a week to the day from her arrival. He'd planned to beg her company for a stroll in the shrubbery and pose his question to her once they were assured of privacy. But now . . . If there was even the slightest chance that Miss Penrose would accept an offer from Harry then he couldn't, in all conscience, ask her. For him it would only be a marriage of convenience. He liked her, but his heart was intact. She would be a suitable bride; he thought that they would contrive to be happy together, but . . .

James watched as Harry bent his head to make some comment in his companion's ear. Miss Penrose's laugh carried clearly. She put her hand on Harry's arm, an affectionate and unstudied gesture, and pointed at something on the water.

James swallowed the last of his wine. He stared at the empty glass. He didn't want to take away a chance of happiness for Harry. To marry the girl his best friend loved would be cruel.

*Arrogant,* he told himself as he put the glass down. There was no guarantee that Miss Penrose would accept an offer from him. She might have no more wish to marry an earl than Kate.

He turned his gaze to Kate, still waiting for the answer to her question. "After the ball," he said. That gave him another week. Enough time to watch Harry and decide if his friend's heart was truly lost. And if it was, then he wouldn't offer for Miss Penrose.

Kate accepted this with a nod. She plucked a stem of grass and twirled it between her fingers. James watched her, conscious that although Miss Penrose was prettier than Kate, it was Kate whom his eye inexplicably preferred. He'd known her for eleven years, but it was only in the past few weeks that he'd truly seen her. Heat rose in his body as he took inventory of the inviting mouth, the delicious breasts, the slender ankles visible beneath the hem of her gown. The freckles didn't jar. They were part of her, nothing more, and the hair . . . A ringlet fell against her throat, beneath the bonnet. It was copper and gold in the sunlight, vivid and unfashionable, glorious.

He wanted to touch it.

James clenched his fingers into a fist before he could reach out and make a fool of himself. He looked away. His heart beat loudly in his ears and his skin was flushed with warmth. Glorious? Had he really thought that word? He'd drunk too much wine. He was foxed. Badly foxed.

His breathing steadied. The heated flush faded. A duck took off from the lake. Harry and Miss Penrose's voices were an indistinct murmur. James risked a glance at Kate. She sat picking daisies. He saw the line of her throat, the curve of her cheek, the ringlet gleaming in the sun. He saw them, and the heat was in his blood again. He inhaled a shallow, unsteady breath, staring at her, wanting to touch his mouth to her throat, to taste the warm skin, to draw that bright, curling ringlet through his fingers.

Kate raised her head. "What is it, James?"

James stared at her dumbly. She was Harry's sister, familiar, ordinary Kate, freckled and red-haired. She was beautiful. And he was going mad.

Her gray eyes became amused. Her mouth curved into a smile. It made him want to kiss her, quite desperately. "James . . . what is it?"

He wondered what she would do if he leaned over and kissed her. Most likely she'd box his ears.

"James?"

"How much wine did I have?" he asked. His voice was slightly rough.

Kate blinked. Her brow furrowed slightly as she thought. "Two glasses, I think."

That was what he'd thought. Only two. Clearly he wasn't as hard-headed as he believed.

"Why?"

He shook his head and managed to drag his eyes away from her mouth. He stared instead at Harry and Miss Penrose.

"Are you feeling quite well, James?"

"Yes."

"You're frowning."

He discovered that he was.

"Is it . . . is it something about Lizzie?" Kate's voice was tentative, worried.

"No," he said, while his brain scrambled for a reason for his frown. "I mean, yes. Has she given you any indication that . . . that she might look favorably on my offer?"

Kate was silent for a moment. He didn't look at her. "No," she said. "She hasn't. But I'm certain she will. Why wouldn't she?"

"You didn't." His tone was sharper than he'd intended. His pride still smarted from that refusal.

Kate didn't speak for so long that he almost looked at her. "That was different," she said finally.

He wanted to ask her how it was different, but a raised voice caught his attention. He turned his head. They weren't the only party enjoying the lake this afternoon. A quarter of a mile away, around a cloth spread on the grass, was another party of picnickers. One of their number now strutted across the grass, his voice high and scolding. He cut a comical figure as he marched towards the water's edge, his paunch out of all proportion to his scrawny legs. James lost his frown. The man clearly had pretensions to dandyism and—just as clearly—no taste. His pantaloons were the most strident shade of yellow James had ever seen.

"Who's that fellow?" he asked, amused. "Do you know him?"

Kate didn't answer immediately. He glanced at her. She was watching the man. There was no trace of amusement on her face.

"Kate?"

"Sir Thomas Granger," she said, in a flat voice.

James looked back at the man, wondering what Sir Thomas Granger had done to earn Kate's disfavor, and wondering, too, why the name was familiar. He was certain he'd never met the man, but he'd definitely heard the name before. Where? And in what context?

A small jetty jutted out into the lake. At the end of it, on hands and knees, a young boy crouched, staring into the water. James watched as Sir Thomas Granger stood on the grass and shook his finger at the boy, his voice squawking. The boy took no notice.

Sir Thomas Granger clambered awkwardly onto the jetty. His face, even at this distance, could be seen to be florid. If they were any closer, James imagined they'd be able to hear him wheeze. He looked a prime candidate for apoplexy.

Sir Thomas Granger strutted down the jetty and stood over the boy, hands on hips, scolding. With the tails of his coat bristling behind him and his head jerking forward with each angry word, he looked like . . . an irate peahen. Suddenly James remembered where he'd heard the name before. Sir Thomas Granger had offered for Kate. He glanced at her. She watched the scene on the jetty, tight-lipped.

The squawking voice rose. James turned his head in time to see Sir Thomas Granger raise his hand to cuff the boy. The boy ducked, and Sir Thomas overbalanced and fell into the lake.

James heard the sharp, gasped intake of Kate's breath. He looked at her. "Oh, dear," she said, a quiver in her voice. She covered her mouth with a hand and glanced at him.

James began to laugh, softly.

"Stop it!"

He couldn't. Not while Sir Thomas Granger splashed and squawked in the water. He lay back on the grass and laughed until his stomach ached, smothering the whoops against his sleeve.

James didn't look at Kate until he'd regained a measure of control. He turned his head, shading his face from the sun with a raised arm. She sat with one hand pressed to her mouth. Her eyes were bright and her cheeks pink. Her expression, as she watched Sir Thomas Granger stagger ashore, was one of delight.

The sodden man was enveloped by his party and bundled

solicitously into his carriage. Kate gave a regretful sigh as he vanished from sight. She lowered her hand to her lap. "What an unfortunate accident," she said, her voice carefully neutral.

James raised himself on one elbow. "You dislike him."

The comment brought Kate's head around. She stared at him and he watched as her expression became blank. There was a pause, and then she shrugged lightly. The nonchalance of the gesture was belied by a slight tightening of her mouth. "Perhaps a little."

*Perhaps a lot,* he thought. "Why?"

Kate shrugged again. "Because of something he once said." Her tone dismissed the matter as unimportant. She made as if to stand.

"When he offered for you?"

He thought that Kate flinched slightly, but it might only have been that she stiffened. "I beg your pardon?"

James felt himself flush. It wasn't his place to know such information, still less to ask such a question. "No, I beg *your* pardon, Kate." He sat up. Embarrassment was hot in his cheeks. He cleared his throat and loosened his neckcloth. "Harry told me that Granger had offered for you, and I . . ." He loosened his neckcloth further. It really was uncomfortably tight. "I'm sorry, Kate. I didn't mean to ask. I beg your pardon."

Kate turned her head away from him. "When I refused him he called me a bran-faced dowd. That's all." Her tone was flippant and light, casual. She stood.

For a moment James was incapable of movement. Anger flared inside him, so intense that he shook with it. "He what? He said *what*?"

"It doesn't matter," Kate said, still in that same light and careless voice. She began to walk across the grass in the direction of the water.

James scrambled to his feet and caught up with her in two strides. He took hold of her elbow, halting her. "The devil it doesn't matter!"

Kate blinked. She seemed surprised by his anger.

"Did you tell Harry?"

"Of course not. Why should I?"

James released Kate's arm and clenched his hands into fists. "So that he could horsewhip him!"

"Don't be ridiculous, James. Sir Thomas only spoke the truth. Why should he be horsewhipped for that?" Kate stepped around him.

James reached for her arm, stopping her. "It was a damned insult, that's why!"

Kate pulled her elbow from his grasp. She crossed her arms over her chest. "You think I haven't been called bran-faced before? I assure you, I *have*. It's a remarkably accurate term. It describes me perfectly."

James stared at her, seeing the golden-brown freckles scattered abundantly across her face. Kate met his look. She raised her chin slightly.

"Tell me who has said it and I swear I'll horsewhip them all," he said, his voice low and fierce. He wanted to hurt the people who'd hurt her. He wanted to make sure they'd never do so again.

Faint amusement replaced the tightness on Kate's face. "Don't be ridiculous, James."

"I'm not being ridiculous."

"Yes, you are."

He scowled at her, knowing she was correct. "Very well. I shall content myself with Sir Thomas Granger."

"No," Kate said, putting out her hand towards him. "You must not."

"Why not?"

"Because you *can't*, James. Think of the scandal!"

James gritted his teeth together. "Then I shall see that he apologizes to you."

"He has apologized, after a fashion. He sent me a letter."

"A letter." James continued to frown at her. "What sort of letter?"

"Oh . . ." A variety of emotions crossed Kate's face. He saw a trace of amusement, a hint of anger. Wryness was predominant. "He begged my forgiveness for losing his temper—and then he placed the blame on me for making him do so!" She smiled, inviting his amusement. The smile didn't reach her eyes; it was a movement of her mouth, nothing more.

James didn't return the smile. "Did he retract what he had said?"

Her lips twisted wryly. "No. He forgot to do so."

"Then I shall remind him!"

"No," she said, laying her hand on his arm. "Please don't, James. It's not worth it."

He was aware of her hand on his arm, a light touch, and aware of an urge to protect her. "Yes," he said. "It *is* worth it."

She shook her head. "Leave it, James. Please."

He looked at her face, lovely beneath the freckles, and saw a silent plea there. He sighed and tried to let his anger go. "If you wish."

She smiled at him again, and this time the smile reached her eyes. "Thank you." She removed her hand from his sleeve.

James glanced over at the jetty and remembered Sir Thomas Granger's plunge. "He deserved it."

"What? Oh," Kate followed the direction of his gaze. "Yes. Perhaps he did. He should not have tried to hit his son."

James thought that Sir Thomas Granger deserved his impromptu dip for quite another reason. "The water is extremely cold at this time of year," he observed, with satisfaction. The sunlight might be warm, but there was frost on the ground every morning. It was, after all, only spring.

Kate nodded.

"Perhaps he'll take a chill." His tone was hopeful.

Kate laughed. "Unchristian, James!"

"Yes." He held out his arm to her. She laid her hand on it again. "I take it he found himself a wife?"

Kate nodded. "The very next day."

James was speechless. He walked in silence for several paces. "The next *day?*" he said, when he had found his voice again.

"Yes."

"A Mr. Collins, no less," he said, contemptuously.

"Yes," Kate said. "A Mr. Collins."

He could have teased her on the subject of Mr. Collins and made her laugh, but his heart wasn't in it. Deep inside himself, he was still furious. How *dared* Sir Thomas Granger say such a thing? How *dared* he insult Kate so? Harry would be livid if he knew. James toyed with the idea of informing him. The punishment would be more fitting if it came from Harry. It was Harry's place, after all, to defend Kate's honor, not his. He was neither brother nor husband; it would look extremely odd if he demanded redress from Sir Thomas Granger.

But no, he'd promised Kate to leave it, which meant not telling Harry. James sighed. He looked across at Harry, feeding the ducks with Miss Penrose by the water's edge. His friend's hair flamed in the sun, the same color as Kate's. Not garish, but quite startlingly rich, full of copper and gold. A fascinating color. He glanced sideways at Kate, but the bright hair was mostly hidden beneath her bonnet. It was a charming bonnet, trimmed with blue ribbon and tiny clusters of flowers. It became her beautifully, as did her gown. But Kate's clothes always looked good. Her taste couldn't be faulted. She had a fine eye for style and color.

"You're *definitely* not a dowd," James said. Sir Thomas Granger must be blind if he thought so.

Kate glanced down at her gown. "No, I don't think I am."

"You're not."

"Thank you." She smiled at him.

"Did you notice the color of his pantaloons?"

Her nose wrinkled. "Yes."

"The ugliest shade of yellow I've ever seen."

Kate laughed. "If you think that's bad, you should see his waistcoats."

"Worse?"

"Dreadful!"

He touched his fingers lightly to the back of her hand, where it rested on his sleeve. "I'm glad you didn't marry him."

"Nothing would have induced me to marry him," Kate said firmly. She was silent a moment, and then glanced up at him, a glimmer of mischief in her eyes. Her tone was demure: "Even if he'd bribed me with Rome and Florence."

James was surprised into a laugh, quickly followed by a twinge of embarrassment. He thought that maybe he flushed. Had he really tried to bribe her? So heavy-handed of him. So clumsy!

They came up alongside Miss Penrose and Harry. Kate removed her hand from his arm.

"Is there any more bread?" Miss Penrose asked, turning her pretty face towards them.

"Say no, Kate!" Harry said, laughing. "The ducklings will sink if they have any more."

"Silly," Miss Penrose said, a giggle in her voice. "They won't sink!"

James looked at her, noting the delicately flushed cheeks and the dimples, the sweetly curved mouth, the wide, long-lashed eyes. She would be a pleasing wife, there was no doubt of that, but—

Miss Penrose was the best of Kate's candidates. Close to perfect, in fact. But was she as suitable as Kate? Would he be happier with Miss Penrose than with Kate?

He glanced at Kate. When it came to compatibility, to being able to talk with someone, to laugh, to share things . . . he'd choose Kate. And if he had to choose between kissing Kate or Miss Penrose, then his choice would also be Kate. *That mouth.* And his body didn't flush with heat at the thought of Miss Penrose in his bed, but when he thought of Kate there . . .

If Harry cared nothing for Miss Penrose, then he could offer for her with a clear conscience. But should he? Or should he reject her, as he'd rejected the other candidates?

Kate had promised to marry him if no one on the list suited him better than she did. And right now, here at the lake, it was Kate he wanted as his wife, not Miss Penrose.

# $C$HAPTER 9

$T$he ball gowns arrived from Harrogate, and that evening it began to rain. It rained and rained and rained, until Kate thought that Merrell Hall might float away. There were no more excursions. Instead they played card games and chess, jackstraws and cross questions and charades. Not all their time was spent frivolously, though. Harry and James discussed estate management for long hours in the study. It was a subject in which Harry was well-versed. He'd managed the Honeycourt land for six years, and in that time made so many improvements that the late viscount would scarcely have recognized it.

Kate knew that James was keen to prove his worth as a landlord. He was concerned about the plight of his tenants in these grim times and determined that they shouldn't suffer through any fault of his. She approved his sentiments and didn't begrudge Harry and James their long sessions in the study; there was plenty of time for courting.

While Harry and James were absent, she and Lizzie read aloud to each other from Henry Holland's *Travels in the Ionian Isles, Albania, Thessaly, Macedonia, &c.,* delighting in his description of bazaars and ruins and natural wonders, and tracing his journey on maps in the library. There was still preparation to be done for the ball, but Kate left those tasks until James and Harry were present to entertain Lizzie. She often returned from the kitchen or cellar or ballroom—the latter now approaching a state of readiness—to find the three of them laughing together in the billiard room, where Lizzie was receiving instruction in the art of wielding the cue. Cousin Augusta would doubtless scold if she knew that Lizzie was alone with the men, but Kate saw no harm in it. She trusted James not to step beyond the bounds of propriety, and Harry too, of course.

After four days of solid rain, Kate began to worry. Sheets of water lay in the dips and hollows and many roads were impassable. What about the ball? Would any of their guests brave such conditions?

When she said as much to Harry, he laughed and said: "Rowing boats."

Kate folded her arms. "Rowing boats."

"Yes. Just the thing!"

"Harry," Kate said. "Be sensible! What if no one comes?"

"They'll come." Harry put an arm around her shoulders. "Don't worry. This weather can't last."

"But what if it does?"

"Rowing boats," he said again. "Can't you just imagine Mrs. Forster in one? That's right, Kate: laugh! And stop worrying. It'll be fine; I promise."

Lizzie, too, had a concern about the ball. "I've never danced the waltz," she confided. "Will you . . . I mean, if you don't mind, Kate . . . will you teach me the steps? Please?"

"Of course," Kate said. And so she did, humming under her breath *one-two-three, one-two-three,* until Harry, coming upon them in the Long Gallery, exclaimed that it wasn't good enough at all—quite shabby in fact!—and proposed a more comprehensive session of instruction with himself and James as tutors.

The furniture was moved aside in the drawing room and the yellow Savonnerie with its pattern of ferns carefully rolled back. A footman lit the candles and Kate sat down at the pianoforte and began to play. Lizzie was uncertain at first in her steps and shy with the intimacy of the dance, but gradually she relaxed under Harry's gentle teasing and James's patient tutelage. Up and down the length of the room she danced, first with James and then Harry and then with James again, while outside the rain came down without cessation.

Kate played, her fingers finding the keys automatically, and watched as James and Lizzie waltzed. James said something to Lizzie, his dark head bent, his hand at her waist, and Lizzie blushed and laughed. Kate's fingers faltered. She dropped her gaze to the pianoforte. There was a pain in her chest, as if someone had taken hold of her heart and squeezed it.

"Are your fingers tired, Kate?" Harry asked cheerfully. "I'll fetch Stewart, shall I? Let's show them how it's *really* done!"

He strode from the room without waiting for a reply and returned several minutes later with the second groom and his fiddle.

Kate stood and took hold of the hand Harry held out to her. He grinned. "Stand back, Miss Penrose, James!" he said, as the groom, Stewart, struck up a tune.

It had been several months since she'd danced the waltz with Harry, and their first turn around the drawing room was sedate. Not so, their second. Kate caught a glimpse of Lizzie watching with open-mouthed delight as Harry spun her into one outrageous turn after another. Up and down the room they danced, while Stewart plied his bow, the notes coming faster and faster. Kate met Harry's eyes and laughed with him as he whirled her into a giddy series of spins. They turned and twirled and spun, and it was impossible to be miserable. There was such pleasure in dancing, in the music and the movement, such exhilaration!

"Enough!" Harry cried, when they were both breathless. They halted in the middle of the floor. The fiddling stopped. "Well?" Harry demanded, panting, turning to face their audience, his arm around Kate's shoulders.

There was an odd expression on James's face, one Kate had never seen before. His eyes were fixed on her and their intensity made her suddenly self-conscious. She looked away from him as heat rose in her cheeks.

"That was marvelous!" Lizzie cried, clapping her hands together.

"Would you like to learn to waltz like that, Miss Penrose?" Harry asked her. "All it takes is a little practice."

Lizzie's eyes widened. "Oh, yes. Please."

Harry laughed and released his hold on Kate. "Very well." He held out his hand to Lizzie and then checked the gesture, glancing at James. "Unless you'd prefer to be the tutor?"

James shook his head. "No," he said. "I shall partner your sister, if she will have me."

His words brought Kate's head around to look at him. He was still watching her. "Well, Kate?" he asked. The expression in his eyes and note in his voice were unsettling. They made her feel shy and—at the same time—more aware of him as a man than she'd ever been before.

Kate swallowed. "Of course," she said, with feigned calmness. She'd never danced the waltz with James. The cotillion, yes, and various country dances, but never the waltz. He came towards her and she felt suddenly as gauche and awkward as she'd been at seventeen. She hoped that he attributed the color in her cheeks to exertion, not embarrassment.

"Another waltz please, Stewart," Harry said. "Slower this time."

The groom nodded and brought the fiddle up under his chin again.

James held out his left hand to her. Kate took it, trying not to tremble. His right hand was at her waist, warm through the fabric of her gown. Gingerly Kate laid her fingers on his sleeve. He was taller than Harry and broader in the shoulder.

The groom began to play.

James tightened his clasp on her hand so that their bare palms pressed together. Kate experienced sudden difficulty breathing. *No gloves,* she thought in panic. *I need gloves if I'm going to touch him.*

"Ready, Kate?" he asked.

"Yes," she said, past the constriction in her throat. It was impossible to meet his eyes. She stared instead at his neckcloth and tried to control the agitated beating of her heart. Her body felt stiff and tense and clumsy. She was afraid that she was going to step on his toes, that she'd trip over her feet, that she'd bump into him, that—

James took her on a slow circuit of the room. Kate had never danced so badly in her life. She was blushing with mortification by the time they were back where they'd started. "I'm sorry," she said, her eyes fixed on the buttons of his striped silk waistcoat. She attempted to pull her hand from his grasp. "Perhaps it would be best if we stopped."

"Craven, Kate," James said, tightening his grip.

A spark of annoyance flared in her breast. She pressed her lips together. The next circuit went slightly better. She concentrated on the sound of Harry's low voice as he talked Lizzie through a spin. If she could just pretend that James was Harry . . .

She didn't notice that she'd lost her stiffness until James had spun her twice. "Much better," he whispered in her ear, as he twirled her backwards down the room.

"A little faster," Harry called to the groom.

The music picked up pace. James executed a daring turn and Kate discovered that she was enjoying herself. Up and down the long drawing room he took her, and now that she'd stopped panicking she was able to follow his movements as easily as if he'd been Harry.

"Faster!" her brother said again.

The groom obliged, and James swept her into a series of twirls and turns that were as reckless as any Harry had ever taken her through. More reckless, in fact, for the spins were tighter and he held her closer than Harry did. Kate felt his heat. Not just the strong clasp of his fingers and the imprint of his hand at her waist, but also the warmth of his body, mere inches from her own. He held her close and took her down the room so fast that she was almost dizzy. He was laughing, and she was laughing too, breathlessly, and she looked up and met his eyes.

"Enough!" Harry cried.

The music stopped. James halted, holding her, steadying her. Her eyes were caught in his. She'd never stood this close to him before. She saw that there were flecks of gold in the brown of his irises. Kate stared, and thought that they were the most beautiful eyes she had ever seen.

James was panting slightly. Color flushed his face. He still held her close, even though they'd stopped dancing. Her body felt his heat. It beat against her.

Kate remembered where she was. She ducked her head and pulled her hand from his grip. She stepped back, smoothing her gown with shaking fingers. *Treat him as a friend. Don't make a fool of yourself.*

She turned to Lizzie, standing flushed and laughing and pretty alongside Harry. "How did you fare, Lizzie?"

"Very well indeed!" Harry answered for her.

Lizzie disclaimed this, shaking her head.

"Fudge!" Harry said.

Lizzie's blush deepened. "You have forgotten that I stood on your foot, my lord."

"Don't worry, Lizzie," Kate said wryly. "I did the same to James—oh, four times, was it not?"

"Three," James said, moving to stand beside her. "So you see, Miss Penrose, you didn't do badly at all."

"Three times?" Lizzie said, her eyes widening. "Really?"

"Yes." Kate managed a laugh. "Poor James! He must have thought he had a lumbering elephant for a partner."

"No," James said. "Merely that you weren't used to dancing the waltz with me." He smiled at Lizzie. "I wouldn't worry about your one misstep, Miss Penrose. We gentlemen are very used to having our toes trodden on, I assure you."

This, said in a teasing tone, won a faint smile from Lizzie. "But I should like *not* to tread on any toes," she said earnestly.

"Then I suggest more practice." James held out his hand to her. "Unless you're tired?"

Lizzie shook her head.

"Again please, Stewart," Harry said. He stepped up to Kate. She took his hand with none of the self-consciousness she'd experienced with James. The music started and Harry swept her into a slow turn. "Three times, Kate?" he said, grinning, his voice too low to be overheard. "How could you be so clumsy?"

"Have care, Lord Honeycourt," she warned him. "Or I shall tread on *your* toes."

"I tremble in terror," Harry said, still grinning, and then he spun her the length of the room.

The rain stopped the day before the ball. James was almost sorry for it when he looked out the window of his bedchamber. The sky was clear and the rain-soaked lawn steamed in the sunlight. From this vantage point, the world looked wet and fresh and clean. He turned away from the window. The rain had been a blessing. Their enforced time indoors had enabled him to observe Harry closely and there was no longer any doubt in his mind; Harry had lost his heart to Miss Penrose. He was trying to conceal it, but James knew him too well to be fooled. Harry's treatment of her might be friendly, not lovelorn, his tone teasing rather than caressing, but he couldn't hide the way his face softened when he looked at her. He was in love.

James walked over to the mirror and tried to concentrate on tying his neckcloth, but his thoughts wandered. The rain had also given him ample time to observe Miss Penrose, and what he'd seen had pleased him. Miss Penrose, he thought, was in a fair way to falling in love with Harry. She, too, was discreet, but there was an expression in her eyes when she glanced at Harry, a shy hopefulness, and her blush came more readily in Harry's company than his own, and her laughter too.

Kate hadn't noticed. He'd spent as much time observing her as he had Harry and Miss Penrose, and he thought she had no suspicions that her plan was unraveling. For himself, he didn't care that Miss Penrose could no longer be a candidate. He wanted Kate as his wife. Not only were they compatible, she aroused passion in him.

He wondered how he could have been so blind for so long. Eleven years, and not once, in all that time, had he thought that Kate had any claim to beauty. Now, whenever he looked at her, she became more beautiful. Yes, she had freckles and red hair, but she was very far from being plain. Her coloring was striking, rich and warm. The freckles accented what was a lovely face, full of intelligence and humor and character. They weren't a disfigurement. On the contrary, they gave a reason to touch her smooth skin—something that his fingers ached to do. And the hair . . . he longed to bury his hands in it, to wind the curling strands around his fingers and make sense of all the colors he saw in it, the differing shades of gold and copper and flame.

"Damn!" That was one neckcloth ruined. He turned to reach for a fresh cloth, but Griffin was already holding it out to him. "Thank you," James said.

Facing the mirror again, he frowned at his reflection. The physical attraction that he felt for Kate—now that he no longer tried to fight it—became more intense with each day that passed. He craved her mouth, her body, her whispered words in his ear, her hands on his skin . . . But Kate, quite clearly, didn't feel the same way about him. Her eyes didn't linger on him. Her manner was friendly, nothing more. She treated him exactly as she did her brother.

He remembered the touch of her hand on his arm,

comforting, when he'd spoken to her about the war. She would have done the same thing for Harry: touched him, comforted him.

"Damn!"

Griffin wordlessly handed him another length of starched muslin.

"Thank you." James cleared his throat and attempted to concentrate on the matter at hand, but thought of Kate intruded. His fingers slowed in their movements as he remembered watching Harry and Kate waltz yesterday. She had danced with grace and flair, but more than that, she had danced with passion. He'd watched and been stunned by what he'd seen.

"Passion," he said, beneath his breath.

"I beg your pardon, my lord?"

James shook his head. "Nothing." He cleared his throat again and frowned at his reflection in the mahogany-framed mirror. But he didn't see himself. Instead, he saw Kate waltzing with Harry.

His curse, this time, was cruder. He stripped the crumpled muslin from his throat and gave it to Griffin.

Griffin said nothing. He merely handed him another neckcloth.

James turned back to the mirror and closed his eyes for a moment. He had to get this damned neckcloth tied.

He opened his eyes and slowly and with utmost care tied the intricate, austere folds of the *Trône d'Amour*—and then he allowed himself to think about Kate dancing with him.

The grace and passion had been there, at the end. It had been a heady feeling to dance down the room with her held close, their bodies moving so well together. Initially, though, she'd been anything but graceful. She'd been as nervous as a débutante attempting her first waltz at Almack's, clumsy in her steps, shy and ungainly and graceless. He'd been surprised, for she had danced beautifully with her brother. Odd, that. He would have expected such behavior from her eleven years ago, but not now.

It occurred to James, quite suddenly, while he stood in front of the mirror, that perhaps Kate wasn't as indifferent to him as she appeared. Why else the nervousness? Why else the self-conscious stiffness?

James stared at his reflection and discovered that there was a tiny smirk on his mouth. He laughed softly to himself.

"Sir?" Griffin asked.

"Nothing." James shook his head. But the smirk wouldn't go away. It sat there on his mouth as he remembered Kate's shyness with him. She had been aware of him as a man. Not as a friend, but as a man.

The ground was too wet for walking, too muddy. Kate and Miss Penrose drove out in the gig, while James and Harry accompanied them on horseback. He thought that Kate would have preferred to ride, too, but there was no hint of this in her manner; she was far too polite to discomfit her friend. But perhaps Miss Penrose also felt that sitting in the gig was a pale substitute for being on horseback, for at luncheon she expressed a wistful desire to learn how to ride. Harry promptly offered to instruct her.

"Oh, yes!" she exclaimed, her eyes wide and eager. "I should like that of all things."

"Then allow me to teach you, Miss Penrose," Harry said. He glanced across at James and hesitated. "Or perhaps you would prefer Arden as your instructor? His skill in the saddle exceeds mine. A hussar, you know!"

James ignored the proffered gambit and continued to eat the cold meats on his plate.

Miss Penrose smiled shyly and shook her head. "I shall be happy with you, my lord," she said, and a faint blush rose in her cheeks. Kate and Harry didn't notice. They were both looking pointedly at him.

James continued to ignore them. Harry waited another second, and then turned back to Miss Penrose. "It would be my pleasure," he said.

Kate frowned at James. He met her eyes with amusement, before glancing back at Miss Penrose.

"Thank you," she was saying. "I have always wished to learn." Then her smile faltered and the enthusiasm faded from her face. "Only . . . perhaps it would be a waste of your time, my lord. I . . . I shall have no opportunity to ride at home. We have no horse." Embarrassment colored her cheeks at this admission of poverty.

"Not a waste of time," Harry said, in an easy tone. "You can ride here, Miss Penrose, when you visit—which I trust you will often do."

This won a grateful smile and another blush, and James could only wonder that Harry and Kate didn't see what was so obvious to him.

Miss Penrose had the first of her lessons later that afternoon, dressed in a blue riding habit that had obviously been hastily altered to fit her. The color didn't become her nearly as well as it would have Kate, but she was glowingly pretty nonetheless, eager and excited. The expression on her face, as she looked at Harry, was close to adoration.

James tapped his whip against his riding breeches and wondered how long it would take for Kate to realize that her friend had fallen for Harry. And for that matter, how long it would take Harry to notice.

Kate came up alongside him, dressed for riding in a habit that was more gray than blue, a color that almost matched her eyes. "That could have been you," she said, her voice low and faintly reproving as she watched Harry explain the intricacies of the mounting block to Miss Penrose.

James contemplated the hours that it would take to make a competent horsewoman of Miss Penrose. "Heaven forbid."

"Whatever do you mean?" Kate asked. Her eyebrows rose. "It would have been perfect!"

He shook his head. "I should be a poor teacher. I haven't the patience."

"Nonsense," Kate said. "You taught Lizzie how to waltz."

"A matter of an hour or two. This," he indicated with his whip, "will take days."

"But—"

"Harry is a much better teacher," he said firmly. "For one thing, he doesn't have my wretched frown!"

The sally didn't draw a laugh from Kate. "Lizzie isn't afraid of your frown."

"No." He shrugged acknowledgement of this. "But Harry is the better teacher. I should get bored." It wasn't the complete truth. He probably wouldn't be bored. He liked Miss Penrose; it would be no hardship to teach her to ride. But the task was far better suited to Harry, who was in love with her.

"Nonsense," Kate said again, but with less certainty in her voice.

Briefly, James considered telling her to look at Miss Penrose and Harry, as they stood together, to really *look*. Then he discarded the notion. Kate was intelligent; she'd notice soon enough. And besides, he was far more interested in the status of Kate's heart than Miss Penrose's. Was Kate indifferent to him, or not? "Shall we ride?" he asked.

"Yes," said Kate. "But I *still* think you should have offered to teach her!"

The disapprobation in her tone made him laugh. "You have such faith in me as a teacher, Kate? I'm flattered!" He tapped his whip against his thigh, grinning. "Groundless faith, too, for I can't recall a single thing *I've* ever taught you."

Kate's eyes narrowed, but her mouth betrayed her, twisting up at one corner. She was more amused than annoyed.

James suddenly lost the urge to laugh. He stared at her mouth and thought that he would like to be her teacher. There were many things he wanted to show her. Kissing first, and after that . . .

His grin faded. He wouldn't mind how long it took. Hours.

Days. Weeks. He'd not be bored. He knew he could teach Kate forever and not be bored. Not once, not ever.

Heat flared low in his belly and he turned away from her and called for their horses. Kate's mare, a lively bay, came first. James waved aside the groom and threw Kate up into the saddle himself. He searched her face for heightened color, for a sign that she had been aware of his touch, but there was nothing. She seemed perfectly unconcerned. He might as well have been her brother, or the groom.

Frowning, he mounted Saladin. They left the stableyard at a walk, then moved into a canter and then a full, stretching gallop. Kate was laughing when they finally pulled up. Mud splashed her habit, and her cheeks were rosy and her gray eyes shining. Bright tendrils of hair had strayed from beneath the peak of her high-crowned riding hat. She looked utterly delicious.

James decided that he must accompany Kate on her rides more often if galloping had this effect on her. He nudged Saladin closer to her and watched for her reaction. No extra color rose in her cheeks. Her smile was friendly and unselfconscious. There was no shyness in her manner, no nervousness. His closeness didn't appear to perturb her in the slightest. James tried not to frown. Kate wasn't behaving as he wanted her to.

"I needed that," she said. "There's nothing better than a good gallop."

"No," James said, although he disagreed. But Kate knew nothing about sex.

The faintest of breezes stirred the loose tendrils against her cheek, issuing an invitation that couldn't be ignored. James reached out and brushed them back, touching her skin with gloved fingertips.

Kate froze in the saddle. Her eyes were startled.

"You hair is coming loose," he said. And he repeated the movement of his fingers against her cheek.

"Thank you," Kate said, as color rose in her face. She turned her head away and picked up the reins. "Shall we ride?" Her voice was brisk.

"By all means," James said, pleased by her blush. He nudged Saladin forward with his knees.

They came back through the woods at a slow pace. The path beside the river was strewn with debris. Trees lurched drunkenly, their roots pulling out of the sodden ground. One had fallen entirely and lay alongside the path. He watched Kate assess the damage. It would be some days before this area of the park could be seen to. There were more urgent repairs to be done closer to the Hall.

Kate's nose wrinkled. "What's that smell?"

James shook his head, but before he'd completed the movement he smelled it. Death. It filled his mouth and nose, ripe and foul. He could taste it on his tongue, he swallowed it when he inhaled.

With the smell came memory. He sat on Saladin, the reins clenched in his fist, and it wasn't Kate he saw, or the woods, it was Waterloo. It had smelled like this when he'd searched for Rupert. He'd stumbled through the bodies, limping from his injury, sliding and falling, his torn uniform smeared with blood and things that were worse than blood, and when he'd found him, when he'd found Rupert—

He slid from Saladin and bent over, trying desperately not to be ill. His hat tumbled from his head to roll in the mud, but he scarcely noticed, didn't care.

He heard Kate's voice, dimly. "James," she said. "James!"

# *C*HAPTER 10

*K*ate stumbled as she went to him, and ended up on her knees in the mud. James looked at her, but she didn't think he saw her. There was wildness in his eyes, blindness, and sweat on his brow and upper lip.

It was more than the smell. She knew it as soon as she saw his face.

Kate rose to her feet and took hold of his arm. "James . . ." She pulled him away from the stench, halting when the air was fresh and clean again. James leaned against a tree, his eyes closed. He breathed in gasps. The tension on his face told her he fought nausea.

Kate glanced around her. A fallen sycamore lay alongside the path. "Here," she said. "Sit down."

James sat with his head in his hands, still breathing in shallow gasps. Kate knelt in front of him, heedless of the mud. "Concentrate on breathing," she said. "Slowly, James. Breathe slowly."

She couldn't see his face, it was hidden in his hands, but she listened to James's breathing as he struggled to control his nausea. She pulled off one mud-smeared glove and reached out to touch his hair lightly, as if he were Harry. "Just concentrate on breathing," she whispered.

Kate stroked his hair while his breathing grew slower, steadier. She wanted to do more. She wanted to rise on her knees and put her arms around James, to hold him, to comfort him. She couldn't, and so she stroked his hair softly, and then after a few moments she stopped doing even that.

Kate got to her feet and sat beside him on the tree trunk. The horses had followed them. She took off her other muddy glove and clasped her hands in her lap.

James took a deep, shuddering breath and let it out slowly. "I'm sorry, Kate." His voice was low, almost inaudible.

"Don't be."

He was silent for several minutes, sitting with his head in his hands. "That smell," he said finally. "It . . ."

She reached out and touched his shoulder. "It's all right, James."

"No." His voice was rough. "It's not all right! I saw him fall, Kate, and I couldn't get to him. I tried, but I *couldn't*—!" Beneath her hand his shoulder was tight with tension and distress. "I went back later. I looked for him. Oh, God, the smell, Kate. The smell!" He almost sobbed the words.

Kate stroked his hair, softly. "Hush," she whispered. Her voice was husky with tears, her throat almost too tight for speech.

James said nothing for several minutes, and then said flatly: "He was dead, of course. It was far too late. He was lying there with his stomach—"

They sat in silence. Kate thought James fought against tears. She touched his hair, thick and black and soft, and stroked it lightly, offering comfort. Slow minutes passed. "What was your friend's name?" she asked finally, quietly.

"Rupert. His name was Rupert."

"Waterloo?"

"Yes."

They sat in silence again. James spoke finally, his voice bleak: "You know what else happened that day?"

Kate knew. "Edward," she said quietly.

James said nothing. His breathing was soft and ragged, unsteady, and she realized with a sense of shock that he was weeping. The tears were soundless. She thought they were for Waterloo as much as for his brother's death. Separately, each event was terrible. Together—

She cupped the back of his head in her hand, stroking his hair, and didn't know how to comfort him. Tears fell down her own cheeks. His grief hurt her. It was like a knife blade in her chest. She would do anything, *anything*, to take the pain away from him.

His breathing steadied. The unseen tears had stopped. Kate continued to stroke his hair. "I wish I could have said goodbye to Edward." James's voice was low and rough and anguished. "Oh, God, how I *wish*—"

"I know," Kate whispered, through the ache in her throat.

"I always thought it would be me. I never thought . . . Not Edward."

Kate said nothing. She smoothed his hair gently with her fingers.

"I miss him, Kate." The whisper was so low that she scarcely heard it. It brought fresh tears to her eyes.

"I know you do." James and Edward had been bound by more than brotherhood. They'd had the same close friendship that she had with Harry. It was a precious thing to have, and a terrible thing to lose.

More long, slow, silent minutes passed. Kate stopped stroking his hair. She clasped her hands in her lap and looked down at them. Another minute passed, then James straightened and pulled off his gloves. He averted his head and wiped his face. "I beg your pardon, Kate," he said. There was embarrassment in his voice, shame. "I didn't mean to—"

"Don't apologize, James. Please."

He turned and looked at her. His eyes were dark, damp, haunted. "I try not to remember that day," he said. "But that smell—" His gaze became unfocused for the merest instant and she thought that he stared through her, seeing remembered horrors. Then he stood in a swift movement. "Forgive me, Kate. I didn't mean to . . . to do that."

Kate shook her head, but James didn't see. He'd already turned to the horses. She watched him, thinking how tall and strong he was, and how hurt inside.

He didn't meet her eyes when he brought her horse to her. "I'm sorry," he said.

The stiffness in his posture and voice told her that he was ashamed of his loss of control, embarrassed by his tears. It distressed her, but at least it was something she could deal with. Kate stood. "If you apologize one more time, James," she said, her tone scolding, "I swear I shall box your ears!"

His gaze flicked to meet hers, startled.

She smiled crookedly at him. "Idiot," she said.

This time, when James looked at her, he really saw her. He stared, and after a moment a faint answering smile showed in his eyes. "Very well," he said. "No more apologies." He reached out and took hold of her hands. He squeezed them gently. "Thank you, Kate." He raised her right hand to his lips and pressed a kiss into her palm. "Thank you."

Kate couldn't help it. She blushed.

James watched the color rise in her face. It flushed her cheeks, tinting them, telling him she was aware of the touch of his mouth on her skin. At any other time he would have pressed his advantage, but not now, while grief was tight in his chest. He released Kate's hands and turned to her mare. He could feel tears drying on his skin, but the shame was gone. Somehow, with a few words and a smile, Kate had made it all right.

"I'll help you mount," he said.

"Thank you." Her voice was calm, as if she'd not blushed. "But first, where are my gloves?"

113

They were trodden into the mud beside the tree trunk. Her whip, though, was nowhere to be seen. Nor was his. Or his hat. Kate began walking back along the track, the voluminous skirt of her habit looped over her arm. James made a move to accompany her, but she stopped him with an upraised hand. "Don't you dare!"

He didn't argue. He had no wish to be physically ill in front of Kate. He waited. The river still ran high. Debris swirled in the brown water. He wondered what the smell belonged to. A dead sheep, perhaps. Whatever it was, its intestines had recently been torn open. It was an unforgettable smell. The accompanying image was in his head: Rupert, gored by a bayonet, trampled by horses, dead. Nausea rose again in his throat and he clenched his teeth. A fragment of a sentence turned in his mind: *one vast carnage bruised.* It took him a few seconds to place it. Homer. Miss Wilmot had quoted it. The description was apt. Waterloo had been a shocking carnage, vast and ugly, a mire of mud and blood, bodies piled upon bodies, a terrible waste of lives.

James stared at the river, not seeing it. He should never have persuaded his father to purchase him a commission. It had seemed the right thing to do. He'd been so bored, kicking his heels around Town, a younger son with nothing to do. He'd finished Cambridge and had no estates in which to interest himself, unlike Edward and Harry. Gambling had held little attraction, and neither had cockfights and other such diversions. He'd wanted a career, an outlet for his restless energy. Not the clergy or the Diplomatic Service, something more exciting. Fool that he was, he'd wanted action.

If he'd known that Waterloo was to come, he would have chosen otherwise. God, if he'd known, he'd have sold out! Then he wouldn't have had to live through that slaughter, wouldn't have seen Rupert like that, wouldn't have been scrambling through a battlefield while Edward lay dying in a carriage wreck. *Edward.* James stared at the swirling brown water and wished, with all his heart, that he could have said goodbye to his brother, that he could have held his hand, done something, anything.

He'd said goodbye to his father, not that the old Earl had been aware of anything; he'd never regained consciousness after the accident. But the few days spent at his father's bedside had been important to James. At least he'd been able to hold his limp hand and talk to him, to say goodbye, even if the words hadn't been heard. He'd not had that chance with Edward. His brother had been two weeks dead by the time he reached home.

Kate returned with both their whips and his hat. Her riding habit, now that he noticed, was filthy. He had a vague memory of her kneeling in the mud, her face pale and grave, tears shining in her eyes. She held his whip and hat out to him.

"Thank you," James said.

He was thanking her for more than his belongings. She had cried for him, or perhaps with him; he wasn't sure if there was a distinction. And she had listened, had understood and said the words he'd needed to hear, had scolded away his shame at letting her see his grief. She was truly his friend, as much as Harry was.

"Thank you," he said again, but Kate didn't hear what he was thanking her for. She smiled at him, a friendly smile that touched her eyes and was at odds with the traces of tears still visible on her face. There was mud, too, smeared across one cheek, as if she'd wiped the tears away with a dirty hand. He looked at her, tear-stained and mud-streaked and beautiful, and knew that he loved her. It was more than friendship and more than desire. It was love.

He didn't tell her. He didn't feel equal to it at this moment. Instead he said softly: "There's dirt on your face," and he took her chin in one hand and carefully wiped the mud from her skin. He wanted to drop a kiss on her lips, but dared not; bile was still bitter in his mouth.

Kate stood quite still while he completed his task, his

thumb rubbing against her cheek, soft and smooth and faintly flushed. She didn't meet his eyes. "Thank you," she said, when he had released her, her tone disappointingly matter-of-fact.

"My pleasure."

Kate pulled on her gloves, while the flush faded from her face. James tossed her up into the saddle and was vaguely disappointed by the unconcern with which she accepted this service. He'd hoped for another blush, for some sign that she was aware of him. Instead, all he got was another polite: "Thank you."

He mounted Saladin, whip in hand. They rode back by a route that avoided the dead animal, although he thought he caught the scent of it, faintly, as they trotted through the trees. That whiff, half-imagined though it was, was enough to take him back. June 1815. Memories of Rupert and Edward and his father tangled in his mind. Good memories and bad ones.

Kate halted so abruptly that James was jerked from his brooding reverie. He blinked and shook his head to disperse the wisps of memory. "What?"

Kate said nothing. Her expression was one of dismay. Puzzled, he followed the direction of her gaze. Merrell Hall was visible through the trees, at the top of a rising slope of lawn. The Hall looked as it always did, large and sprawling, handsome, with warm brickwork and climbing ivy and windows glinting in the sunlight. He could see nothing amiss.

"What?" he asked again, and then he noticed the traveling carriage drawn up in front of the Hall. Foreboding tightened the skin at the nape of his neck. "Is that . . . ?"

"Cousin Augusta," Kate said.

# $C$HAPTER 11

$C$ousin Augusta didn't start scolding until she had Kate and Harry alone, but once she started, there was no stopping her. Out of long experience, neither of them tried to do so; it would be over more quickly if they allowed her to vent her spleen without interruption.

"How could you have been so lost to the impropriety of it? I had thought *better* of you, Harold, I really had. And Kitty! If you had only written to me and asked my guidance, I should have come home instantly! I am *shocked*. Truly shocked! What were you thinking?"

Cousin Augusta allowed them no time to explain what they'd been thinking. She continued, unabated, in the same vein, for twenty minutes. Kate knew precisely how long it was, because the clock on the mantelpiece told her. The clock was made of satinwood, with four carved ebony feet. She sat watching it while the words flowed over her, and she watched Harry, as he leaned tight-lipped against the wall, and she watched Cousin Augusta, whose pale features were animated by her outrage. The crêpey skin at her neck was flushed, as were her usually pallid cheeks.

"I was never so *shocked* in all my *life* when I received dear Mrs. Forster's letter!" Cousin Augusta exclaimed for what

Kate thought was the eighth time. Or maybe it was the ninth. "I lay the blame *entirely* at your door, Harold. So *ill-judged*!"

This last censure, targeted at Harry alone, was too much for Kate's forbearance. She opened her mouth to defend her brother, but he beat her to it. "You make a great fuss about nothing, cousin," he said. "There was no reason in the least for you to return."

"But the *impropriety*—"

"Nonsense!" Harry said. "Kate is perfectly capable of acting as my hostess. As capable as you—" He closed his mouth abruptly and Kate knew he'd bitten back the words *if not more so.*

Cousin Augusta took a swelling breath. "The earl's presence—"

Harry's eyes kindled dangerously. He straightened away from the wall. "If you are implying, Cousin Augusta, that anything improper has happened under this roof, then I must tell you that you are more foolish than I had thought!"

Cousin Augusta bristled. "Mrs. Forster—"

"Has been far too busy! You would have done well to ignore her letter, cousin."

"She was *shocked*," cried Cousin Augusta. "And quite rightly! I was never more shocked myself when—"

"Mrs. Forster was not so shocked as to refuse an invitation to our ball," Harry said, his tone cynical. "Was she, Kate?"

Thus appealed to, Kate shook her head.

"And *that* is another thing!" cried Cousin Augusta.

"No," said Harry, his patience clearly at its end. "It is *not* another thing. Whether we have a ball or not is none of your concern!"

"But it *is* my concern! When your poor mama asked me to take care of you, on her deathbed—"

"*Enough!*" Harry said, between his teeth.

The rigidity of his expression alarmed Kate. She stood hastily and extended her hand to Cousin Augusta. "You are doubtless tired from your journey, cousin. May I suggest that you rest?"

The light of battle was in Harry's eyes. Cousin Augusta cast a glance at him, folded her lips together disapprovingly, and allowed herself to be coaxed from the room.

"I'm sure I'm very fond of your brother, Kitty," she said, as Kate escorted her up the wide staircase. "But his conduct is *quite*—"

Kate interrupted this diatribe before it could start. If there was one thing she could not tolerate from Cousin Augusta, it was criticism of Harry. "He dislikes being scolded, cousin."

"Kitty, if *anyone* is entitled to scold him, it is I! I stand in your dear mother's stead."

It was on the tip of Kate's tongue to answer hotly in the negative. Instead, she swallowed her anger and said mildly: "He is thirty years of age. Surely you must understand that he is too old to be scolded. It only serves to make him angry."

Cousin Augusta refused to understand this. She was excessively vexed. Her voice grew more agitated and by the time she reached her bedchamber she was in the throes of one of her spasms. Since these dreaded—and all too frequent—occurrences were accompanied by palpitations and mild hysteria, more than an hour passed before Kate could extricate herself from the room and leave her cousin to the ministrations of a maid.

Harry was waiting outside in the corridor. He leaned against the wall, his arms folded across his chest, one booted foot resting against the oak paneling. A heavy frown was on his face.

He straightened when he saw her and uncrossed his arms. "I'm sorry, Kate. I should have held my tongue."

Kate smiled faintly and shook her head.

Harry said, "When she talks of Mother like that—"

"I know." She reached out and took hold of his hand.

Harry gripped it tightly. "She goes too far, Kate. If Mother hadn't asked us to give her houseroom—"

"I know," Kate said again. She sighed. "I must change for dinner or else I'll be late." She managed a glimmer of a smile.

"At least we shan't have Cousin Augusta's company at the table."

Harry's laugh was short and flat. "A blessing!"

Augusta Stitchcombe didn't make an appearance that evening. James was relieved, but unsurprised. He concluded, from Harry's tense jaw, that she'd been foolish enough to come to cuffs with him. That she had, subsequent to this event, suffered a spasm, he'd known after one glance at Kate's weary face. What surprised him—and had surprised him since his first meeting with Miss Augusta Stitchcombe—was that so mild-looking a female could have such an effect on a household. Miss Stitchcombe's appearance was entirely forgettable. She was a woman in her late forties, of slight build and with graying hair and pale eyes and no chin to speak of. When he'd initially met her, some five or six years ago, he had dismissed her at a glance as a meek little dab of a woman, a cipher. He'd been wrong. Miss Stitchcombe was possessed of an entrenched belief that she alone knew best and an inability to prevent herself from giving unwanted advice—her comments to Kate about matters of household management were—in his opinion—close to impertinence. Even worse, Miss Stitchcombe had a pronounced tendency to hypochondria. If she wasn't laid up in bed with the migraine or the vapors or a touch of the influenza, then she was suffering from a nervous tic or, more likely, a spasm. James didn't understand how Harry and Kate had managed to bear her presence at Merrell Hall for so long. He'd have got rid of her years ago.

Kate and Harry both made valiant attempts to appear cheerful over dinner, and later in the drawing room, but James didn't think Miss Penrose was fooled. He certainly wasn't. His own thoughts preoccupied him, but not so much that he failed to recognize the forced note in Harry's laugh or see that Kate's smile rarely reached her eyes. He knew whom to attribute their low spirits to, and heartily cursed Miss Stitchcombe.

He was glad to seek his bed, but it took him several hours to find sleep. There was too much to think about. He lay awake, turning the events of the day over in his mind, recalling how Kate had looked in her filthy riding habit, with mud and tearstains on her face, and remembering the moment when he'd realized that he loved her.

It seemed incredible that when he'd offered for her he'd felt trapped and angry, resigned to his fate, and yet now, less than three weeks later, he loved her. It was beyond belief. But it was real. He knew deeply, in his heart, that it wasn't a passing fancy. The foundations for his love had been laid over eleven years. They were solid. There was no one—*no one*—whom he would rather marry than Kate.

But . . . would Kate want to marry him? She liked him, he was certain of that, and she blushed sometimes when he touched her, but was it possible that she could come to love him? She hadn't loved him three weeks ago. But then, he hadn't loved her three weeks ago, either. His own feelings had changed, swiftly and profoundly. Could Kate's?

He fell asleep wondering how to win Kate's heart and woke, with his lungs heaving, at Waterloo. Cannons boomed and muskets cracked and popped. The scene was smoky, a vision of Hell, with grappling figures and screaming horses.

James sat upright before he was fully awake. He dragged air into his lungs and fought back a shout. The well-remembered taste of cannon smoke was in his mouth. His heartbeat was as loud as the shells had once been. *Breathe,* he told himself. *Breathe.*

When his breathing had steadied, he unclenched his hands and rubbed his face with hard fingers, wiping away the sweat that slicked his skin. It had been more than a month since he'd woken like this, with his heart thundering, drenched in the sweat of his terror. At least he hadn't cried out this time; the sound of his shout didn't echo in the room. He'd woken when the dream had barely begun. He hadn't seen the faces, black with smoke, filthy with mud and blood, contorted in fear and savagery, as his own face must have been.

And then there was Rupert's dead face—

James swore, a short and ugly cavalry oath, and threw back the bedclothes. He went to the window and jerked the heavy, fringed curtains open. The moon was almost full. It cast shadows on the ground, turning the pleasure gardens into a strange and almost unrecognizable landscape. He fisted his hands on the windowsill and leaned his forehead against the cold glass and closed his eyes. If he was married, he could turn to Kate in the darkness and find comfort in her soft, warm body. She would whisper to him, calming, soothing, and touch him as she had that morning, stroking his hair, taking him away from his memories.

He imagined framing her face in his hands, tracing the lovely lines of her eyebrows and cheekbones and jaw. And then he imagined kissing that delicious mouth and losing himself in it. He opened his eyes as his body stirred and tightened. Heat flushed his skin. He saw the dark gardens through the shadowy, ghostly reflection of his own face in the windowpanes.

James turned away from the moonlit scene and leaned against the windowsill. He raised a hand to his shoulder, fingering the scar through his nightshirt. It wasn't his only wound, merely the one that had come closest to killing him. There was another on his arm, a third scored across his ribs, a fourth on his thigh. But he'd been lucky. He had all his limbs. He had his life.

James stood in the dark, stroking the scar and eyeing the dim shape of the bed. He wanted a love match. He wanted Kate. She had agreed to marry him if none of her candidates were suitable and he had every intention of holding her to her word, but . . .

He frowned at the empty bed. The ormolu *appliqués* on the

mahogany bedhead glinted in the moonlight. He and Kate were friends, but—friendship aside—she was extremely reluctant to marry him. If he forced her to honor her agreement, then she'd insist on a separate bedchamber. He didn't want that. He wanted Kate alongside him, every night. He wanted her to *want* to share his bed.

Somehow he had to gain her love.

# CHAPTER 12

Kate and Lizzie shared their *toilette* for the ball in Kate's bedchamber, a spacious room decorated in blue and cream. Kate watched with pleasure as her maid, Paton, transformed Lizzie from a pretty young lady into a ravishing one. The rose-pink satin slip with its overdress of gauze became Lizzie to perfection. Ribbon of the same deep shade of pink graced her dark hair, which was dressed in an elaborate and extremely becoming style with ringlets framing her face. She needed no enhancement in the form of cosmetics; her cheeks and lips were rosy and her skin clear. She had refused Kate's offer of jewelry, accepting only a slender gold chain on which she hung a cross of pink topaz.

Lizzie stood and gazed at herself in the mirror. Paton's expression was smug, as well it might be; Lizzie was a vision of loveliness.

"Oh," Lizzie said, staring at herself. "Oh!"

Kate thought James would be similarly speechless when he saw her. She smiled at her friend's wide-eyed delight in her appearance.

Lizzie turned to her. "Oh, Kate!" she exclaimed. "How can I ever thank you?"

Kate laughed as she accepted her impulsive embrace. "You can thank me by enjoying the ball."

"How can I not!" Lizzie's eyes shone with excitement. She turned back to the mirror, her hand straying over the bodice of the gown, smoothing the expensive fabric. "I've never . . . It's so beautiful."

A tap on the door signaled Cousin Augusta's entrance. She came into the room without waiting to be invited, as was her habit.

Kate suppressed a flicker of irritation.

"Hurry along, girls!" Cousin Augusta cried. "We shall be late, and that would *never* do. Oh! My dear Miss Penrose! So *exquisite.* I declare I have never seen *such*—! Oh, you shall be quite the belle of the ball!"

Lizzie flushed with shy pleasure.

"And you look very well, too, Kitty," Cousin Augusta said.

"Yes, doesn't she?" Lizzie agreed eagerly. "Quite beautiful."

Cousin Augusta tittered. "My dear Miss Penrose! No one as bran-faced as my poor, dear Kitty can be beautiful. And that hair! But she is passable. Quite passable, indeed."

Lizzie's flush deepened. "I *like* freckles," she said.

Cousin Augusta tittered again. "My dear Miss Penrose, it wasn't a criticism, I assure you. Why, I *dote* on Kitty."

Lizzie looked unconvinced.

"Kitty doesn't mind, do you, dear?" Cousin Augusta said gaily. "Why, if anyone has the right to say such things, it is I!"

Kate held her tongue. It stung, always, to be called bran-faced, however apt the description might be, but it was pointless to correct Cousin Augusta; although she was adept at giving criticism, she was quite impervious to it herself. Memory of James's threat to horsewhip all those who used the term came to her rescue, and Kate summoned a small smile. "We shall be down in a minute, cousin. Don't let us delay you."

"Well, *do* hurry, Kitty," Cousin Augusta scolded. "The

dinner guests will soon be here. So *discourteous* if you were to come down late!"

Kate lost her smile. The admonishment was quite unnecessary. There was ample time before the guests arrived, and if Cousin Augusta thought her capable of such a breach of good manners—

"Don't worry," she said, biting back a sharp retort, telling herself that her cousin didn't mean to give offense. "We will be down shortly."

Cousin Augusta hurried out of the room. Lizzie looked at Kate. There was a spark of anger in her eyes. Then she glanced at Paton. Whatever she wished to say, she was too well-bred to do so in front of the maid. She contented herself with a mild question: "Does your cousin always call you Kitty?"

Kate grimaced. "Yes, always. I have asked and asked and *asked* her not to, but—" She pressed her lips together. She wouldn't mind Katherine, but Kitty? She wasn't a Kitty.

Paton uttered a sound that was suspiciously like a snort. "Begging your pardon, Miss Kate," she said, with the confident familiarity of one who had dressed Kate since she was a girl. "But Miss Stitchcombe hears only what she's wishing to."

Kate grimaced again. Paton was quite correct. "Are you ready, Lizzie?"

Lizzie nodded.

"Well, Paton? Do we meet with your approval?"

Paton's approval being gained, they left the bedchamber. Kate glanced at Lizzie as they crossed the Long Gallery, where generations of Honeycourts gazed down on them, red-haired and freckled. "Nervous?" she asked.

"A little," Lizzie said, but the sparkle in her eyes and color in her cheeks hinted at excitement rather than nerves.

Kate was nervous, if she dared admit it to herself. She would have to open the ball by dancing with the highest-ranking gentleman present: James Hargrave, Earl of Arden. Of course it wouldn't be a waltz. Merely a minuet. She blew out a shallow breath and smoothed the long gloves up her arms and told herself that it would be a pleasure to dance with James. But in her heart of hearts she knew it wouldn't be pleasurable. On the contrary, it would be quite painful.

"And your cousin is wrong," Lizzie said as they descended the staircase. "You do look beautiful!"

Kate smiled, not believing her for an instant. "Thank you," she said.

Miss Stitchcombe unfortunately emerged from her bed-chamber in time for the ball. James had hoped, when she didn't appear for either breakfast or luncheon, that she would continue in her bed for the rest of the day. That hope had been dashed as evening approached. He'd heard her voice when he came in from his ride—and had promptly avoided her. Now though, as she entered the saloon, there was no chance of escape. She was dressed for the ball, in brown crêpe and with a lace cap on her head. She looked exactly what she was: a spinster.

James made his bow to her, a courtesy she accepted with an irritating titter. She then, coyly, compared his appearance to that of the elegant and impecunious Beau Brummell. James listened to the long-winded compliment and managed not to grit his teeth. There was some truth in Miss Stitchcombe's words; a few points of similarity did exist between himself and Brummell—aside from the obvious one of having served in the same regiment—namely an emphasis on personal hygiene and a dislike of the ostentatious in one's apparel. But many others shared those traits. Harry, for example, and Kate. And if Miss Stitchcombe had ever met Beau Brummell, as she was implying, then he'd eat his neckcloth!

Miss Stitchcombe reached the end of her compliment

and turned to Harry, praising his dress while at the same time deploring the Honeycourt coloring. James listened in grim silence, his jaw clenched, wondering whether she'd said similar things to Kate. He suppressed the urge to snap at Miss Stitchcombe. His mood was not the best. He'd seen little of Kate today. He'd talked to her briefly at the breakfast table and even more briefly over luncheon. She had been busy, immersed in a welter of final preparations for the ball that included such things as refreshments and flowers and seating for the musicians.

The door opened a second time. James turned his head and his bad humor vanished abruptly. There was Kate. Miss Penrose was with her, looking extraordinarily pretty, but he only had eyes for Kate. She wasn't pretty. The quality that she possessed was more than mere prettiness, rarer and more precious. It was beauty, and right now Kate was the most beautiful woman he'd ever seen.

She was tall and graceful in a gown cut on simple, elegant lines, with a crossover bodice and tiny puffed sleeves trimmed with seed pearls. The teal blue silk perfectly complemented her rich, bright hair. Her shawl was of ivory tulle, sheer, and woven with a delicate pattern of silk flowers, and the fan dangling from her wrist had gleaming sticks of mother-of-pearl. James stared at her, seeing the clear gray eyes, the slight smile on her full mouth, the modest silk-covered swell of her breasts, the shapely ankles beneath the scalloped hem of the gown. Pearls gleamed in her glorious hair and around her slender throat.

He had to look away, or gape at her like a smitten fool. He glanced at Harry. Harry was paying no attention to his sister. He watched Miss Penrose as she and Kate came across the room. There was admiration in his eyes and, beneath that, something close to anguish.

James almost winced. He'd planned to keep his own counsel for a few more days, but what he saw in Harry's eyes made that impossible. It was too cruel. He had to tell Harry he had no intention of offering for Miss Penrose. As soon as possible. Tonight.

He failed to speak to Harry alone before the meal, but managed several exchanges with Kate at the dinner table, protocol having put him at her right hand.

"I see Miss Stitchcombe has been restored to health," he said in a low voice.

"Yes." Kate looked down the crowded table at her cousin. "I'm pleased she felt well enough to join us."

James sent her a narrow glance. "Really, Kate? I had thought you'd be wishing her to Jericho."

Kate's gaze flicked to him, startled, faintly shocked. Then her mouth curved into a rueful smile. "I confess that I do wish she was in Bath, but—" a glimmer of laughter came into her eyes, "—I had not gone so far as to wish her to Jericho!"

James had, most definitely.

Kate must have seen this on his face, for she said: "She is difficult, James, but there's no malice in her."

"I concede your point." Miss Stitchcombe's tongue was sharp, but not deliberately nasty. "I merely wish that your cousin, well-intentioned or not, was—"

Kate shushed him hurriedly as the gentleman seated on her left turned towards her. James swallowed a laugh, and applied himself to his veal. He snatched one more brief conversation with her before the meal was over, and asked her to save him a waltz.

Kate heard him out with her eyes fixed on her plate. "Brave of you, James," she said, glancing up at him. The color in her cheeks was slightly heightened. "Are you certain you dare?"

"Do you intend to tread on my toes again?" he asked, smiling. Was it memory of her clumsiness that made her blush, or shyness at the thought of waltzing with him again? He chose to think it was the latter.

"I should, of course, endeavor not to," she said. "But I can make no promises. You would be safer to take a country dance."

"For shame, Kate," he said, grinning. "Do you take me for a coward?"

This drew a smile from her. "Very well," she said. "A waltz. But it is your fault entirely if I step on your toes!"

He managed to speak with Harry before the ball started, detaching him from his other guests by asking for a private and urgent word with him.

"Of course," said Harry, in that easy, laughing way of his. "But make it quick. You have to open the dancing, you know."

James checked to make sure that no one was within earshot, then turned to Harry. "I shan't be offering for Miss Penrose."

The laughter vanished from Harry's face, leaving it blank. There was a moment of silence. "I beg your pardon?"

James repeated himself.

Harry's eyes were serious, gray and steady. "Why not?"

"Because I don't wish to marry her."

"You . . . don't?"

James shook his head.

"But . . . but . . . *why not*?"

James shrugged. "I don't wish to."

Harry looked as if this concept was entirely beyond his comprehension. "You don't?" he asked again.

"No," James said, amused.

Disbelief was prominent on Harry's face, but beneath it was rising hope. "Are you quite certain?"

"Quite certain," James said. He smiled at his friend. "I'm not in love with her, whereas I think you are. Why didn't you tell me?"

Color rose in Harry's cheeks. "I thought—"

"You're a cod's head, Harry," James said, with great affection. "What kind of friend do you take me for? As if I'd offer for the girl you love!"

Harry said nothing. His flush deepened.

"She's in love with you, you know."

"Me?" Harry shook his head. "Oh, no. Couldn't possibly be."

James laughed. "Are you blind? She adores you!"

Harry blushed almost scarlet. Anxiety pinched his eyes. "Do you think so?"

"Yes, you idiot," James said, grinning. "Without a doubt." He held out his hand to Harry. "I wish you luck—although I don't think you'll need it."

Harry took his hand. His grip was strong. "Thank you."

James turned away. Harry's voice halted him: "Have you told Kate?"

"No. Not yet." He looked back at his friend.

Worry creased Harry's brow. "But what about you? If you don't have Miss Penrose, who will you have for a wife? There's less than a month left."

"I shall have your sister," James said.

Harry's face became blank again. "Do you want to?" His tone was diffident.

"Yes," James said. "Very much."

Harry stared at him, searching his face. "How much?" he asked bluntly.

"As much as you want Miss Penrose."

Harry frowned. "You do?"

"Yes."

Harry's frown deepened. "Dash it, James! I'm not *that* much of a cod's head! I remember very well what you said about Kate in the library."

James stepped close to his friend and met his eyes squarely. "Harry, I know what I said. But you must believe that my feelings for Kate have undergone a profound change."

Harry shook his head. "How can I believe that? You've known Kate for eleven years. How, in three weeks, can you *possibly*—"

"When have I ever lied to you?" James asked quietly.

There was silence for a moment. "Never," Harry answered.

"Then trust me now. I love your sister."

The frown didn't fade entirely from Harry's face. His gray eyes were still worried. "Does Kate know?"

James shook his head.

"I know you have an arrangement with her," Harry said. "But . . ."

"But will she be happy to marry me?"

"Yes."

James managed a wry smile. "I don't know. That is where the difficulty lies."

Harry regarded him for a moment longer, his expression sober, and then smiled. "I wish you luck," he said. "You know that nothing would make me happier than you and Kate—" He held out his hand.

"I know," James said, gripping Harry's hand. "Thank you."

Kate was enjoying her role as hostess. The opening minuet with James was behind her and her guests were disporting themselves with every sign of pleasure. Beneath the sound of violins were laughter, the murmur of scores of voices, and the rustle of silk and satin as the dancing couples made their bows to each other. The crystal drops of the chandeliers sparkled like diamonds and the air was scented with perfume and pomade and beeswax from the candles.

There were as many couples standing up for the latest country dance as the room could comfortably hold, and she congratulated herself that one of those couples was Mr. Renwick and Isabella Orton. It was a pairing that had taken some effort on her part to achieve, Mr. Renwick being a bashful young man and Isabella handsome enough to not want for dance partners, but she had prevailed in her mission. They made a fine couple as they went through the dance together and Kate was pleased to observe that Mr. Renwick's shyness had not rendered him tongue-tied. His words, whatever they were, brought laughter to Isabella's face. There was an unmistakable warmth in Mr. Renwick's eyes, and if Isabella had previously been unaware of his *tendre* for her, Kate was certain this was no longer the case.

Kate hoped there would be a match made between the pair, and turned her attention to procuring a dance partner for Amelia Hart who, having torn a flounce during the last dance, had missed the beginning of this one.

Amelia's eyes were bright with amusement and her mouth was pursed in an effort not to laugh. "Oh, do listen, Kate!" she said, in an undertone. "Mrs. Forster has started."

Mrs. Forster's voice was clearly audible. "A scandalous dance. Quite scandalous! I hope Miss Honeycourt has no intention of allowing it. Why, in *my* day—"

Kate wished that James was within earshot of Mrs. Forster's penetrating utterances, but he was on the dance floor with Lizzie. If Mr. Renwick and Isabella made a fine couple, then James and Lizzie made the finest. They were well-matched: Lizzie with her glowing prettiness, and James, tall and elegant in his formal dress. The austerity of his black satin knee breeches and dark blue coat, the stark white of the silk waistcoat and neckcloth and stockings, became him better than any man on the dance floor. He was strikingly handsome.

"To be touching in such a manner, and so close!" exclaimed Mrs. Forster to her acquaintance. "*Far* too intimate."

Kate, dreading her waltz with James, could almost agree. She slipped an arm through Amelia's and began to stroll around the perimeter of the ballroom, looking for a dance partner for her friend. The chandeliers were ablaze with candles, making spangled gauze shimmer and expensive fabrics gleam with rich luster. Potted palms and ornamental plants from the succession houses were arranged prettily at either end of the long room, their leaves dark and glossy. Mrs. Forster's voice became lost beneath the energetic fiddling of the musicians and a burst of masculine laughter from the card room.

Kate's eye alighted on Mr. Wood. She ignored him. She was still of the opinion that he and Amelia would suit very well, but it appeared that he had no intention of being married for a second time. His interest had been nothing more than a flirtation. Poor Amelia.

She turned her attention from Mr. Wood. Spying the eldest Charnwood boy, she drew him into conversation with Amelia and had the satisfaction of seeing them paired for the next dance.

A glance around the ballroom assured her that no young ladies languished neglected and ill at ease; having been a wallflower so often during her Seasons in London, it was a fate she wished for no one. Kate fanned herself idly. The combined heat of the scores of guests and hundreds of candles made the room almost too warm, but the tall French windows were open onto the terrace, allowing a cool breeze to enter and preventing the atmosphere from becoming stifling. Torches flamed outside, although the strong moonlight made them almost unnecessary. The coachmen need have no fear of overturning their vehicles on the country roads tonight.

"Do you intend to have the waltz, Miss Honeycourt?" came a familiar voice.

Kate turned her head and found herself confronted by Mrs. Forster, a formidable figure in purple silk. She quelled a cowardly urge to reply in the negative. "Yes," she said, with a smile. "Have you come to scold me, ma'am?"

James anticipated his waltz with Kate with pleasure. He watched her out of the corner of his eye. She was talking to a square dowager dressed in purple. Harry had taken one look at Kate's companion and steered James and Miss Penrose away. "Oh, Lord," he'd said, under his breath. "It's Mrs. Forster."

It had been James who'd danced with Miss Penrose, but Harry who escorted her to the room where the refreshments were laid out. James had ceded this duty to his friend without protest and stood now watching the assembled guests. Many of the faces were familiar. He saw Miss Ingham, giggling, and the Misses Bellersby in the company of an elderly gentleman who must be their father. Miss Orton had vanished into the refreshments room, her hand on the arm of a tall and bashful young man, and he'd seen the bloodthirsty Miss Wilmot in the crush, too. The entire Charnwood family was present, including Miss Horatia, who'd been minding her dance steps with painful concentration, and her eldest sister, who had, as far as James had observed, not stopped talking since she'd entered the ballroom. There, in the corner, was Miss Hart, with her ample figure and pretty dimples—

James realized he wasn't the only gentleman with his gaze on Miss Hart. A stout, pleasant-faced man of perhaps his own age was watching her with more than casual interest. James wondered who he was.

He asked Harry, when he'd returned from liberating Kate from Mrs. Forster.

Harry followed his gaze. "Mr. Wood. He owns Brede Hall. He's a widower. Nice chap."

James watched Mr. Wood watch Miss Hart, and thought that Kate's imagination hadn't been overactive. If he wasn't mistaken, Mr. Wood was contemplating a second marriage. James wondered if Kate had noticed the man's intent interest in her friend. A glance in her direction told him she hadn't; she was laughing with Miss Penrose, several paces distant.

"She's lovely," he said involuntarily, under his breath.

"Miss Penrose?" Harry said, his voice equally low. "Yes, isn't she just!"

"I meant your sister," James said, amused, careful that his words weren't overheard by a young buck who stood nearly at his elbow.

"Eh?" said Harry, in a startled tone. His eyes narrowed with sudden suspicion. "James . . . are you bosky?"

James laughed. "No," he said, shaking his head. And then: "You don't see it, do you?"

"But . . . she has the Honeycourt coloring."

Harry's tone was so baffled that James almost laughed out loud again. He grinned at Harry, and saw in his friend's face everything that he liked so much in Kate's. They were very similar in appearance, Harry and Kate, with their freckles and red hair, their slim build and gray eyes. Harry's features were arranged as felicitously as Kate's and, like his sister, his intelligence and humor and innate integrity were obvious in his face. It was no wonder that Miss Penrose had fallen for Harry.

"I like the Honeycourt coloring," James said. "And," he dropped his voice to a whisper, "I think Miss Penrose does too."

Harry flushed.

James waltzed with Miss Penrose, who acquitted herself creditably, and then danced a *cotillion* with Amelia Hart and a *boulanger* with Isabella Orton. He stood up with Marianne Charnwood next, and was reminded of how lively a companion she was. It was with regret that he bowed to her and turned to her duller sister, Caroline, for the *contredanse*. Kate was correct. It was a shame that Marianne Charnwood was unmarried. But—rack his brain as he might—he could think of no gentleman of his acquaintance who would suit her.

After Caroline Charnwood came Fanny Bellersby, and after her, Dorothea Ingham. James, bored by these partners, was utterly relieved when it came time to take Kate onto the dance floor. He was only sorry that the music was more sedate than the romping tune they'd waltzed to in the drawing room. He couldn't spin so fast or hold Kate so close when the musicians played with such decorum. He was sorry, too, that they both wore gloves; holding Kate's bare hand had made the dance seem much more intimate.

There was no hint of shyness in her this time, nor clumsiness as he took her through sophisticated turns. Her manner was perfectly unruffled. "Look," she said, her tone pleased.

"Isabella and Mr. Renwick are dancing a *second* time—and it's a waltz!"

"So are we," he pointed out.

He thought that Kate almost faltered in her step. "Oh, but that's quite different," she said.

James didn't agree, but he refrained from saying so aloud. He wanted Kate graceful in his arms, not stiff and self-conscious. Harry and Miss Penrose were also dancing together for a second time, but he didn't draw Kate's attention to that either. "Have you seen Miss Hart's partner?" he said instead.

"No. Where is she? Oh! Mr. Wood! Just look at the expression on his face!"

James didn't bother looking; he'd already seen the warm intentness in the man's gaze. He took advantage of Kate's distraction to draw her slightly closer to his body. He wished he could press himself against her. He glanced down at the smooth curve of her cheek, seeing the freckles and liking them. Nothing short of maquillage would hide them and Kate had the sense not to try that. She wore no cosmetics. The rosy lips were unrouged. "James, do you think . . . ?"

"Miss Hart and Mr. Wood? Yes. I think it quite likely."

He watched her mouth shape itself into a delighted smile. The urge to kiss her became almost overwhelming. Fortunately the music came to an end.

"How marvelous!" said Kate, as he escorted her from the dance floor. "It would be perfect if—" Her voice stopped abruptly.

James glanced at her and halted. Kate's expression was dismayed. He followed the direction of her gaze, to where Harry and Miss Penrose stood. Miss Penrose's hand was on Harry's arm, and her face was turned up to him. Her expression was shyly adoring. Harry's face was less revealing of his feelings, but the tenderness and admiration in his eyes were unmistakable.

"A match, I think," James said, keeping his tone light.

Kate's voice aghast: "But I meant Lizzie for you!"

"Would you begrudge your brother a love match?" he teased her gently.

"It's not funny, James!" Kate turned to him. "It's a disaster!"

There was a general movement towards the refreshments. James steered Kate in the opposite direction, out onto the terrace. The night air was cool and refreshingly clean after the scents of so many people. Torches flamed, casting warmth and light. He took her around the corner of the house, so their *tête-à-tête* wouldn't be overheard.

"It's not a disaster," he said, stopping in shadows cast by the full moon.

"But it is!"

"If Harry and Miss Penrose are happy, how can it be a disaster?"

"But—"

"Don't you want them to be happy?"

"Of course I do."

"So it's not a disaster. Quite the opposite in fact."

"But James, I thought . . ." Kate's voice was troubled, tentative. "Don't you want to marry Lizzie?"

"No," he said. "So don't picture me with a broken heart, Kate."

"But—"

"Kate," he said. "I like Miss Penrose, certainly, but I *don't* want to marry her."

"Oh," Kate said, clearly bewildered. "Why not?"

"Does it matter, Kate?"

"No, perhaps not." Her tone was worried. "Oh, but it *is* a disaster! We've lost two whole weeks. There's so little time left. Less than a month until your birthday!"

James stepped closer to her. "And I keep telling you, Kate, that it's *not* a disaster. I've found someone I'd very much like to marry."

The words were out of his mouth before he realized he'd spoken them—and for a brief, panicked second he wished them unsaid. He'd not meant to declare himself tonight. It was too soon. He had no real idea of what Kate's feelings for him were.

She stood silently for a moment. He'd chosen the shadows so they'd be unobserved, but wished now that they stood in moonlight. He wanted to see her face more clearly.

"Who?" she asked finally, her tone cautious. "I thought you disliked the other candidates."

"You, Kate."

"*Me?*" She stepped back. "Oh, no, James! Not me."

"Why not?"

"Why not?" She echoed his words, her face a pale and indistinct oval. "The question is *why,* James, not why not."

James stood in the dark, watching Kate. The answer to her question was on his tongue, but he found himself afraid to utter the words. It wasn't the fear that had accompanied him in battle. That had been a silent whine in the back of his throat, thin and sharp, shortening his breath and quickening his heartbeat, bringing cold sweat to his skin. This was a different fear, an apprehensive emotion that was centered in his chest, a painful clenching. He took a low, slow breath: "Because I love you."

"No," Kate said, her tone fierce. "Don't be absurd!"

He asked quietly: "Why is it absurd?"

"Because it *is!*"

"But Kate, I do." He stepped closer to her again. He wanted to reach out and touch her, but dared not. "I do love you."

"As a friend, perhaps, but nothing more than that."

"No?"

"No. It is inconceivable!"

"Why?"

"You know why!" she cried angrily. "You only have to look at me to know why!"

He considered her words for a moment. A breeze stirred his hair, bringing strains of music with it. A *cotillion* was starting. "You're talking about more than affection, aren't you, Kate?"

"I don't wish to discuss this."

"But I do." James stepped even closer, until mere inches separated them. "You're talking about desire, aren't you, Kate? About passion." He raised a hand to her cheek, touching it lightly. "Is it inconceivable that I could desire you?"

She jerked her head away, leaving him with his fingers outstretched. "Yes."

He was sad—and at the same time furiously angry. Not with Kate, but with everyone who'd ever confirmed her belief that she was undesirable: the young men who'd not stood up to dance with her, the girls who'd laughed at her freckles, the ladies who'd bemoaned her hair, Sir Thomas Granger, *everyone.* He closed his hand into a fist and lowered it to his side.

"You think I don't desire you." He made it a statement, not a question.

"I *know* that you don't."

James stared at her shadowy figure, wondering how to convince her. The only tool he had was the truth. "You have the most beautiful mouth I've ever seen, Kate," he said softly. "So full and sweet. Do you have any idea how much I want to kiss you?"

Kate took a step back.

"And your hair." He stepped towards her. "Do you know how many colors are in it? So bright and rich. So glorious. I want to unpin it, Kate. I want to touch it."

He reached out as if to do so and she took another step backwards, moving from shadow into moonlight. Her eyes were wide and staring. James moved one pace closer to her. Kate stepped back again, until she was pressed against the ivy-covered wall.

"And your throat," James said, closing the distance between them. He stripped his right glove off and touched bare fingers to her throat, stroking lightly. The skin was as smooth as he'd imagined.

Kate flinched, inhaling in a gasp. "James!"

He rested a fingertip on the pulse at the base of her throat.

Her heart beat wildly. "If I kiss you here, Kate," he whispered. "What will you do?"

"Stop it, James! You're being absurd." Her voice wasn't frightened or angry, it was breathless. He felt her pulse and heard her voice and smiled to himself. No, Kate wasn't indifferent to him.

He removed his fingertip from her skin and stepped even closer, until his body almost brushed hers.

"Stop it!" Kate said again. She pushed her hands against his chest. Her fan swung between them, dangling from her wrist.

James bent his head until his mouth was by her ear. "Are you certain you want me to stop?" he asked, and then he placed a kiss on her skin.

He closed his eyes and inhaled her scent. There was no heavy, cloying odor of perfume, nor could he distinguish the lighter scents of rose or orange-flower water. Instead there was an elusive fragrance, a hint of something fresh and clean, as if she bathed with herbs in her water.

"Of course!" Kate said.

James ignored her words long enough to kiss his way down the line of her jaw. The kisses were feather-light, the merest brush of his mouth against her skin. He held her, his hands at her waist, and felt the faint quivering of her body. It wasn't the cool breeze that made her shiver; her skin was warm.

"Do you still doubt that I desire you, Kate?" he whispered, when he reached her chin. He licked lightly below her lower lip, a small and delicate movement of his tongue. It was the prelude to a kiss, but that kiss never came. He laid his mouth on hers for the briefest instant, the merest fraction of a second, and then Kate jerked her head aside and pushed at his chest, hard.

"Yes!" she cried. "I *do* doubt it!"

Frustration coiled in his muscles. He didn't want to stop. His desire for her was intense. He wanted to hold her tightly, to press himself against her, to feel her body against his, warm and soft. To open her mouth and kiss her properly, to taste her.

James released her and stepped back. He was trembling. "But I do, Kate," he said, struggling to keep the frustration from his voice. He wanted her more than he'd ever wanted any woman. How could she not believe him? "I do desire you."

"No!" Her tone was low and fierce. "You *don't*." She pushed past him roughly. Her dancing slippers slapped faintly on the flagged stone as she ran back to the ballroom.

James was left on the terrace in the moonlight, alone and dismayed. A cool breeze slid over his face, bringing with it laughter and music. He squeezed his eyes shut and cursed under his breath. Kate had been wrong. *This* was the evening's disaster.

# $C$HAPTER 13

$\mathcal{K}$ate had been lucky enough to avoid James at the breakfast table, having come down very late, but she knew an interview between them was inevitable after what had happened last night. She'd spent long hours thinking about it, sleepless, while the sky had lightened into dawn, remembering the words he'd said and the soft touch of his mouth on her skin. His hands had been at her waist, warm and strong, and she'd felt hot, as if she blushed all over. His kisses had been so light and delicate down the line of her jaw that they could have been the whisper of a butterfly's wings, and when he'd touched his tongue to her skin she'd felt a sensation, deep inside herself, that had been hot and sweet and almost painful. And then he'd tried to kiss her properly, his mouth against hers, and her heart had almost leapt from her chest.

He'd said that he desired her, that he loved her, and if she hadn't overheard his words to Harry in the library, she might almost have been fooled. But she *had* heard them and could remember them quite vividly. And because of that, she knew he was lying.

She thought she knew why. With Lizzie no longer a candidate and time running short, James had decided to go with his first choice: herself. And being a kind man, he'd decided to give her the love match she wanted. Well, *he* may have given up, but *she* hadn't! James deserved a wife he could feel desire for, one he could love. There were still three potential brides he hadn't met. Any of them would be better than she was.

Kate sat at the little writing desk in the morning room, waiting for Lizzie to join her for their daily walk. She unfolded the two lists, looking at them for the first time since Lizzie's arrival. She studied the requirements and then the names. The three remaining candidates had been at the ball last night. She would have shown them to James if she hadn't been so shaken by what had happened on the terrace.

"Kate."

She started, nearly dropping the lists, and turned her head. James stood in the doorway. His face was closed and unsmiling. As always, when the smile was absent, his features arranged themselves into a sternness that would daunt the uninitiated. Kate, not one of their number, was still daunted. Dread tightened her chest. This was one conversation she wished was over.

"James," she replied, and was pleased to discover that her voice was calm.

"I beg your pardon for my conduct last night."

"You were foxed," she said, smiling slightly, giving him an opportunity to retract the statements he'd made on the terrace.

"I was not foxed!" he said, stepping into the room. His slanting black eyebrows drew together in one of his ferocious frowns. "I meant what I said. I *do*—"

"Please!" Kate said sharply, panicked, cutting him off. "Don't." She didn't think she could bear to hear those false words of love again.

James's mouth closed in a tight line. He shut the door and advanced into the morning room. Kate watched with growing alarm as he came towards her. He halted, several feet distant, and stood looking down at her. "Very well," he said. "I won't." He stared at her for a taut, silent moment, his eyes intent on her face. "Kate, may I ask you a question?"

Her trepidation increased. He was going to ask what her own feelings were. She would have to lie. "Of course," she said, her tone light and cool. If he could prevaricate about such matters, then so could she.

"Why do you want a love match?"

Her mouth almost dropped open. She blinked and stared at him, unprepared for such a question. "I beg your pardon?"

"Why do you want a love match?"

Kate dropped her eyes to the lists in her hand. She felt herself blush. She moistened her lips nervously, unsure whether she should even answer such a question. It was *not* the sort of subject she should discuss with a gentleman, even one she knew so well as—

"Kate?"

"Because . . ."

"Because?"

Her cheeks burned. "Because I don't think I could endure a marriage without affection and . . . and—" She bit her lip and stared at the lists. She *couldn't* say it.

"And passion," he said. "Affection and passion. That's it, isn't it, Kate? You want what your parents had."

Highly embarrassed, Kate managed a minuscule nod. She kept eyes on the lists in her hand. Her cheeks were acutely hot. She wished that Lizzie would hurry.

"Don't you think we could have passion, Kate? If we married?"

The words, spoken mildly, brought more heat to her cheeks. She knew the answer. "No," she said, still not looking at him.

"Why not, Kate? We have affection. Why not passion?"

"Our affection is that of friends. Quite platonic! Not . . . not—"

"Mine isn't."

"Well, a brother for a sister, then," she said desperately. "There can be no passion there!"

He was silent for a moment. "Is that how you feel, Kate? That I'm a friend? A brother?"

"Yes!"

"And there can be no passion between us?"

"No! It's impossible!"

"And you don't wish to marry me?"

"No!"

At that answer he made a sound that was half laugh, half sigh. "Would it be so very distasteful to marry me, Kate?"

"If we do not love each other, yes!"

"But—"

"You promised to look at all the candidates." She overrode him, panicked by his persistence. "There are still three left on the list."

There was a long moment of silence. "And you promised to marry me if none of them suited me," James said finally, quietly.

"And you promised to give them a fair chance! I shall hold you to that promise, James!"

"And I shall hold you to your promise."

Kate glanced up. James's voice had been mild, but his expression was annoyed. He held out an impatient hand. "Who's left?"

She handed him the lists.

"Miss Cecily Mornington," he read. "Miss Sarah Durham . . . Mrs. Emmeline Hurst?"

"A widow."

He said nothing. He turned to the second list and read, his eyebrows rising. "That," he said, pointing, "is *not* one of my requirements."

"What?" Kate asked, reaching for the list, wondering why he sounded angry. "Oh, that. Well, you should have a pretty wife, not a . . . an antidote such as I."

"Take it off the list," James said, articulating each word clearly. His voice was hard and, glancing at him, she saw that his jaw was clenched. "And you are not an antidote!"

Kate didn't bother to reply. They both knew she was one. Pressing her lips together, taking refuge in anger, she dipped a quill in ink and drew a line through the word *Pretty*. "You should set your standards higher, James," she said crossly.

"I like your looks!"

She ignored this blatant lie. "*And* I'm old. You should have a wife who's younger than I."

"You're hardly in your dotage, Kate."

"Nor am I in my first bloom." She laid down the quill and looked up in time to see James grit his teeth. His fearsome frown was back.

"Neither am I," he said, biting out each word.

"Raise your standards, James!" she snapped. "You can pick and choose! Any lady would be pleased to have you as a husband."

"Except you."

Sudden heat flushed her cheeks. She lowered her eyes before he could see the truth in them: that if he truly loved her, there was nothing she would like more than to be his wife.

"This is a change of tone, Kate." She heard anger in his voice. "First I'm too nice in my requirements, and now I'm not nice enough! Which am I to be? Mr. Collins or Mr. Darcy? Do, pray, tell me!"

Kate remained silent, knowing she'd earned this reproof.

James said nothing for several seconds. When he spoke again, his voice had lost its hard, angry edge. "Kate," he said softly. "I love you."

Kate stood so abruptly that she almost overturned the chair. It hurt to hear him utter such lies. "You're talking nonsense, James!"

"Am I?" His face was tight.

"Yes! And I wish you would stop it." Kate picked up the lists and walked past him to the door. "We can visit Miss Durham this afternoon." She halted with her hand on the handle and glanced back. He hadn't moved, but merely turned his head to watch her. "I suggest we take a groom this time," she said.

James's eyes narrowed. "No," he said flatly. "We will not take a groom."

"Then I won't—"

"It's not a closed carriage." He cut the words off tightly with his teeth.

"But—"

"If you wish to show me these candidates of yours, then we will *not* take a groom."

Kate was tempted to argue the point, but common sense told her that James couldn't continue last night's caresses while he drove, however skilled he was with the ribbons.

"Very well." She opened the door and walked through it, leaving him in the morning room. She was trembling. "Oh, there you are, Lizzie!" Kate managed a smile. "Are you ready?"

James had been unable to find fault with Miss Sarah Durham's appearance or manner. The short visit, mostly spent in discussion of the ball—which Miss Durham had greatly enjoyed—told him that she met his requirements for a suitable wife. Not as well as Miss Penrose, perhaps, but still well enough. And yet Miss Durham was completely unsuitable, for the simple reason that he was no longer prepared to settle for a marriage of convenience. He wanted a love match, and he could have that with only one person: Kate.

He declared Miss Durham unsuitable. "She has a lisp," he told Kate once they were back in the curricle. "An irritating speech defect, don't you agree?"

Kate hadn't agreed. She'd not been pleased.

James refrained from embellishing his falsehood. He had the feeling that Kate would box his ears, given the slightest provocation. She was very cross with him.

Back at Merrell Hall, Kate avoided any chance of a *tête-à-tête*. She retired early, claiming a headache, although that may not have been a lie; she looked very weary.

Now, seated alongside her in the curricle on the way to view Mrs. Emmeline Hurst, he thought that she looked much less heavy-eyed. Her manner, though, was distant and edgy. James refused to be discouraged. His birthday might be little more than three weeks away, but he would have Kate as a wife before then. He'd view the remaining candidates, as she had asked, and then he'd hold her to her word and marry her. And he'd make damned sure that she thought of him as a lover, not a friend or a brother!

James gritted his teeth as he remembered her words: *There can be no passion there.* Well, Kate was wrong, and he'd show her. He was no callow youth. He knew how to give a woman pleasure so intense that she cried out. He'd rouse a desire in Kate that was equal to his own. He'd make her *want* to share his bed—and there'd be no more of this nonsense about passion being impossible.

Love, though, was more difficult. He couldn't make Kate love him. He could only hope that she would come to do so.

He glanced at Kate, seeing her fine profile, noting that the blue kerseymere pelisse with its dark sable trim became her beautifully. It was on the tip of his tongue to tell her how lovely she looked, but he bit back the words. He was resolved not to court her until he'd viewed, and rejected, the final candidates. He had made the decision in light of Kate's anger in the library. He'd never heard her speak so sharply in all the years he'd known her. For a moment he'd been afraid she would renege on her agreement to marry him. That fear kept him silent now, although his frustration grew with every second that passed. This wasn't how he wanted to spend his time, looking over ladies he had no intention of marrying.

James frowned at his horses. Kate felt affection for him—*that,* she hadn't denied. And she'd responded to his touch on the terrace. There'd been passion there. He had felt it in the quiver of her body and the beating of her heart, he'd heard it in her breathless voice. She was wrong and he was right—and he would have her for a wife.

But first, Mrs. Hurst.

Mrs. Hurst was almost as suitable as Miss Durham—if he'd been looking for a *mariage de convenance*. He thought she wouldn't be a widow for long. She had the demeanor of a lady who liked men, who knew about passion and who enjoyed the pleasures of the flesh. Her features and figure weren't as fine as Lizzie Penrose's, but she had something else, a sensuality that Miss Penrose, in her innocence, lacked. Mrs. Hurst's hazel eyes were bright and knowing, and she made it quite clear, in her flickering, sidelong glances at him, that she liked what she saw. She was very much a lady. There was nothing vulgar about her; the flirting was subtle and discreet. She parted her lips slightly and let him see the tip of her tongue between her neat little teeth, she touched her necklace to draw attention to her breasts—her ploys were numerous and, to his eye, unmistakable, although Kate seemed unaware of them. But they weren't directed at Kate; they were directed at him.

James watched it all with a faint smile on his face, appreciating Mrs. Hurst's tactics, enjoying the display but wanting nothing of what was offered. The demure glances through dark and curling eyelashes, the flick of glossy nut-brown ringlets over a shoulder, the pouting of full lips, the slight arch of her back to bring the full breasts into prominence—it was all well done, and it left him cold. But when he looked at Kate . . . then the heat came.

Mrs. Hurst was the type of lady with whom he could have had an entertaining interlude in years past, the type of lady he could easily have married for convenience, *if*—and he knew that the if was there—*if* he was prepared to turn a blind eye to her dalliances with other men. She would enliven his bed *and* the beds of other men. Her laugh was rich, her eyes inviting, her heart fickle.

Kate wasn't as dashing as Mrs. Hurst, but there were dozens

of Mrs. Hursts, hundreds. And only one Kate. Kate had integrity. She was someone who would bestow her love only once. If he could convince her to bestow that love on him, she'd make him happier than Mrs. Hurst and her ilk ever could. He felt nothing when he looked at Mrs. Hurst, not even the faintest pricking of lust, but when he looked at Kate . . .

If he had Kate, he would never want anyone else. She would be everything to him: lover, friend, wife. There'd be no need for opera dancers, no need for anyone but her.

"Well?" Kate asked in the curricle, her tone cool.

"Too . . ." he almost said *fast,* but substituted a more polite term, ". . . dashing for my taste."

Kate's lips pinched together. "Dashing."

"Yes."

"I thought you'd like that: a dashing widow. Most men do." Her voice was sleek and barbed, angry.

"I prefer you," he said bluntly.

"Nonsense!"

He met her eyes. "You would never take a lover, would you, Kate?"

The anger fled, chased away by shock. "Of course not!"

"Mrs. Hurst would."

Kate said nothing more after that. She sat silent and frowning. James concentrated on his team. A curl had strayed from beneath Kate's bonnet and lay against her cheek, vivid in the sunlight, absolutely begging to be touched. He held the reins tightly between his fingers and paid great attention to the road, and cursed himself for a coward.

*The hell with it,* he thought, as they began the drive through the park. He slowed the horses to a walk and reached across and brushed the curl back from Kate's cheek with his gloved fingertips. It was something he'd done once before; unfortunately, this time, her reaction was less gratifying. She flinched from him.

"What are you doing!" Her voice was sharp and hurried, slightly panicked.

James lowered his hand. "Your hair has come loose," he said, mildly.

There was a moment of silence. Then: "Oh," she said.

A quick glance told him that a flush had risen in her cheeks. James took note of that telltale color, and smiled. The smile was short-lived. He lost it when Kate edged slightly away from him on the seat, as if he was a leper, and tucked the errant curl firmly behind her ear. James clenched the reins, restraining his temper as he restrained the horses. He wanted to shake her, to rip off the bonnet and throw it away and kiss her. He did none of those things. Instead, he allowed the horses to pick up their pace. His only sign of anger was the breath that hissed between his teeth.

They accomplished the rest of the drive in silence. Back at Merrell Hall, Kate avoided him again. She was polite and cool and distant during dinner, and afterwards in the drawing room. She retired early. Harry caught his eye, and James waited until Miss Penrose and Miss Stitchcombe had also departed the drawing room. Then he asked Harry: "Well?"

"That's *my* question," Harry said, lounging on a green-and-yellow striped couch. "Well?"

James laughed, but it was without humor. "I made a mull of it."

"I thought so," Harry said, with no satisfaction in his voice. "Kate's not happy with you."

"No." He didn't tell his friend just how much of a mess he'd made of the proposal, how grossly he'd overstepped the bounds of propriety. He didn't think Harry would be pleased to hear that he'd backed Kate up against a wall and tried to kiss her. He said, instead: "She doesn't believe me."

Harry's mouth twisted into a smile. "Frankly, I don't blame her."

James thrust to his feet. The lyre-back chair almost toppled, its legs thumping on the carpet. "Damn it, Harry!"

Harry waved him down. "I believe you," he said. "I'm just saying that I can't blame Kate for not doing so."

James steadied the chair and sat again.

"So . . . what are you going to do?"

James rested his elbows on his knees and stared down at the carpet. A green fern leaf curled against a pale yellow background. "I have a plan."

"Tell me."

James laughed. The sound was hollow. "It's nothing fancy. I'll hold Kate to her word and marry her, and then I'll *prove* it to her . . ."

Harry was silent. Finally he spoke: "Do you think you can?"

"Prove it to her? Yes. Make her love me? I don't know, Harry. I don't know. She did eleven years ago, after a fashion."

"A long time ago."

"Yes."

"So . . . you'll have Kate as a wife, whether she wants it or not?" Harry's tone was neutral.

James looked up and met his eyes. "Yes."

There was no amusement on Harry's face. Instead, there was censure.

"You don't approve."

"James . . ." Harry leaned forward on the couch. "She's my sister. I don't want her to make an unhappy match."

"I'll do everything in my power to make her happy. You know I will!"

Harry sighed. "James . . ."

"Trust me."

"All right," Harry said, rising to his feet. "All right! I won't interfere. Just—"

"She will be happy. Trust me."

Harry sighed again, and shook his head. "All right." He turned towards the door.

"What about Miss Penrose? You haven't asked her yet, have you?"

Harry halted. He turned to face James. "No. I haven't."

"Why not?"

Harry blushed. "It's only been seventeen days. I thought . . . don't you think it's too soon to ask?"

"No," James said. Then he managed a grin. "You've been counting the days?"

Harry's flush deepened.

"Ask her," James said. "She won't refuse you."

Harry looked down at his boots. He scuffed one gently against the green and yellow Savonnerie. "I thought . . . three weeks is more fitting."

"*Ask* her!"

"Three weeks," Harry said firmly.

"Kate," Lizzie said, as they took their morning walk through the park together. "There is something . . . that is to say . . . I would like to ask you . . ."

Kate smiled and glanced sideways at her friend. Although she was an energetic walker, Lizzie's cheeks were unaccountably flushed. "Is it about Harry?"

The color in Lizzie's cheeks grew deeper. "Yes," she said, not meeting Kate's eyes.

"You will be very happy together."

"Oh, no!" Lizzie cried. "I mean— He hasn't asked me . . ." Her words trailed into miserable confusion.

Kate stopped and turned to her. "Then he is being shockingly slow."

"Perhaps . . . but I have no fortune, Kate, and my birth isn't noble—"

"As if Harry cared about that!"

Lizzie raised her eyes. "Do you think so, Kate?"

"I know so," she said firmly. "Honeycourts have always married for love, not consequence."

"But—"

"My mother was no noblewoman, Lizzie. She was a gentleman's daughter like yourself, with no fortune or title. A very ordinary Miss Stitchcombe."

"Oh."

"So don't think you aren't good enough for Harry, for I assure you, *he* doesn't think so!"

"Oh," Lizzie said again, twisting her gloved hands together.

Kate softened her voice: "Lizzie . . . Harry will be very lucky to have you as a wife."

Lizzie blushed scarlet. "I . . ."

Kate took hold of her friend's hands before she could ruin the kid gloves with her wringing. "I must confess that I asked you here with marriage in mind." Her smile was rueful. "Only, I thought James, not Harry . . ." She looked at Lizzie. "Why not James?"

"Oh," Lizzie said, flushing even more deeply, if such a thing was possible. "I like Arden well enough—he is very nice! But . . ."

"But?"

"But . . ." Lizzie's brow crinkled, as if she searched for words. "But he has . . . shadows inside him that your brother doesn't have. A . . . a darkness."

Kate was silent a moment, remembering. "He wasn't always that way," she said, her voice low in memory. "If you could have seen him when he was younger. There was such laughter in him. Such *joie de vivre*."

She looked at Lizzie, but her eyes saw James as he'd been when she'd first met him, so young and merry. Lord, but she'd made such a fool of herself, with her blatant, puppy-dog adoration! There had been no shadows in him then, no darkness. It was the Peninsular War that had done that to him, and Waterloo, and his brother's death. They'd left scars on his soul.

"I like Arden very well," Lizzie assured her. "Indeed I do! But . . . I like your brother so much more. He's . . . he's lighter in his heart."

"Yes," Kate said. "He is." She wanted to defend James, to

point out his essential kindness, his willingness to laugh, but she knew Lizzie had seen these things—and chosen Harry. "You must like freckles very much."

Color rose in Lizzie's cheeks again. "Your brother is exceedingly handsome."

Kate could only shake her head and laugh. Harry, handsome? Lizzie was more besotted than she'd thought. "I shall be glad to have you for a sister," she said, releasing Lizzie's hands and embracing her friend.

"He hasn't asked me yet," Lizzie said, a quiver in her voice.

"He will," Kate said. "Or else I shall have something to say to him!"

Lizzie laughed, shakily. Her eyes, when Kate stepped back enough to see them, were bright with unshed tears, anxious and eager to believe. "Do you think so?"

"I know so," Kate said.

Kate found Harry alone in the library before luncheon. She closed the door behind her and eyed him, trying to understand what Lizzie had meant by handsome. Harry certainly looked well enough. Like James, his clothes were distinguished by their understated elegance, and, like James, he disdained the fripperies of fashion. He wasn't quite as tall as James, nor so strongly built, but his legs were well-shaped and his shoulders needed no padding. If not for the hair and the freckles, he could conceivably be called well-favored. But handsome?

Harry looked up from the *Gazette*. "Do you want something, Kate?"

Prompted by memory of Lizzie's anxiety, Kate sat down alongside him on the couch. She fingered the smooth mahogany of the scrolled arm, aware that she was inviting a sharp set-down. "Harry, if you don't mind me asking . . . what are your intentions towards Lizzie?"

Harry blushed to the roots of his hair.

"Are you intending to offer for her?"

"Dash it, Kate!" he said, folding the *Gazette* briskly. "I don't have to explain myself to you!"

"I know, and I'm sorry, but Lizzie is my friend. If you are merely amusing yourself—"

The words brought a flash of anger to Harry's eyes. "Amuse myself? As if I would!"

"Good," Kate said, smiling at him. "That's what I thought." She held out her hand to him. "Don't be cross with me, please."

Harry put down the *Gazette* and took hold of her fingers. His smile was wry. "Are you disappointed, Kate? I know you meant Miss Penrose for James."

"Of course I'm not disappointed! I am very, *very* happy. I should love to have Lizzie for a sister."

Harry continued to hold her hand. His eyes searched her face. "What about James?"

Kate felt heat rise in her cheeks. She removed her hand and stood, walking towards the windows. "I shall find him another bride. I have several in mind."

There was a moment of silence. "Not yourself?" Harry's voice was diffident.

"Oh, no!" Kate said, looking out over the park. "Someone much more suitable."

"Define suitable, Kate."

"Oh . . ." She shrugged, staring at the stands of trees and soft undulations of the lawn. "Someone prettier than I, younger—"

"Do you think that's what James wants?"

"Of course!"

# CHAPTER 14

*M*iss Stitchcombe had an attack of the vapors after luncheon. This required Kate's presence in her bedchamber for much of the afternoon, so the viewing of Cecily Mornington was necessarily postponed until the morrow. But Miss Mornington wasn't at home when they drove past on the following day, a circumstance that brought a worried frown to Kate's brow. "There's so little time," she said, her tone anxious.

James said nothing. His goal, now, was different from Kate's.

Miss Mornington and her mother returned their visit the next afternoon, and sat down to light refreshments with Kate, Miss Penrose, and himself. Harry had grimaced when he'd identified the carriage and swiftly absented himself. James, forming a rapid and deep dislike of Mrs. Mornington, soon wished he'd done the same. Mrs. Mornington was quite the most ferocious snob he'd ever met. The granddaughter of a duke—a fact she very quickly let drop—she spoke authoritatively about London, claimed intimate acquaintance with numerous members of the *ton,* and dropped names in a manner that was as ludicrous as it was pretentious. James, torn between amusement and irritation, tried to catch Kate's eye, but she assiduously avoided looking at him. Perhaps it was as well; Mrs. Mornington would doubtless be offended if he started laughing.

Cecily Mornington was an attractive young lady of two-and-twenty years, with fair coloring, aquiline features, and a gracious manner. Her conversation was smooth, her laughter polite, her posture excellent. She would be a marvelous society hostess—a circumstance her mother brought to his attention. From Mrs. Mornington's repeated mention of his earldom and her interest in his estates and his house in Mayfair, James was given to understand that he met her requirements for a suitable husband for her daughter. This condescension had the effect of raising his hackles. His smile became a mere baring of his teeth, tight and insincere. Mrs. Mornington, proud granddaughter of a duke, didn't notice.

Mrs. Mornington's pride led her into another mistake: she all but ignored Miss Penrose, having swiftly ascertained that her birth wasn't noble. This, in James's opinion, was an unforgivable piece of rudeness. Cecily Mornington, whose manners weren't as arrogant as her mother's, deigned to converse with Miss Penrose. For this politeness, James could like her, but not enough to marry.

Mrs. Mornington and her daughter left, issuing an invitation for dinner next week. Kate accepted, to James's annoyance. Miss Penrose, with a glance at the clock on the mantelpiece, blushed and excused herself to change for her riding lesson with Harry. James looked at Kate. Anticipation thrummed in his veins. This was the last refusal. Nothing stood between him and Kate now.

"Well?" she asked.

He decided to skirt the topic. "What a dreadful woman."

"Yes."

Some of his affront made it into his voice: "She was appraising me!"

"Did you dislike it?" Kate asked, with cool amusement. There was a faint glimmer of laughter in her eyes, the first he'd seen in days.

"Yes! Dashed condescending of her. Granddaughter of a duke, indeed!"

"Mrs. Mornington places great weight on such matters."

"So I noticed. She's exceedingly high in the instep."

"Yes," Kate said. "Poor Cecily."

"Poor Cecily? She seems nearly as proud as her mother."

"Oh, no," Kate said. "Not at all. She's a little proud, to be sure, but nothing like her mother."

"Hmph," James said. In his opinion, even a little was too much when it came to snobbery.

"Cecily's becoming very anxious, poor girl. She's had quite a number of offers, but her mother has refused them all on the grounds of—"

"Let me guess! Snobbery!"

Kate nodded. "Yes. Poor Cecily. And now her father's put his foot down and said she may have no more Seasons—they are dreadfully costly, you know, James—and she's nearly on the shelf and it's all her mother's fault."

"Very well, Miss Mornington has my sympathy—but I must tell you, Kate, that I'm *not* going to offer for her."

Kate became quite still and stiff as she sat on the couch. "No?"

"No."

"Why not?"

"Quite apart from Mrs. Mornington—whom I *refuse* to have as a mother-in-law—Miss Mornington's manners are too proud."

"Only a little," said Kate earnestly. "And Mrs. Mornington need not concern you. You would hardly ever see her!"

"No," he said firmly. "Mrs. Mornington aside, I have no wish for a top-lofty bride." He was harsh in applying the term to Cecily Mornington; her manners lacked the arrogance and condescension of her mother.

"But—"

"I prefer you to Miss Mornington," he said. "You're not high in the instep."

"I've been accused of it."

"What?" He frowned at her. "Gammon! Who said so?"

"Sir Thomas Granger."

James experienced a very strong urge to plant his fist in Sir Thomas Granger's face. "Well, you're not!" Kate's manners were easy and unassuming, and not at all top-lofty.

Kate appeared not to hear him. "James," she said. "Are you quite certain that—"

"I will *not* be offering for Miss Mornington."

Kate was very pale. The freckles stood out starkly on her skin. He saw distress in her eyes.

Silence hung between them for a moment. "Kate," he said softly, watching her, hating that thought of marriage to him was making her look like this. "We have to talk."

The door opened. Miss Penrose stepped into the room. She was dressed in her made-over riding habit. "I forgot to ask . . . Honeycourt and I are going for a ride in the park. A very gentle one! Would you care to join us?"

"Yes!" Kate rose abruptly to her feet. "I should very much like to." She almost ran from the room.

Miss Penrose smiled at James. "And you, my lord?"

James stopped frowning at the door through which Kate had vanished. "I beg your pardon?"

"Will you join us? It's my first proper ride, so we'll be very slow, and perhaps you'd rather not . . ."

"On the contrary," he said, rising to his feet. "I should like to join you. Thank you."

He'd hoped to engineer a *tête-à-tête* with Kate while they rode, but no opportunity arose. Nor was it possible to speak with her afterwards, nor at dinner or later in the drawing room. Miss Stitchcombe was still laid up in bed, so they were only four, but Kate stayed close to Miss Penrose and all his attempts to detach her from her friend were futile. Her face was pale and her manner distracted. Harry and Miss Penrose, with eyes only for each other, didn't appear to notice. James could only wonder at their blindness.

When the time came to retire to bed, every muscle in his body was rigid with tension. He submitted to Griffin's assistance in removing his boots and coat, and then sent the valet away, knowing he'd bite the man's head off if he stayed any longer. Frustration clenched his jaw and drew his eyebrows together in a frown. And more than frustration, there was anxiety. Kate was very reluctant to discuss this marriage with him. He was afraid—

But no, she'd given her word. She wouldn't renege on her agreement. And however reluctant she was now, he *would* make her happy. He'd make certain of it. He wouldn't be merely her husband, he'd be her friend and her lover. He would strive to fill her life with joy.

And maybe one day she would be able to return his love.

Kate lay awake for a long time, compiling a mental list of new candidates. James might have given up hope of finding a suitable bride, but she hadn't. He deserved a love match, or at the very least a wife he could desire. Not herself. Someone with a claim to beauty, someone whose bed he'd enjoy sharing and who would make him happy. She'd have to widen her search, that was all. It would mean longer drives, but James would surely have no objection.

Or . . . she could host another entertainment. James could meet several candidates at once, and Lizzie would enjoy it, too. Perhaps a picnic. Yes, a picnic would be just the thing!

Accordingly, after breakfast, Kate canceled her daily walk with Lizzie and sat down at the rosewood writing table in the morning room with her lists. She picked up a quill and dipped it in the porcelain inkpot.

She took the list of requirements first, since it was the easiest. *Not proud,* she wrote. *Not . . .* she finally settled on *fast* as a description of Mrs. Hurst. James had said that she was too dashing, but fast was what he meant: of loose morals and easy virtue. Kate wasn't at all sure how he knew Mrs. Hurst was fast, but he'd seemed very certain of it and he was more experienced in such matters than she was. She would trust his judgment on this.

*Doesn't lisp,* she wrote, then looked at that last requirement and frowned. It seemed to her that James had rejected Sarah Durham very hastily. The lisp was barely noticeable. How could he refuse her on such flimsy grounds?

Still frowning, Kate turned to the list of possible brides. She put a line through Cecily Mornington's name and began to write down the candidates she'd thought of during the night. There were eight. She had just finished when the door opened. "Kate?"

She tensed, and then turned her head and made herself smile. "Yes?"

James entered the room and closed the door behind him. "We need to talk."

"Yes. We do." She laid down the quill.

He stood with his back to the door. "Where's Miss Penrose?"

"Riding in the park with Harry."

"And your cousin?"

"In bed with the vapors."

"Still?"

He echoed her own sentiments, but Kate made no reply.

163

"So we shan't be interrupted?" James moved away from the door.

Kate shook her head.

"Good. Kate, we must—"

"I have more candidates," Kate said.

James halted in the center of the room. His eyebrows lowered slightly. "You do?"

"Yes," she said, glancing down at her list. "Miss Ellerslie and Miss Thorpe and the Misses Gregory and—"

"No," he said, flatly.

Kate stiffened. She raised her head to look at him. "What do you mean, no?"

"No more candidates. We're getting married. You and I."

"But . . . but you promised to view all my candidates." She stared at him, confused. Didn't James want to make a love match?

"I promised to view all those on your first list."

"No! We never said that!"

"It was understood."

Kate shook her head. "No."

"No more candidates," James said, in an uncompromising tone. "No more lists."

"But you *promised*." Anxiety tensed her muscles and she felt the first stirrings of panic in her chest. She'd not thought that James would refuse.

"I promised to view everyone on your *first* list, Kate, not whatever list you have now."

"But—"

"And you said you'd marry me if no one on the list suited me. And no one has."

"Miss Durham would, I'm sure! It's only a tiny lisp, James."

"It would drive me mad within a day."

"Nonsense!"

James took a step closer to her. "You promised, Kate."

"And you promised to give them a fair chance!" she said, the panic rising higher in her chest. James couldn't give up now. He *couldn't*.

"I have given them a fair chance." He took another step towards her. "I've kept my word . . . are you reneging on yours, Kate?"

"But Miss Ellerslie—"

"Is not on the first list."

"But she's—"

Exasperation crossed James's face. He advanced on the writing table with something approaching violence in his stride and snatched the lists up. He tore them in half, and then in half again. "No more candidates, Kate! No more lists!" He crumpled the scraps of paper in his clenched hand.

Kate stared at him, speechless. The panic was in her throat now, constricting it, making it impossible to utter a protest.

James opened his fingers and let the torn lists fall back onto the little table. His frown had gone. "Now," he said, more calmly. "Let's discuss our marriage."

Kate shook her head.

"Yes," James said. He pulled up a silk-covered chair and sat beside her. "Kate . . ." He reached for one of her hands. His grip was warm and strong. "I love you, Kate. I do."

The words, if they had been true, would have been precious beyond anything. Kate snatched her hand away and stood, nearly knocking her chair to the floor. It was bad enough that James had to marry her for convenience; it was intolerable that he felt he had to pretend to love her. She found her voice: "I have to go to my cousin. I promised to sit with her." She brushed past him.

"Kate!" James rose to his feet. "We have to talk."

"Not now!" she cried, picking up her skirts and running from the room.

James almost put his fist through the rose-tinted wall. "Damn it, Kate!" he said to the empty room. "Damn it!" There was bitterness in his mouth and something painful in his chest. He flung himself out of the morning room and up the stairs to find his riding gloves. If he wasn't going to punch holes in Harry's walls, then he needed a damned good gallop on Saladin.

He met a housemaid in the corridor outside his room. She shrank back from him, dropping the tray that she carried. He saw fear on her face and begged her pardon, wishing—not for the first time—that his frown wasn't quite so ferocious. He entered his bedchamber at a slower pace. A glance in the mirror showed a dark and savage face. He scowled at himself and couldn't blame the housemaid for being terrified.

He found his riding gloves and stood at the window, twisting them between his hands, frowning. Kate was—

Kate, rather than sitting with her dreadful cousin, was taking a walk. James watched as she crossed the lawn at a rapid pace and vanished into the trees. She had lied to him! He gritted his teeth and cast the gloves on the bed. The housemaid dropped her tray again as he launched himself precipitously out of the bedchamber. James begged her pardon a second time and strode down the corridor. He took the stairs two at a time and exited the house through a side door, opening it so hard that it slammed against the wall.

His hot fury ebbed to mere anger as he crossed the lawn, but his determination didn't falter and his pace didn't slow. Kate had to talk to him. She *had* to. His birthday was only three weeks away. Arrangements for their marriage had to be made. She couldn't keep avoiding the issue!

It had rained during the night. The lawn squelched beneath his boots, and if he'd been in less of a hurry he would have gone around by the path. Not only the gardeners would be displeased with him, but Griffin also; his top boots lost their polished gleam before he reached the trees and he had splashes of mud on his breeches. Once beneath the trees, the going became worse. The path he'd seen Kate take was little more than mud and puddles. His boots rapidly became filthy.

James was beginning to think that he'd taken a wrong turning when he finally caught sight of Kate. She was walking briskly with her head down. She'd thrown a shawl of Norwich silk over her gown and exchanged her shoes for sturdy kid half boots, but she'd forgotten both bonnet and gloves. Her gown was heavily splashed with mud and its embroidered hem was dripping. She seemed to be making no effort to avoid the puddles.

He had to stretch his legs to catch up with her. She heard him when he was still several yards behind her and whirled to face him.

"James!"

"Kate." He made her a bow. "Fancy meeting you here. I had thought you were with your cousin."

Faint color rose in her cheeks. She said nothing.

James crossed the ground between them. Kate watched him with wide eyes, clutching the shawl about her shoulders.

"How is your cousin?"

"She's . . . she's asleep."

"Oh?" he said, raising his eyebrows. There was disbelief and a thread of anger in his voice.

The color in Kate's cheeks deepened. She said nothing. He thought that she shrank slightly into herself. Her gray eyes were apprehensive and wary, her posture tense. It struck James, suddenly, that she almost looked afraid of him.

His anger fled abruptly. "Forgive me, Kate," he said softly, ashamed and contrite. "I didn't mean to—" He bit back the words *frighten you* and held out his arm to her. "Will you walk with me? Please?"

Kate hesitated, clearly reluctant. James waited. After a moment she laid her hand on his arm. He was unaccountably relieved by that small gesture of trust.

Kate held herself stiffly as they began to walk. Her tension was contagious. The muscles in his shoulders tightened as he cast about for a topic of conversation that would ease the constraint between them. "You appear to be in need of an escort, Kate," he said, striving for a teasing note. "Your gown is filthy. You must have stepped in every puddle between here and the Hall!"

Kate glanced down at herself. "Oh," she said. "I hadn't noticed . . ." She brushed at a fleck of mud on her gown. "Paton will scold me."

The path was in shade for the most part, but here and there sunlight came down through the boughs. They passed through one such sunny patch. Kate's hair shone with glints of flame. "She will scold you for more than that," James said, thinking how lovely her hair was in the sunlight. "You have forgotten your bonnet."

"I have?" Kate raised a hand to touch her hair. It was dressed quite simply, in a knot on top of her head and ringlets falling down. "Oh." She laughed. The sound, usually so merry, was faint and hollow, forced. "How odd. I can't think how I came to forget it! Excuse me, James." She disengaged her hand from his arm. "I must go back and fetch—"

"You will survive without it," he said.

"But—"

"Please, Kate. Walk with me. *Talk* with me."

"But my bonnet." She took a step away from him, a second step, a third.

"Don't run away from me again, Kate!" He let her hear some of his frustration. "Please!"

Kate halted.

"We have to talk about this," he said, more calmly.

She remained stationary, silent, her eyes fixed on his face.

"We must discuss our marriage, Kate."

"But what about Miss Ellerslie? James, you really should see her! She's very lovely. I think you'd—"

"No. No more candidates."

"But Miss Ellerslie—"

"No!"

She closed her mouth.

"You gave me your word, Kate."

She said nothing.

He held her eyes, willing her to believe him: "I love you, Kate."

She jerked back as if he'd struck her across the face. "No," she said. "You *don't*. And if you keep pretending, then I won't marry you! It was not part of our agreement."

James clenched his jaw. "I am not pretending."

"Yes, you are!" Kate cried, her voice sharp and angry. "I had thought better of you, James!"

"Damn it, Kate!" he said, too annoyed to moderate his language. "I am *not*—"

"Let me find you someone else! Please!"

He looked at her beseeching face. If he was a gentleman, he'd say yes. "No," he said. It was a flat sound.

"But—"

"I am not pretending," he said, biting out the words. "And you're wrong, Kate. We can have passion."

She shook her head.

"Yes." James gritted his teeth together, infuriated by her refusal to believe him.

"No."

The word was firmly spoken, and it was the final straw. James decided, abruptly, to prove to Kate that she *was* wrong. He took a step towards her. "What do you know about passion, Kate?"

"What?" Confusion crossed her face, followed by alarm.

"Passion, Kate. Tell me about it."

Kate backed away from him. "James . . ." she said uncertainly. "What are you doing?"

"Proving a point."

Kate took a sideways step along the path. "James—"

He followed her, moving slowly, strolling, his eyes intent on her face. "You seem so certain that we can't have passion."

"Of course I'm certain!"

"Then you'll not object to a little . . . experiment, will you?"

Kate's eyes narrowed warily. "What kind of experiment?"

He gave her a tight smile. "To determine whether or not there can be passion between us. We shall test your hypothesis against mine."

"No," she said, taking two rapid steps backwards in the mud. "Absolutely not!"

James halted, watching her through narrow eyes, wondering how to make her agree to his suggestion. "Afraid you'll be wrong, Kate?"

She flushed faintly. "No!"

"Then why the reluctance?"

"Because it's not . . . it's not—"

"You're afraid you'll lose."

Kate's flush deepened slightly.

"A little experiment," James said, resuming his strolling advance on her.

"No!" she cried. "I'm not doing that . . . that *thing*!"

James halted, standing in a puddle, enjoying the rising color in Kate's face. "What thing?" he asked, although he had already guessed.

Kate became extremely pink.

James grinned, and in doing so lost his bad humor. The tension in his muscles eased. "You surprise me, Kate. What do you know about . . . ah . . . that thing?"

"Charlotte told me," she said stiffly, not meeting his eyes.

"Charlotte?" James stepped out of the puddle and tried to remember where he'd heard the name before. "Oh, yes. Your married friend. The one who lives near Miss Penrose."

"Yes," she said, avoiding his gaze.

"I'm shocked, Kate," he said, his grin widening. "Truly shocked! I had no idea that ladies discussed such matters." He eyed her for a moment, feeling laughter rise in his throat. "Were you curious, Kate? Did you ask her about it?"

"I am not going to answer that question."

James laughed out loud. Her tone had told him the answer: Yes. She had asked.

He could have teased her about it, but he didn't. Instead he said, still grinning: "Don't worry, Kate. I wasn't proposing that we . . . do that thing. Merely that we attempt a kiss or two."

Kate looked at him directly. Her expression was horrified. "No!"

"Why not?"

"Because . . . because we *can't*."

"Actually, we can," James said, smiling at her. "Quite easily."

"But—"

"Afraid that you'll be wrong, Kate?" It was no taunt this time, merely a mild question.

She opened her mouth and then shut it again without speaking. She moistened her lips, drawing his attention to their soft fullness. Her lower lip was really the most delicious—

"No," she said. "Of course not!"

"Then what have you to lose?" He made his voice smooth and persuasive, coaxing. "A little experiment. Your hypothesis, that there can be no passion, tested against mine, that there can."

"And . . . if I'm correct, you'll see Miss Ellerslie and Miss Thorpe and—"

"If you're correct, I'll see them all," James said, confident of his ability to rouse passion in her. "You have my word."

Kate twisted her hands together. There was a worried crease between her eyebrows. Sunlight gilded her hair. He reached out and touched one of the long curls that framed her face. She flinched, and then held herself very still.

"Relax, Kate," James whispered, drawing the ringlet slowly through his fingers.

Kate didn't relax. If anything, she stiffened. "Just hurry up and do it!" she said, her tone cross and flustered.

James stepped close to her, until their bodies almost touched. "Hurry?" He shook his head. "Oh, no, Kate. I'm not going to hurry."

# CHAPTER 15

It was worse than it had been on the terrace, for Kate could see his face clearly. He stood so close that the gold in his irises was visible. There was an odd smile on his mouth, the faintest curve to his lips.

James released the curl. It sprang back against her cheek. Kate held herself rigid, anticipating his kiss, determined not to betray herself. But James didn't kiss her. Instead he drew a fingertip down her jaw. He traced a path from her ear to her chin, the same route his mouth had taken on the terrace. Her skin tingled at the light caress. She concentrated on holding herself extremely still.

His fingertip lay beneath her lower lip now, in the soft indentation there. He was still staring at her. That intent gaze and the fingertip on her skin unnerved her. "Well, get on with it!" Kate said tartly. She had things to do, a picnic to plan, invitations to write. James might have given up all hope of his making a love match, but she hadn't. If she could just survive the next few minutes then she could show him the new candidates. And really, after Lizzie, Georgina Ellerslie was—

"Impatient, Kate?" James removed his finger.

Heat rose in her cheeks. She lowered her gaze. His riding coat was open and she fastened her eyes on his waistcoat. The cream-colored silk was embroidered in a muted shade of moss green. She began to count the buttons. They were covered in fabric of the same discreet pattern.

James touched her again, raising both hands to her jaw and drawing his fingers slowly down her throat until they rested on her collarbone. Kate couldn't help trembling with pleasure. She lost count of the number of buttons on his waistcoat. "That tickles!" she said, hoping he hadn't noticed her quiver.

"Does it? My apologies." His words were polite, the tone bland, but his voice was lower than it usually was, slightly husky. It almost made her shiver again.

James pushed the shawl back from her shoulders. Too late, she clutched at it. It fell to the ground. "James!" she said, indignant.

He bent his head and whispered in her ear: "Tell Paton it was my fault."

Kate trembled again as she felt his breath against her skin. "I shall!" she said, taking refuge in annoyance. Anything was better than panic, and she was very close to panic. "Have no fear of that!"

James's hands were still at her shoulders, but they weren't motionless. His fingers moved from cambric gown to muslin *fichu* to skin, stroking lightly, raising more tremors in her. She felt his fingertips in the hollow where her pulse beat, on her collarbone, lower, brushing aside the soft, white muslin—

"Stop that!" Kate grabbed hold of his wrists, wishing she'd worn a gown with a high neckline instead of the *fichu* crossed at her breast.

James didn't raise his head. Instead, she felt his teeth close gently on her earlobe. Her body jolted at that intimacy. "Stop!" she cried again.

He released her earlobe. "Stop what?" he whispered.

"That! Everything!" Kate let go of his wrists and took several steps backward, into a puddle. "You said a kiss! Nothing more!"

James stood watching her. He didn't look annoyed. Rather,

he appeared to be pleased. His eyes were very dark and he was smiling. "Very well," he said. He held out his hand. "Come out of that puddle, Kate. Unless you wish me to join you there?"

The ripple of laughter in his voice brought even more heat to her face. Kate came out of the puddle with what she hoped was dignity. "One kiss," she said primly.

"Two," James said.

"No! You said—"

"I said a kiss or two. I've decided on two."

"But—"

"Afraid I'll win, Kate?" His voice held a challenge.

*Yes.* "No," she said. "Of course not."

"Then I fail to understand your objection."

Kate set her teeth together and smiled at him. "Fine," she said. "Two kisses. But nothing else!"

There was amusement in James's face. "Very well."

Stiff with reluctance, Kate stepped close to him again. Her heart pounded with panic. James placed his hands on her shoulders, his eyes holding hers. She jumped as his fingers moved along the soft edge of the *fichu,* stroking her skin. "No hands!" she cried.

James laughed. "How am I to hold you then?" His tone was reasonable, but what his hands were doing was not. His fingertips moved slowly, caressingly, tracing light paths across skin that was suddenly acutely sensitive. Kate shuddered deep inside herself. Heat flooded her body.

She snatched at his wrists. "No hands!"

James made a sound that was half laugh, half sigh. "Spoil-sport," he said.

Kate pressed her lips together, holding his hands away from her. He made no resistance.

His eyes dropped to her mouth. "Very well. No hands."

Kate released his wrists.

James stood looking at her for a moment. "In fact . . ." He began to smile.

"In fact, what?" she asked warily. That growing smile made her nervous.

"In fact . . . why don't *you* kiss *me*?"

Her heartbeat faltered. "What?"

"Why don't you kiss me?" James said. There was a wide smile on his mouth, and a dark and glittering one in his eyes.

Kate stared at him. She *couldn't* . . . could she?

"Well?" he asked.

Kate thought of Georgina Ellerslie. James deserved a bride he could desire, and Georgina was young and pretty, almost as pretty as Lizzie, and she was—

"Well?" he said again.

Kate was so nervous she could barely speak: "You'll have to bend your head."

James lowered his head slightly.

Kate raised herself on tiptoe. Her heart beat wildly and her throat was tight with panic. She couldn't do this. She *had* to do this.

With Miss Ellerslie firmly in mind, Kate rested her fingertips gingerly on his chest, avoiding the waistcoat and choosing instead the thicker superfine of his coat. "You're using your hands," James pointed out in a very reasonable voice, his mouth mere inches from her own.

Kate stepped back, heat rushing to her face. "You know, James, sometimes I dislike you intensely!"

James, far from being chastened, laughed. "I'm sorry, Kate," he said. "I couldn't resist . . . it was very childish of me. I beg your pardon." He held out a hand to her, grinning.

Kate folded her arms across her chest.

"Stop glaring at me, Kate, please," James said, a glimmer of laughter still visible in his eyes.

"If you are going to make a joke of this—"

He lowered his hand. "No joke." The last of the laughter faded from his face, leaving it serious. "Forgive me, Kate. I was only teasing." He offered her his hand again, palm up, placatory. "Come, try again. I promise to behave myself."

His contrition was clearly sincere, but Kate couldn't bring herself to move. It had taken all her courage to approach

175

him the first time. His laughter had destroyed that courage. Perhaps James saw this in her face, for he took those few steps himself, walking through the mud to stand in front of her. "Forgive me, Kate," he said again, softly. And then he bent his head until his mouth hovered over hers. "Kiss me," he whispered.

Kate took hold of her courage and pecked primly at his lips. The contact lasted a bare half-second, brief and far too intimate. "There," she said, taking a hasty step backwards. Her heart hammered high in her chest and her throat was so tight that the word almost came out as a croak. She had touched his warm lips, had inhaled the scent of his skin.

James tutted under his breath. "No, Kate," he said, stepping closer. "Like this."

His mouth covered hers.

Kate's heart leapt in her chest. She panicked and jerked back.

"What?" James asked, raising his head. His eyes were very dark. The glitter was back in them.

"That was one," she said stiffly. Her heart beat fiercely, trying to batter its way out of her ribcage.

"No, Kate," he said, exasperation in his voice. "That was *not* one. We'd barely started." He pulled her towards him. "Trust me, I'll tell you when the kiss is over."

"But—"

"It's just a kiss," he said. "What is there to worry about? After all, you're so certain you'll win."

Kate wasn't at all certain. But she pictured Georgina Ellerslie in her mind and managed not to flinch when James bent his head.

She closed her eyes, unable to bear seeing his face so close to her. He brushed her mouth lightly with his several times, as if teasing her, then she felt the tip of his tongue against her lips. Her eyes flew open and she tried to step back. James halted her with his hands on her shoulders. "Kate," he warned her in a low voice. She saw that his pupils had dilated. His eyes were almost black.

"All right!" she said, flustered, trembling. "All right. Get on with it!"

He removed his hands without being asked, and bent his head again. Kate closed her eyes. His mouth covered hers and she felt the light touch of his tongue again. She didn't flinch. Instead, her body quivered. She thought frantically of Georgina Ellerslie. That didn't work. She groped instead for memory of Sir Thomas Granger's proposal. But even that failed to quench her response to James.

"Open your mouth," James whispered, against her lips.

Kate hesitated for a moment. Her heart beat so loudly that it drowned out all other sounds. Panic and apprehension twisted inside her, but there was also a treacherous flicker of anticipation. Charlotte had told her about this type of kissing. At the time, she'd thought it sounded disgusting. She was no longer quite so sure.

"If we're going to do this properly, then you have to open your mouth."

Kate tensed.

"Kate . . ."

She parted her lips slightly. She was afraid and—to her shame—eager.

She'd feared that James would thrust his tongue inside her mouth; he didn't. Instead, he licked her lower lip and then bit gently into it. Pleasure flared inside her. She inhaled on a gasp. James must have heard it for he made a sound of satisfaction, deep in his throat. He bit her lip again, very gently, and then licked it. Kate shuddered and clutched at the lapels of his riding coat.

He teased her like this for some time, licking, biting, while heat built in her body. It prickled across her skin and rushed in her blood and swirled like smoke in her mind, stealing reason. When he finally entered her mouth, Kate was in no state to protest. Instead she quivered and opened herself to him, desperate for what he offered and past all thought of consequences. His hands touched her, cradling her face, tilting her head, his fingers tangling in her hair, but she didn't care. All her attention was focused on his mouth. His tongue touched hers, and there was a sensation inside her that was so urgent and so sweet that it could almost be called pain.

Kate had no idea how long they kissed. It could have been minutes, it could have been hours. Finally James brought it to an end.

"Don't you wish we didn't have to stop, Kate?" he whispered against her mouth. "Don't you wish we were married and somewhere private, just the two of us, where we'd not be disturbed . . ."

His words slid over her skin, sweet and delicious. Kate opened her eyes, dazed. There was a tight fullness to her skin, an urgency in her blood. There was *heat.*

James raised his head and looked at her. His eyes were very black and his cheeks were flushed with color. "One," he said softly.

Kate realized that she was pressed against him. Horrified, she pushed herself away. James's fingers slid from her hair. He let her step back, his hands falling to his sides.

Kate stared at him. James smiled. It was a sharp, gleaming, triumphant smile. "I appear to be winning," he said.

His smug tone brought heat to cheeks that were already hot. "Nonsense!" Kate said, trying to gather the shreds of her dignity around her. It was a futile task. She knew that her face was flushed and her hair tangled and her gown muddy and wet. Dignity, under such circumstances, was impossible.

James shook his head. "Kate," he said, in a chiding, teasing tone. "If ever I heard a bouncer, that was it."

Kate bent to pick up her shawl. The tasseled border dripped with muddy water. "Nonsense," she said again.

"Are you telling me that, right now, you don't feel passion?"

"Yes," she lied firmly.

His eyebrows rose. "But I can see it in you."

"What? Nonsense!"

"It's in your eyes," James said, stepping close and touching a light fingertip to the corner of her eye. "And in your face." The fingertip moved to her hot cheek.

She moved her head so that he no longer touched her. "That's not passion."

His eyebrows rose again, in a mocking movement. "What is it then?"

"It's . . . well, it's . . . it's discomfort!"

"Really?" Laughter flashed across his face. "How odd. It looks just like passion. And so does this." His finger was suddenly on her pulse, where it beat frantically in the hollow at the base of her throat. "Such a *passionate* pulse, Kate."

Kate stepped back hurriedly. She crossed her arms. "It is not passion!"

James stopped teasing her. "Yes, Kate, it is," he said, his voice quite serious. "Admit it. We both feel passion. We both desire each other."

His words chased the heat from her body. Kate stared at him. "You don't desire me," she said flatly.

"What? Of course I do! You just have to look at me to know that."

"Do I?" His cheeks were flushed and his eyes glittered blackly. It could conceivably be desire, but having overheard his words in the library, Kate knew it wasn't. He hadn't desired her a month ago and he didn't desire her now. "You're pretending, James. Don't bother to deny it."

A subtle change came over his face. His eyes were still hot and dark, his cheeks still flushed, but she knew he was angry.

Kate moistened her lips nervously. His eyes fastened on the movement.

"The second kiss," he said.

She flinched. James must have seen the involuntary movement, for his face tightened. His voice was almost bitter: "I wish you would believe me, Kate."

Kate wished she could believe him, too. But she'd be a fool to do so. She fixed Georgina Ellerslie's image in her mind and stepped forward. "Very well," she said. "The second kiss."

He looked her up and down. "Like that?"

Kate uncrossed her arms. The embroidered silk shawl, already filthy, fell to the ground again. She put her hands on her hips and raised her chin. "Better?" Belligerence edged her tone.

She saw amusement flicker in James's eyes. "Marginally."

Kate pressed her lips together.

"You're not going to make this easy, are you?"

"Just get on with it!"

James made her a bow, somehow instilling the movement with irony. "As you wish." He stepped close, careful to keep his hands away from her, and lowered his mouth to her throat.

Kate let out a noise that was very close to being a squeak. It took all of her willpower not to jerk away. "What are you doing?"

"Merely trying something different," James said, his breath warm on her skin.

Heat came roaring back into Kate's body as he opened his mouth against the curve where her neck met her shoulder. She felt his tongue and then his teeth, and closed her eyes, clutching at his arms. Her fingers dug into the cloth of his coat.

James's tongue moved across her skin. He was kissing her throat now, tasting the feverish jump of her pulse. His hands were no longer held away from her, but at her waist, steadying them both, hot through the fabric of her gown.

Kate opened her eyes and stared blindly past James. *He's pretending,* she told herself. *He'll be happier with Georgina Ellerslie than with me.* But her breath was coming in unsteady gasps and that hot, sweet, painful sensation was rising in her again. She swayed against him and tried, desperately, to concentrate on the scene she'd witnessed in the library. What had James said? Oh, yes, that was it: *You think I can't give a woman pleasure, even if I feel no desire for her?*

Memory of his words and the bleak expression on his face as he'd uttered them quenched the rising pleasure in her body.

She stiffened. The thought of him counterfeiting passion was sickening. It made her feel ill. "Enough," she said, releasing her grip on his arms.

James paused, his lips against her skin. Then he straightened to his full height and took his hands from her waist. Her skin felt cold where his mouth had been. He looked at her with hot, dark eyes.

"*That* is the second kiss," Kate said firmly. "And I win."

James's eyebrows snapped together. "Kate . . . are you breaking your word?" His voice was soft and dangerous.

"No," she said. "Because I've won."

His breath hissed between his teeth. "You have not won." Each word was hard and flat and carefully articulated. "Damn it, Kate. Can't you *see*—"

"I see that you're angry. But I can't see any passion." She bent to pick up her shawl again. "Miss Ellerslie—"

"Damn it, Kate!"

It was almost a yell. It shocked her upright. The shawl slipped from her fingers. James's anger was palpable. She could almost taste it, black and hot and bitter. It raised fine hairs on her skin.

She was suddenly aware of the sheer size of him. James was so much larger than she was, so much stronger. Without moving, he managed to tower over her. She stared at him, seeing clenched teeth and flared nostrils, and remembered that he was a man who had killed.

She took an involuntary step backwards.

James turned his back on her abruptly. He put his hands to his face. For long seconds he stood stiff and motionless and silent, then he lowered his hands. "I'm not going to hurt you, Kate," he said in a low voice, his back still to her. "Don't be afraid. Please."

He turned around. Seeing his face, Kate was ashamed of her reaction. James had killed men, but she knew with deep certainty that he would never raise his hand against her. He didn't have it within him to do so.

"Kate," he said, distress in his eyes, "I would *never* hurt you."

"I know," she said. "I'm sorry. I . . . I wasn't thinking." She could be wary of his words, could wish to avoid the conversation they were now having, but she could never be afraid of him.

"I love you, Kate." His voice was as weary and defeated as his face. "Why won't you believe me?"

Kate picked up her shawl. Water dripped from the tasseled hem. She shrank from revealing herself as an eavesdropper, but something in James's voice made prevarication impossible.

"I heard you in the library," she said, looking at the shawl and not him.

"What?" James said. "Whatever are you talking about?"

Kate raised her head and met his eyes. "The day you arrived, I . . . I overheard you in the library. I heard what you said about me. That's why I know you're pretending."

His look of stupefaction would have been comical under other circumstances. "You *what?*"

"There's a priest's hole," Kate explained, looking down at the shawl again, rubbing mud off it. "I keep my diary there. I was there when . . . I didn't mean to eavesdrop, I truly didn't! But . . ."

James was silent. She risked a glance at him, expecting to meet embarrassment or even anger. Instead, he looked aghast. "Oh, God," he said.

Kate shrugged with one shoulder, a small, awkward movement. "So you understand why I don't believe you."

"Yes. I understand very well." His face was part in sunlight, part in shade, and wholly shocked. "Kate, how can I prove—"

"You can't," she said briskly. "Which is why I think you should meet Miss Ellerslie." She smiled at him. "I'll make the arrangements, shall I?"

James stared at her. He made no answer. His face was pale.

"Excellent," Kate said, forcing her mouth into another smile. "I'm sure you'll find her suitable." She folded the shawl over her arm. "Now, if you'll excuse me, I must change my clothes. Good day to you, James."

He said nothing. His expression was quite blank.

Kate walked with careful briskness until she'd passed around the first bend in the path, then she picked up her skirts and ran. Tears fell down her cheeks. She ran through mud and puddles alike. Dirty water splashed up, on her gown, her face, her hair, but she was past caring. She ran, and wept.

James stood for long minutes, stunned and appalled. Then he swore and punched a tree. And then he swore again because it felt as if he'd broken every bone in his hand. He understood, finally, what Kate had meant when she said there could be no passion between them. It hadn't been that it was impossible for her to feel passion for him, rather that it was impossible for *him* to feel passion for *her*.

Lord, what a mess!

James almost punched the tree again, then thought better of it. He stood in the mud and tried to recall what he'd said in the library, from beginning to end. What exactly had Kate overheard? The conversation had started with talk about débutantes and then moved on to Maria Brougham and Bella, his opera dancer, and then . . . Oh, yes. James winced. How could he have forgotten? He'd said that he'd chosen to offer for Kate because he could tolerate her. Tolerate! That had been an arrogant choice of word. He would have been well served if Kate had thrown it back in his face.

What had he said after that?

James shut his eyes to concentrate. Memory returned, grudgingly. He'd said that he could tolerate Kate and then he'd said . . . He grimaced in recollection: he'd said—no, he'd *stated*, quite clearly—that he neither loved nor desired her.

James opened his eyes and gave a sour grunt of laughter. No wonder Kate didn't believe him. How could she if she'd heard him say that?

He wanted to hit something, but there were only trees. He settled for a fierce expletive. It didn't help.

More memory returned of what he'd said to Harry. There'd been that statement . . . he couldn't recall the precise wording, but he'd said some nonsense about all women being the same in the dark—a suggestion as offensive as it was untrue and one that Harry had, quite rightly, pulled him up on. And then . . . oh, yes, he'd made a remark about Kate having been on the shelf for years. And even worse than that piece of crudity, he'd scoffed at the thought of her turning down his offer and implied that she'd be grateful for it. An insufferable piece of conceit! For that comment alone, he'd deserved that Kate refuse him.

James exhaled a hissing breath between his teeth. He'd wanted to horsewhip Sir Thomas Granger. He should horsewhip himself! He deserved it far more than that strutting peahen of a man!

James flexed his aching hand, feeling something close to hatred for himself. He raised his knuckles absently to his mouth and tasted blood. What else had he said? He searched his memory and then narrowed his eyes in a wince. There had been more, a comment about Kate's infatuation for him eleven years ago. He'd said . . . ah, yes, how could he have forgotten? He'd expressed relief that she'd outgrown her partiality for him and said he was thankful she didn't make sheep's eyes at him anymore. If any remark had been calculated to make Kate deny that she desired him, that was it!

James lowered his bleeding knuckles from his mouth. He swore again, words he'd used in battle and not since, fierce, ugly words.

When he'd finished swearing, he shoved his hands through his hair and clenched his fingers. There was despair in his heart, a fast-spreading and numbing sensation. He couldn't have made a greater mess of things if he'd tried. Kate had heard everything he'd said. *Everything.* It was no excuse that what he'd said hadn't been intended for her ears or that he'd been too angry to care what he was saying. What mattered was that the words had been insulting and hurtful and cruel and should never have been spoken. It was no wonder that Harry had looked so black while he listened, and no wonder that Kate had refused him.

Nor was it any wonder that she didn't believe he loved her. Or would admit to her desire for him. No one with an ounce of pride would after hearing such comments.

James released his death grip on his hair. He turned slowly and began to trudge back to Merrell Hall. Kate had heard every bitter utterance he'd made to Harry.

It was more than a mess. It was a catastrophe.

# *C*HAPTER 16

*K*ate met her cousin in the corridor outside her room. She thought it was typical that Augusta should choose now, of all times, to emerge from her bedchamber.

"Kitty! Good gracious. Look at the *state* of you. Your *clothes*!"

"Don't worry, cousin," Kate said, opening the door to her bedroom. "I assure you I'm all right."

Unfortunately Cousin Augusta followed her. "But your gown! And your *boots*. What have you been doing? You look like a wild woman! And where's your bonnet?"

Paton came through from the adjoining dressing room. "Miss Kate!" she said, her eyes widening.

"Yes, Paton. I'm quite a mess." Kate managed a smile. "I do apologize. And . . . I believe I need a bath."

"I should say that you *do*, Kitty!" cried Cousin Augusta. "You are filthy beyond imagining. The *state* of your clothing. I have never seen anything like it!"

Kate removed her sodden boots and unpinned the brooch that held the disarranged *fichu* at her breast. With Paton's assistance she extricated herself from the dripping, muddy gown and petticoat and the tightly laced short corset. She thought that both boots and gown were ruined, and perhaps the petticoat. The shawl most definitely was, and her knitted silk stockings too. She stood in her damp chemise and drawers, shivering in front of the fire, while Paton supervised the filling of the copper bathtub. Harry had been talking for months about installing one of the modern bathing chambers, but until that event, copper hip baths in their private dressing rooms sufficed.

"Quite shocking! Really, Kitty, I had thought better of you. Your clothes are *ruined*. Such a waste. So careless!"

Kate bore it in silence until the bath had been filled with hot water brought up from the kitchen, then she turned to Cousin Augusta. "If I may have some privacy, please, cousin."

For a moment she thought Cousin Augusta would refuse to leave, then her cousin gave an angry titter and let herself out of the room. Kate heard the words "*in your mother's stead!*" uttered, but chose to ignore them.

Paton sniffed. "That woman," she said, under her breath.

Kate ignored that, too. She turned to Paton with a faint smile. Her maid had maintained a tight-lipped and loyal silence during Cousin Augusta's scold. "Your turn, Paton," Kate said, as she stripped off the clammy chemise and drawers.

But instead of scolding her, Paton said, her brow knitted with concern: "Are you quite all right, Miss Kate?"

Kate almost burst into tears. She managed—barely—not to. "Perfectly," she said, with an attempt at gaiety. "And I shall be even more perfect once I'm clean!"

Paton didn't smile at this sally. If anything, her frown deepened. She sprinkled herbs into the bath water and said nothing.

James spent the day thinking. At least, that's what he told himself he was doing. In reality, he was brooding on his mistakes. Luncheon came and went. He noticed that Kate was clean again and Cousin Augusta present at the table, but that was all. There was a limit to his ability to brood, though, and by early evening he had begun to emerge from his black gloom. Arriving in the saloon before dinner, he was relieved to find Kate the sole occupant.

Kate paled and looked as if she wished she'd not been so punctual. James was glad he had been.

"Kate," he said, halting just inside the door. "If you had *any* idea how deeply I regret what I said to Harry. Or how much I hate myself for doing so!"

The tension in Kate's face dissolved. "Hate? Oh, no! There's no need."

"There's every need! I should never have said such things. I was angry, Kate, and I . . ." He took a deep, slow breath and said quietly: "I can only apologize."

"Of course I know you were angry," Kate said, astonishingly. "You think I didn't realize that?"

He stared at her. "You don't hate me?"

"Of course not."

He blinked. "But what I said—"

"Was never intended for my ears."

"Should never have been said at all!" he corrected her fiercely.

Kate made a light, shrugging movement with her shoulders. "It was said, James. And I heard it—for which I apologize. But there is no need for *you* to apologize."

There most definitely was and he would have said so, but Miss Penrose entered the room, putting an end to private conversation. That brief exchange lightened his mood, though. Kate had every reason to despise him, and yet apparently she did not.

The flush in Miss Penrose's cheeks and spring in her step made him look twice at her. When Harry followed soon after, the glance the two exchanged told James a betrothal had been made. He counted the days silently in his head. Yes, it was three weeks since Miss Penrose's arrival at Merrell Hall. He eyed the besotted pair and, astonishingly, after the day he'd had, a laugh came to his throat.

The announcement was made after dinner, in the drawing room. Kate was unsurprised and pleased; Miss Stitchcombe was both surprised and displeased. "Oh," she exclaimed, putting her hand to her chest. "Such news! Oh, I do believe . . . Oh, I can feel a spasm coming on!"

Kate was too well-bred to roll her eyes, but James thought she wanted to. "Come upstairs with me, cousin," she said, smiling and holding out her hand to Miss Stitchcombe. "Such wonderful news has come as a shock to you. You'll feel better once you have lain down."

James doubted that. He watched Kate escort her cousin from the room and then turned his attention to Harry and a glowing Miss Penrose, giving them his heartfelt congratulations.

Cousin Augusta was excessively vexed—again. "I blame you *entirely,* Kitty!" she said, as she climbed the stairs. "If you'd only written to tell me of her arrival! I could have *stopped* this."

"Why would you wish to, cousin?" Kate asked mildly.

"Such a *dreadful* match!"

"Dreadful? How so?"

"Her birth and fortune are not equal to dear Harold's. Not in the slightest! Oh, it is a very advantageous match for *her,* to be sure. But not for Harold!"

Kate halted outside her cousin's bedchamber. "Cousin," she said. "Lizzie doesn't care about Harry's title, or his fortune. It is a love match."

"A love match? Don't be so naïve, Kitty! Miss Penrose is a scheming little hussy—"

"Take care what you say, cousin!" Kate said sharply. "And if you have any sense, do not utter such sentiments to Harry. He will tolerate them even less than I do."

"He will listen to *me*," Cousin Augusta cried. "Why, I stand in your dear mother's stead—"

"No," Kate said. "You do not!"

"I most certainly *do*," Cousin Augusta declared, in tones of affronted outrage. "Look after my children, she said on her deathbed! Take care of them for me—"

"Words which you have interpreted a great deal too liberally!" Kate said, cutting this recollection short. "Mother never scolded Harry, or told him what to do, and if you think she wished *you* to do so, then you are quite mistaken!"

"*Well*," said Cousin Augusta, in a dangerous tone. An ugly flush rose in her cheeks. "I know who to attribute *this* to! That creature has poisoned your—"

"No," Kate said. "She has not. What you fail to realize, cousin, is that you have *never* stood in Mother's stead—and you never will!"

"She would not have wished for such a *mésalliance*," said Cousin Augusta, ignoring Kate's words. "I shall tell Harold so!"

"No, you will not!" Kate said, her voice quivering with anger.

Cousin Augusta bristled and opened her mouth.

"Not another word!" Kate said. "Your foolishness is beyond bearing!" She took a deep, steadying breath, and spoke with calm firmness: "Cousin, I must give you warning that if you continue to speak against Lizzie—especially to Harry!—then you will no longer be welcome at Merrell Hall."

There was a moment of silence. Cousin Augusta pressed a limp hand to her temple. "Oh," she moaned. "I feel a spasm . . ."

Kate turned on her heel and walked away. "Ring for a housemaid."

The trembling anger subsided by the time she reached

the drawing room. In its place was shame. She shouldn't have spoken like that, however great the provocation. To threaten her cousin, indigent and dependent on the charity of relatives, with eviction had been grossly wrong of her. But, equally, she couldn't have let her speak against Lizzie. That, too, would have been grossly wrong.

Kate sighed. She fastened a smile on her mouth and opened the door to the drawing room. She wished that the day was over.

After Kate and Miss Penrose had retired, James and Harry moved to the library. "Brandy?" Harry said, holding up a decanter.

"Thank you."

Harry poured and handed him a glass, and then sprawled on one of the couches. James chose a comfortable leather armchair. "To your happiness," he said, lifting his glass in a toast. The brandy was smooth and well-aged, with subtle spicy undertones.

Harry flushed a faint pink, a color that couldn't be attributed to the warmth of the fire. "Thank you." He drank and then stared into his brandy, a smile on his face.

James eyed him. "How old is the Hall, Harry?"

Harry blinked. "How old? Oh, two hundred years or thereabouts. Why?"

"Just curious." James swirled the brandy in his glass. "Are there any priest holes?"

Harry grinned. His eyes lit up. "Supposed to be one! Lord, Kate and I spent months looking for it when we were younger. Never found it, though."

"Hmm," James said, regarding the walls with a frown. Paintings in ornate frames hung above book-filled shelves, and beneath the shelves was oak wainscoting, the panels carved with flowers and scrolling foliage and fruits.

Harry sipped his brandy and sighed. It was a beatific sound.

James abandoned his study of the paneling. "So, is it to be a special license?"

"I wish!" Harry said. He sighed again, hollowly. "No. August, at the very earliest."

"August isn't that far off. A couple of months."

"No," Harry said, cheering. "It's not, is it?" He said nothing more, but slid into a state of blissful contemplation of his marriage, his gaze on the brandy and a slight, dreamy smile on his mouth.

James envied him. "You'll be very happy," he said, wishing he could be certain of a future with Kate.

"She's perfect, isn't she?" Harry said. "Quite perfect."

"For you, yes," James said, drinking deeply from his glass. "For me, no."

The smile slipped from Harry's face. His gaze sharpened as he looked across at James. "What about Kate?"

James twisted his mouth into a rueful grimace. "It's not going well," he admitted.

Harry grunted. "I'm sorry."

James was sorry, too.

"Your parents . . . it was a marriage of convenience, was it not?"

James nodded, while logs shifted in the fire, sending out warmth.

"It wasn't for mine."

James nodded again, remembering the fondness that had existed between the deceased Viscount Honeycourt and his wife. It was another reason to envy Harry. His own parents had been ill-matched, suited in rank and fortune, but not temperament. His mother had died when he was twelve. He remembered her as aloof and untouchable, scornful of sentiment and levity, and possessed of an inflexible will. His father had been as hot as his mother was cold, a short-tempered and volatile man who'd delighted in the ridiculous, a man given to passionate rages and equally passionate laughter—and great obstinacy.

James frowned into his brandy. The mess he was in now, having to marry in haste, was typical of his father: an explosion of anger, a decision made in rage, and subsequent refusal to admit fault. He raised his glass and drank a silent, bitter toast to the old earl. *Thank you, Father.*

James sighed again and swallowed the last mouthful of brandy. He didn't hate his father, he just wished . . .

He sat up in the armchair and reached for the brandy decanter. Harry's parents had been happy together. His own hadn't. What he remembered most about his parents' marriage was the silence. Days and weeks of silence.

"I think . . . I never said anything to Kate, but . . ."

"But what?" James asked, glancing up.

Harry was frowning.

For a moment there was silence except for the muted crackling of the fire, and then Harry shook his head. "Nothing."

"Rubbish."

Harry was unoffended. The frown vanished. He smiled faintly, and shook his head again.

James shrugged. He wasn't going to pry. He picked up the decanter.

"I think my mother may have died of a broken heart."

James paused in the act of pouring, startled. He looked at Harry. "You do?"

"She died so soon after . . ." Harry shrugged. The frown was back on his face. "Maybe I'm wrong."

James finished pouring his drink, slowly. "She missed him?"

"Very much." Harry stared into his glass as if he saw more than brandy in it. Then he looked up. His smile was crooked. "May we both be as happy in our brides as my father was in his." He lifted his glass in a toast.

James drank to that. The brandy slid smoothly down his throat. "So, an August wedding."

"I hope," Harry said, his expression becoming dreamy again. "I'll write to her father tomorrow. Should really drive down and speak with him . . . not that he can refuse consent! She's four-and-twenty."

"If I succeed with Kate, we shan't be here in August," James said. He cupped the glass in his hands, warming it. In the candlelight and firelight the brandy was the color of mahogany, dark and luminous. He faintly caught the scents of oak and vanilla and raisins.

Harry blinked. His eyes became alert. "What?"

"A honeymoon on the Continent," James said. "A very long honeymoon. Italy, Greece . . . Of course, you and Miss Penrose are welcome to join us, if you're married. Or," he frowned, "even if not. Kate would be a proper chaperone for Miss Penrose—there could be no objection on that score! How would you like a wedding in Rome, Harry?"

Harry narrowed his eyes. He held out a hand for the decanter. "That," he said with dignity, pouring carefully, "is bribery!"

James shrugged and grinned. The grin was a trifle forced, but Harry didn't notice. It was all very well to talk of a honeymoon with Kate, but after today's disaster—

"A special license," Harry said, staring into the fire. "It's too late for anything else for you."

James didn't bother to speak; he merely nodded.

"I wonder if Lizzie . . ." Harry lapsed into thoughtful silence.

James stayed in the library after Harry had gone to bed, frowning at the wainscoting and thinking gloomily of Kate's new list of candidates. He didn't want to meet any of them, but he could see no escape. Kate would keep throwing eligible brides at him until the last possible minute. Three weeks of viewing young ladies whom he had no intention of marrying, and then a hasty marriage to a reluctant bride—if Kate didn't cry off. She had threatened as much. *If you keep pretending,* she'd said this morning, furious, *then I won't marry you. It was not part of our agreement!* And she was correct. Their agreement had been one of convenience only. Love and desire had no place in it.

He could do it. He could hold his tongue and make no protestations of love until she wed him. The irony was that then he *would* be pretending. But if that was what it took to marry Kate . . .

James drained his glass and sighed. Kate thought he was dissembling—a perfectly reasonable assumption given what she'd overheard—and he didn't know how to prove her wrong. He put down the glass and sat with his head in his hands and indulged in a brief moment of black despondency. Then, with a groan, he stood. A glance at the clock on the mantelpiece told him that the hour was late.

James sent Griffin away after his boots and coat had been removed. He stood at the window in shirt-sleeves and stockinged feet, scowling at his reflection in the dark rain-spotted panes of glass. He had no wish to look over another batch of pretty little misses. All he wanted to do was marry Kate.

There was no doubt in his mind that they could have a passionate marriage. Kate had responded very satisfactorily to his kisses this morning. She'd claimed it was discomfort, but it hadn't been. He was no green youth; he knew the signs of passion when he saw them. But Kate wasn't experienced in such matters and she hadn't been able to recognize those same signs in him.

James stood, brooding, at the window. Memories of kissing Kate coiled like silk in his mind: the sweetness of her mouth, the clean scent of her skin, the way she'd quivered, her rapid pulse . . .

His body stirred in response, flushing with heat. James closed the curtains and turned away from the window. He stripped off his clothes and pulled on his nightshirt. He caught a glimpse of himself in the tall mirror in the corner of the room. His expression was grim.

*I can't do another three weeks of this.*

He turned away from the mirror. It was a farce: sipping tea and making polite conversation with ladies he had no interest in. If he could just talk with Kate, convince her—

*Then talk with her. Convince her.*

He'd faced Napoleon's army at Waterloo. Why was he afraid of this?

James hesitated a moment, and then snatched up his dressing gown and thrust his arms into the sleeves. He belted it roughly around his waist and picked up the candle.

# CHAPTER 17

The betrothal made matters easier, Kate realized with relief. A dress party was clearly in order. She could invite every young lady she knew, with the double purpose of introducing them to Lizzie *and* to James. It was better than a picnic, especially with the weather so unsettled; rain pattered against the windowpanes even now.

Kate sat on the window seat in her bedchamber with her legs curled under her. She wrote carefully, so as not to spatter ink on her nightgown. A single candle stood on the dressing table, casting barely enough light for her to see the growing list of names. *Miss Georgina Ellerslie, Miss Lucilla Thorpe, Misses Clara and Amabel Gregory.* Who else had been on the list James had torn up? Kate frowned and pulled her plait through her fingers as she thought. Oh, Maria Ormsby, of course, and the Honorable Jane Chalmers. And Elinor—

Someone entered her bedchamber. Kate started, almost flicking ink onto her nightgown. She turned her head. Her mouth fell open. James stood inside her room, leaning against the closed door, wearing a dressing gown of crimson and gold brocade. He held a candle in one hand. His feet were bare.

"James?" she said, in disbelief.

"Good evening, Kate." James put his candle down on the

shelf beside the door. "What are you doing? I thought you'd be asleep."

"What am *I* doing?" She gaped at him. "What are *you* doing?"

"We need to talk." His eyes focused on the paper in her lap. He frowned. "Is that another list, Kate? Because I've had enough of viewing candidates—"

"We can discuss this tomorrow!" She put aside the invitation list and scrambled to her feet.

"No, Kate. This has gone on long enough."

"You can't be in here." She was aware of how little she was wearing, how foolish she must look in her nightgown. "James, it's absolutely—"

He continued as if he hadn't heard her, his tone conversational. "I've come to explain about passion. If you knew what to look for, Kate—"

"I do know." She reached hurriedly for her wrap. "Charlotte told me."

James eyebrows rose. "She did?"

Kate flushed. She pulled the wrap around her tightly. "Please leave, James."

"Not yet. You needn't be afraid, Kate. I'm not going to—"

She lifted her chin. "I'm not afraid. But James, you can't be in here. It's absolutely—"

"What exactly did Charlotte tell you?"

Heat came to her cheeks. She took refuge in haughtiness. "I have no intention of repeating what Charlotte said."

Laughter lit James's face. He began walking towards her. "She told you about the overt signs, didn't she, Kate?"

She stepped back, colliding with the window seat. "This conversation is most improper! I must ask you to leave."

"Not yet," James said again. He halted a mere two feet from her. His eyes were as dark as they'd been in the woods that morning, almost black. "Look at me, Kate. What do you see?"

"Nothing," she said. Her heart was beating far too fast.

James opened the collar of his dressing gown. "Look, Kate."

"Really, James—"

"Look." His voice held an implacable note.

Kate lowered her gaze. She saw crimson and gold brocade, white linen, and the bare skin of his throat. His pulse beat in the hollow of his collarbone, rapid.

"Can't you see what you do to me?"

She glanced up at his face.

"I'm not pretending, Kate. This is real." James stepped even closer. His eyes seemed to darken.

Heat rose sharply in her body. He'd stood this close when he'd kissed her in the woods. She looked away from his dark eyes, his mouth, and stared at his pulse again.

"Can't you see?" he said again, his voice soft and low.

She swallowed past a constriction in her throat. The room was extraordinarily hot; it was quite difficult to breathe. "James, I think you'd better go."

"Not until I know you believe me."

"I'm sorry, James, but—"

His hands closed around her arms. He pulled her gently towards him. His voice was in her ear, a whisper. "What did Charlotte tell you?"

Heat burned in her cheeks. She tried to pull away. "James!"

"No." He held her against him, firm, gentle. "I know it's grossly improper, but Kate, I really must insist . . ."

The sound of his voice faded in her ears. It was impossible to concentrate on his words, impossible to think, to breathe. She was conscious of James's strength, his warmth . . .

She became aware of a slow change in his body.

She knew what it meant. Charlotte had told her.

Her response was instinctive, physical. She had no control over her body. It felt as if every muscle clenched. Sensation swept through her, sweet and eager, so intense that it almost hurt. *I want*—

"Feel what you do to me," James whispered.

Kate jerked back. Her pulse hammered in her throat.

"Now do you believe me?"

She stared at him. His cheeks looked as hot as her own. His eyes were black, glittering. His hands were still warm on her arms.

"Kate?"

Her mouth was too dry for speech. She nodded.

James released her. He stepped back. She was aware of tension in his body. "Good." It was a short, satisfied word. "Then we'll have no more nonsense about passion being impossible!"

She stood immobile, speechless, hot and agitated.

"Will we?" His voice challenged her. "Because it wasn't discomfort this morning, was it, Kate? It was passion."

She opened her mouth to deny this charge, but James's expression stopped her. The knowledge and certainty on his face told her that he knew the truth. More heat came to her cheeks, embarrassment upon embarrassment.

He waited a moment for her denial. "Good," he said, when it didn't come. He turned and walked across the bedchamber. "No more candidates."

"Oh, but—!"

James turned his head to look at her, one hand on the doorknob. His eyes narrowed. "But what?"

"But . . . Miss Ellerslie!"

James released the doorknob. "I beg your pardon?"

Kate stared at him, desiring him, loving him, and above all, wanting him to be happy. "I . . . I concede that you may feel . . . some passion for me, and . . . and I for you, but Miss Ellerslie—"

"Not another word about Miss Ellerslie!"

"But you haven't seen her, James! You will surely feel more passion for her than you do for me. She's dark, and you know you said you preferred dark ladies!"

His eyebrows drew together in a frown. "I have changed my mind."

"Nonsense! You really must see her, James. She—"

James clenched his jaw. "Enough!" he said. "That's enough, Kate!"

"No." She drew breath, determined to list Georgina Ellerslie's many virtues.

"Yes!" James turned the key in the lock and pocketed it.

"What . . . ?" Kate watched nervously as he advanced towards her. "James, what are you doing?"

James halted. "What am I doing?"

The answer to her question flickered across his face; an intention, a decision made, a hot and dark anticipation.

"Oh, no." Kate shook her head. "No!"

James grinned. "Oh, yes. My dearest Kate, I am about to compromise your virtue."

"No! You cannot!"

His grin widened. "Yes," he said. "I most definitely can."

"I mean—I mean, you *must not*!"

"Oh, but I must, Kate. If only to stop you from showing me more candidates. For I must tell you—" his voice flattened, "—I have had enough of that."

Kate scrambled sideways and reached for the bellpull. The wrap slid from her shoulders, falling to the floor.

"Think, Kate. What will happen? To be found with a man in your bedchamber." James smiled. "Of course, as a plan it has its merits. We would have to marry. But I must point out that *my* plan will be less embarrassing for us both. And more enjoyable."

Kate stared at him, grasping the bellpull. James waited, watching her. "Don't be afraid, Kate," he said softly. "I won't hurt you. It will be as it was in the woods this morning, only better. I promise." He took a slow step towards her, and another. "I don't want to see Miss Ellerslie." His voice was little more than a whisper. "I don't want to see any more candidates. I just want you."

He halted, so close that she felt the heat of his body. He made no attempt to take the bellpull from her fingers. "You liked it this morning, Kate. I know you did. I saw it." He touched a light fingertip to the corner of her eye, her cheek, the pulse at the base of her throat. "I felt it . . ." His voice trailed into silence as he bent his head. His kissed her where his finger had touched, the merest brush of his lips across her skin.

Kate stood frozen, clutching the bellpull. She didn't know what to do. There should have been horror, but there wasn't. Instead there was heat, so much heat, rising in her body.

"You may call for a servant if you wish," James whispered in her ear. "But I beg that you will not." His hands were at her waist, warm and strong. He kissed his way down her throat, biting lightly, licking. He stopped when he reached the lace-trimmed neckline of her nightgown. His mouth left her skin and he raised his head.

Kate stared at him, panicked, eager, unable to order her mind. She didn't know what to do. James watched her. His face was in shadow, his eyes black in the dim candlelight. "Well, Kate?" he asked, as his hands began to move up her body, slowly. "What will it be?"

She released the bellpull and clutched at his wrists before his hands could climb any higher. His fingers lay just beneath her breasts, their warmth burning through the thin linen of her nightgown. "Well?" James asked again, watching her.

Kate stared at him. All thought of Georgina Ellerslie was gone. Her heart beat wildly in her chest. There was such heat in her body, such trembling urgency, such confusion. "I don't know what to do," she whispered in a choked voice.

James smiled at her. "I do," he said. "Kiss me, Kate."

"But—"

"Then I shall kiss you."

His mouth was as marvelous as it had been in the woods. He teased her with light kisses until she ached for more, almost desperate enough to beg, and then he gave her what she wanted, entering her mouth, tasting her, letting her taste him. His hands were on her breasts, caressing. She was awash with heat. She wanted—

James broke their kiss. His cheeks were flushed and his eyes were hot and dark, glittering with passion. "The bed," he said, his voice hoarse.

A measure of sanity returned to Kate. She stared at him, tasting brandy in her mouth and feeling his hands on her breasts. James must have seen something in her face. He stepped back, breaking the contact between them. He was trembling and she was aware of tension in his body. "Please don't change your mind, Kate." He stood looking at her, panting slightly. "Please, Kate. I . . . I *need* you."

Her response was visceral, strong and primitive: a craving, a wanting that shocked her in its intensity. *I need you, too.*

When he reached out and took her hand, Kate didn't resist. She allowed him to pull her to the bed.

James released her hand. He dropped his dressing gown to the floor and stripped, letting her see all of him. He stood in front of her, naked and aroused, entirely unselfconscious, without shyness. His body was strange in its maleness, but beautiful too, strongly-muscled and graceful. There were scars at his shoulder and across his ribs, on his arm and thigh. She saw them now that the robe was gone. James caught her flickering glance. "Do they bother you?"

Kate shook her head. She wished the scars weren't there, not because they marred the perfection of his body, but because each one was a declaration of blood spilled and pain endured.

"Your turn," James said, reaching out to remove her nightgown.

She flinched. "Must I?"

James lowered his hand. "No," he said. "Not if you don't wish to. But . . . I beg you, Kate. Please."

"But—"

"I want to see you, Kate," he said, his voice husky and low. "Please."

Kate bit her lip, cringingly aware of her plainness. Panic began to chase away the hot passion in her body.

"Ah, Kate . . ." James said softly. "Don't look so distressed."
He stepped up close to her and took her face in his hands
and kissed her gently. "It can wait," he whispered, against her
mouth.

The panic faded as he kissed her. Heat returned as his
teeth grazed her lower lip. Urgency came rushing back with
the touch of his tongue. Kate opened her mouth and let him
kiss her, and then she allowed him to draw her onto the bed
and to stretch his long, strong body alongside her on the blue
and gold counterpane. A curious combination of anticipation
and apprehension shortened her breath. She was afraid and
eager and excited, all at the same time.

They lay side by side in the dim candlelight, facing each
other. Her eyes were caught in his. She was unable to look
away from that dark, intent gaze. "Touch me, Kate," James
said, and he took her hands and placed them on his chest.

He shuddered and inhaled deeply. She felt both the inha-
lation and the shudder through his hot skin, and responded
with a quiver and a sharp, inhaled breath of her own. Her
pulse gave a leap. James smiled, watching her with black eyes,
his face very close to her own.

"Kiss me, Kate," he whispered.

She did, moving her head until her lips touched his. He
released her hands, then, and took hold of her face and kissed
her hungrily, licking into her mouth.

They were both breathless when he stopped. James pulled
his head back slightly and she saw the heat in his face, the
dark glitter in his eyes. "Your nightgown," he said hoarsely.
"Please, Kate."

Shyness surged over her, but not panic. When her refusal
didn't come, James stripped the nightgown from her with
haste that was almost frantic. He kissed her skin as he bared
it. "Kate," he said, against her shoulder, her midriff, her hip.
"Oh, God, *Kate.*" There was something close to reverence in
his voice, something that made self-consciousness impossible.

When she was naked, he kissed her mouth again. From

her mouth, he moved to her throat, his fingers straying across her skin ahead of his lips. He kissed the crook of each arm, open-mouthed, causing her to shiver. He kissed the insides of her wrists. He drew her fingertips into his mouth, one by one, and bit them lightly. He licked beneath the curve of her breasts and took her nipples into his mouth, making her gasp for breath. He moved lower, kissing, stroking. He spread her legs, sliding his hands over her skin, and then kissed his way down one leg and back up the other. Kate trembled as he licked the hollows of her knees and bit gently at her calves and placed light kisses on her ankles. She panted and tried not to writhe as he licked his way up the length of her inner thigh. Her body quivered and throbbed, was so *hot*—

Her eyes, which had been heavy-lidded with pleasure, opened wide. "Oh!" she said, as his fingers slid between the private curls at the junction of her thighs. She tried to say it again when she felt his mouth there, but speech had become impossible. Charlotte hadn't said anything about *this*.

He brought her to a mindless pleasure. Her body tried to arch, but James held her hips down, using his mouth to give her a long moment of pure ecstasy. Kate lost all thought of who and where she was. Pleasure rode her, hot and urgent, sweet and wild, as ruthless as his mouth.

James held her in his arms afterwards, pressed close to the heat of his naked body. She trembled and gasped against his shoulder and heard the solid beating of his heart beneath her ear. With each breath, she inhaled the scent of his skin. It was intensely and deliciously male.

Endless seconds passed. Her heartbeat slowed. James released her and leaned back on one elbow and looked at her. His face was in shadow, but the candles cast sufficient light for her to see that his gaze was dark and satisfied. "I predict that you and I are going to be very happy together, Kate," he said. "That was an extremely passionate response."

Kate felt a blush rise in her face.

There was laughter in James's eyes, but he didn't tease her.

Instead he reached out and tucked a straying tendril of hair behind her ear. "May I undo your hair, Kate? Please?"

She blinked. "If you wish." His request confused her. Why would he want to do such a thing? Her hair was a ghastly color, as unfashionable as was possible.

"I do wish." James undid the plait with slow care and then ran his hands through her hair, spreading it over her shoulders and across her breasts. "Look at all the colors, Kate," he said, holding up a long, loose curl for her to see. "It's amazing." And then he laughed at the expression on her face. "You don't agree."

"No."

He grinned and released the curl and pulled her close to him, pressing their bodies together, letting her feel the heat and hardness of his need for her. "It's time, Kate," he whispered, against her ear.

James had never had a virgin before and despite his promise to Kate that he wouldn't hurt her, he was afraid he might. He brought her back to a heat of passion and then entered her body carefully. He watched her face as he did so. She gasped. Her eyes widened. "Oh."

James gasped, too, and trembled. It was a strain to take it so slowly. It took all his self-control. She was so hot, so slick, so tight, so perfect.

Her body welcomed him inside. He thought she felt little pain. Emotions crossed her face. He saw curiosity, a flicker of uncertainty, surprise. Her eyes narrowed slightly in discomfort and then widened with the beginnings of amazement. A flush of pleasure rose in her cheeks.

When he was fully sheathed in her, James paused. He braced himself above her, panting with the effort of holding his passion in check. "Is it . . . comfortable?"

Amusement gleamed in Kate's eyes. "Is it meant to be? Charlotte says—"

James gave a grunt of laughter and nearly lost his precarious control. He closed his eyes for a moment and gasped for breath, his head bowed, his muscles bunching as he held his body still.

He felt a light touch on his cheek. He opened his eyes to find Kate watching him, her face flushed and shy and serious. "Do it," she whispered.

So he did, with one long, straining thrust after another, striving for gentleness and not knowing whether he quite achieved it. Sweat beaded on his skin and his breath came in hoarse gasps. Kate moved with him, her innocent passion stoking his arousal. His pleasure built until it was intolerable. His skin was bursting with it, exquisite and painful and beyond anything he had ever experienced.

Release, when it came, was shattering. He couldn't breathe for the ecstasy of it. "Oh, God," he said afterwards, as he lay dazed and trembling, holding Kate close to him. "God." Even in his wildest flights of fancy he'd not imagined it could be like this. The pleasure had been searing.

Kate made no attempt to pull away from him. She was trembling too. He recalled that her beautiful, sweat-slicked body had arched up to meet him at the end, and smiled to himself. Kate had had her pleasure, too. They were well-matched in passion. Once she overcame her shyness, she would be no passive bed-partner.

Finally, with a groan, James stretched out an arm and groped for the silk handkerchief in the pocket of his dressing gown, on the floor. "Here," he said. "We don't want your maid to find out."

Kate blushed shyly as he cleaned up the evidence of their lovemaking before it could stain the embroidered counterpane. There was a hint of blood on the damp handkerchief when he finished, evidence of her lost virginity.

James returned the handkerchief to his pocket and

gathered her in his arms again. He stroked her hair. It wound around his fingers, soft and buoyant, too curly to be sleek. Kate touched his shoulder with light fingertips, exploring the scar there.

"Musket ball," he said. "At Toulouse. And this one . . ." He pulled back from her slightly and touched his fingers to the thin line that scored his right arm from wrist to elbow. "This one I did myself at Sahagún, when I came off my horse. Fell on my own sword."

He didn't tell her that he'd fallen because his mount had been shot from beneath him. It wasn't a detail she needed to hear. He stroked the scar with his fingertips, remembering. Sahagún had been his first experience of battle, the one that had taught him the meaning of fear. The wound had been minor, little more than a scratch, but the terror he'd experienced upon regaining his feet in the midst of that *mêlée* had been anything but minor . . .

James pushed the memory aside. "This one was from a *chasseur's* saber," he said, tracing the narrow, curving slash across his ribs. "At Benavente. On the retreat to Corunna." More memories intruded. Such a miserable, ignoble retreat. The British Army had become nothing more than a starving rabble of men scrambling over frozen roads. He was horrified, even now, by the acts of pillage and violence he'd witnessed. The images were there, if he cared to remember—

"And that," he said briskly, pointing to the ragged scar on his thigh, "was from a shell fragment, at Waterloo." The shell had maimed his mount, the second one he'd lost that hideous day.

Kate touched that last scar. "You have no limp."

"It wasn't a serious wound." The surgeon had allowed him to return to the battlefield in search of Rupert. His leg had borne him well enough . . . and Rupert had been dead. He flinched from that memory and concentrated on Kate. Such a lovely face. Such glorious hair.

Her mouth twisted slightly. She raised her fingers to the

scar at his shoulder. "Toulouse," she said. She lightly traced the scars across his ribs and arm. His skin shivered beneath her fingertips. "Sahagún. Benavente." She touched his thigh again. "Waterloo." Something close to sadness shadowed her face in the flickering candlelight. He thought that tears shone in her eyes. She smiled at him, a lopsided movement of her mouth. "You are a geography lesson, James."

He leaned over and kissed her, cupping the back of her head with one hand, winding his fingers into her hair. There was no place in his mind for memories when he kissed Kate. The sweetness of her mouth made it impossible to think of anything but her. He closed his eyes and clutched her to him and kissed her. He wanted to tell her that he loved her, but was afraid to. If she thought he was lying . . .

He'd proved his desire. But desire was more easily proven than love. Love would have to wait. He had Kate as his bride, warm and passionate. That would have to suffice for now.

He opened his eyes and released her mouth. Kate sat back on the rumpled counterpane. James looked at her, aware of deep contentment. She was going to be his countess. She would share his bed every night for the rest of his life. And not merely every night. He had no intention of confining his lovemaking to nighttime hours, or even to beds. He didn't think Kate would object. There was much passion in her.

He'd have to tell her about the nightmares; he didn't want her to be frightened if he woke up screaming. But those dreams didn't loom so dreadfully now that he knew Kate would be beside him. When he woke, frantic with remembered terror, she'd be there. He'd be able to turn to her, and she'd hold him, and her warmth and her voice would chase the memories away.

He gazed at Kate, loving her. Such a beautiful body, with its slim curves. Such fascinating hair. It gleamed in the dim candlelight, glinting with gold and copper and flame. "Shall I replait your hair?" he offered.

She shook her head, causing long, disheveled curls to tumble over her pale shoulders. "I can do it."

"I'd like to do it," James said, his tone hopeful. He loved her hair, so bright, so soft.

"Do you know how?"

He shook his head.

Laughter crossed Kate's face. "Then I decline your handsome offer."

"You could teach me."

"Not tonight. Look at the clock, James."

He did, turning his head and glancing across the room. He had to squint to read the clockface in the dim light. What he saw made him wince.

With a sigh, James climbed off the bed. He wished he could stay with Kate. There were all manner of things that he wanted to teach her, so many different ways to enjoy each other. And as much as that—if not more—he wanted to fall asleep with her. He wanted to know that if he woke, he could reach out in the dark and touch her, that she'd be there, warm and soft and sleeping, alongside him. He sighed again and told himself it would be reality soon enough.

James pulled on his nightshirt and shrugged into the dressing gown. He leaned over to kiss Kate, holding her face in his hands. "Don't *ever* doubt that I desire you," he said fiercely, against her mouth. "All right?"

"All right," she whispered. Her cheeks, when he drew back enough to see them, were faintly flushed. Her eyes were shy.

He stroked a finger over one high, round, rosy-nippled breast.

"James!" Kate said, her flush deepening.

He ignored her protest and continued to caress the smooth, soft skin. He wanted to taste it again, so fragrant and delicious, he wanted—

He removed his hand before desire could overcome sense. "Good night, Kate," he said, and pressed a brief kiss into her hair.

"Good night."

James walked across the room. His feet made no sound on

the blue and cream carpet. He unlocked her door and picked up his candle. It was nearly burnt out.

He cast one last hungry glance at Kate, kneeling naked on the rumpled bed, her hair loose about her shoulders, and left the shadowy bedchamber. He very much wished that he didn't have to leave her.

# $C$HAPTER 18

$J$ames came down to the breakfast table several minutes after Kate. He moved with a relaxed grace that made her realize how tense he'd been lately. Riding clothes of elegant cut and somber color concealed his body, but she could remember how it had looked in the candlelight, strong and bold in its lines, beautiful.

Kate blushed and lowered her eyes to her plate. Last night had been marvelous beyond anything Charlotte had described. Having James touch her like that, having him inside her—

Her throat tightened and she nearly choked on her buttered roll. Hurriedly she swallowed a mouthful of tea. The amber liquid with its hint of lemon cleared her throat and she was able to breathe again. Calmly she replaced her cup, listening as James greeted Harry and Lizzie and Cousin Augusta.

Her turn came: "Good morning, Kate."

The cup rattled in the saucer as her fingers shook slightly. Kate raised her eyes. James was watching her. He smiled slowly and she saw memory of their lovemaking on his face.

Heat rose in her cheeks. She looked hastily away. "Good morning."

"Did you sleep well?"

Kate's throat constricted again. "Yes," she managed.

"Are you certain, Kate?" She heard teasing solicitude in his voice. "You look as if you slept . . . poorly."

"Oh," Kate said, aware that every eye was suddenly on her. "Well . . . perhaps a little."

"I slept poorly myself," James said, in a conversational tone.

"Were you too cold?" Cousin Augusta asked. "*I* was. The fire in my chamber was quite insufficient! I swear I scarce slept a *wink* for all my shivering. I do hope I shan't catch a chill. Or even the influenza! For you know, my lord, my constitution is exceedingly frail."

"My difficulty was quite the opposite," James said. "I was too hot, Miss Stitchcombe. *Far* too hot." His words were directed at Cousin Augusta, but his eyes were focused on Kate.

"Hot?" Cousin Augusta said. "How odd. It was such a cold night!"

"And you, Kate?" James asked, ignoring this comment. "What was the source of your disturbed sleep?"

If Harry and Lizzie hadn't been looking at her, Kate would have glared at James. It was quite dreadful of him to tease her in this manner!

"Well?" James asked.

Heat rose in her face.

"Too hot?" he asked smoothly, lifting a forkful of ham to his mouth.

"No," Kate said tartly. "Too cold."

Laughter sprang into his eyes and she watched in satisfaction as he momentarily choked on his food.

"I think that perhaps I have a touch of the influenza," Cousin Augusta said. "For my dreams last night were *quite*— Although, of course, it could have been the pork. Pork frequently gives me nightmares! My stomach is *extremely* sensitive. Why, I feel ill if the merest morsel of lobster passes my lips. And as for mushrooms, I cannot eat them at all!"

No one made any comment to this.

Kate chewed slowly, remembering. It had felt so strange to have him inside her, so very odd. The tight fullness had been

213

uncomfortable at first, and then the discomfort had faded and only pleasure had remained. James had watched her, his eyes intent on her face. He'd been concentrating on her utterly. She thought he wouldn't have noticed if Paton or even Cousin Augusta had burst into the bedchamber and demanded that they stop.

It had been primitive: the movement of their bodies, the heat and the sweat and the panting gasps. She'd seen his pleasure in the shadowy candlelight, had watched it flare on his face while his body had shuddered in release. That had been a deeply intimate moment, perhaps the most intimate moment of all—when physical gratification had overcome him.

Kate laid down her knife and fork. Her cheeks were hot again.

". . . a walk on the terrace," Harry said, rising from the table.

"But Miss Penrose has no bonnet! Surely she won't wish to accompany you?"

"A mere stroll on the terrace, cousin. There's no need for a bonnet."

"But the sunlight! So terrible for one's complexion! I'm sure Miss Penrose does not care to have a *freckle.*"

Lizzie glanced at Harry. "I like freckles," she said shyly.

"Oh!" Cousin Augusta gave an angry titter. "*Surely* not. No one could!"

Harry opened the door to the terrace. His jaw was tight.

"But—" cried Cousin Augusta, in an agitated voice, rising in her chair, clearly determined to allow no *tête-à-tête* between the betrothed couple. "It is *cold.* Miss Penrose may catch a chill!"

"I think not," Harry said. He offered his arm to Lizzie. She took it, her eyes upraised shyly, her cheeks delicately flushed. Harry placed his hand over her fingers and smiled at her, as the late Viscount had been used to smile at his wife. Lizzie's flush deepened.

"But—"

"No, cousin," Harry's voice was firm.

A bow, and he and Lizzie were gone.

"*Well,*" Cousin Augusta said, hurrying to the door, her tone outraged. "Did you ever? *Such*—"

James sent Cousin Augusta a narrow-eyed glance, then leaned across the table. "We must talk, Kate," he whispered. "Meet me in the library in five minutes."

Kate nodded, her attention partially on her cousin.

"It will serve her right if she *does* get a freckle!" Cousin Augusta cried.

James's mouth tightened and for a moment Kate was afraid he'd snap at her cousin. He didn't. Instead he pushed back his chair. "Five minutes," he reminded her in a low voice. With a black glance at Cousin Augusta, he left the breakfast parlor.

Ten minutes passed before Kate was able to join James in the library. She had apologized to Cousin Augusta for her sharp words last night—then narrowly avoided pulling caps with her again. It had been a very close thing, particularly when Augusta informed her that she'd advised Harry to retract his offer of marriage. Only the fact that Harry had clearly ignored this advice prevented Kate from losing her temper. That, and the recollection that her cousin's state was to be pitied.

James stood at one of the tall windows. He turned as she entered the library and watched as she closed the door behind her. "You look cross," he remarked.

"I am."

"With me? Or with your cousin?"

"With my cousin. Although *your* behavior—"

Laughter leapt into his face. "I know. Terrible, wasn't it!" He walked towards her. "I can scarcely believe I had the effrontery. Like the villain in a gothic novel!"

Kate had been referring to his teasing at the breakfast table; he was clearly speaking of last night's events. She tried to feel affronted that he'd compromised her. It was difficult when she'd experienced so much pleasure. "Worse than any villain I've ever read of!" she said, managing to insert tartness into her tone. "It was very bad of you, James."

"I know." He smiled wryly as he came up to her. "I've come to the conclusion that I'm not a gentleman. It's very lowering." He took hold of her hands. "Kate, do you mind very much?" She heard anxiety in his voice and saw it on his face, beneath the laughter.

Kate looked at him. She didn't mind that he'd taken her virginity; she did mind that he wasn't getting a love match. This wasn't the marriage she had wished for him.

"Affection and passion, Kate," he said, still holding her hands. "That's what you said. Remember? And we have both. You know that, don't you?"

Kate nodded.

"I wish . . ." James laughed. It was a flat sound. "Oh, Lord, how I *wish* you'd never heard what I said to Harry!"

"Some of it was very interesting," Kate said, trying to lighten his mood. "I had no idea Harry had offered for Maria Brougham. Or that he'd fought a duel over her . . . her eyebrows, wasn't it?"

James's mouth formed a humorless smile. "Her eyelashes." His clasp on her hands tightened. "Kate . . . some of the things I said . . . You can have no idea how much I regret them!"

"James, please, forget it."

"I can't." He stared at her. "What I said about women and . . . and the dark. Oh, I can't remember exactly what I said, but—"

"One woman is like another in the dark," Kate quoted.

A flush rose in his cheeks. "You know that's nonsense, don't you, Kate?"

She didn't need his earnest voice to tell her so; she'd always known. She nodded.

Relief crossed his face. He loosened his grip. "And you know that I don't want to marry you because I merely tolerate you, don't you, Kate?"

Kate looked at him. She remembered the expression on his face when he'd made love to her. She nodded again.

The tense line of his jaw relaxed. He released her hands. "Kate . . ." He reached out to touch her hair. "I know what I said about you, but you must believe me—you *must*—when I tell you that my feelings have undergone a profound change. I never saw you properly before. I never . . ." His fingertips brushed lightly over her cheek. "You're beautiful, Kate."

Kate jerked her head back. *That* was a lie. She spoke sharply: "Don't, James!"

"It's the truth," he said quietly, his hand still outstretched.

"You know it's not. I have freckles, James—and red hair!" Her voice, although she tried to prevent it, was slightly bitter.

"I like them," he said simply.

"But—"

James sighed. He lowered his hand. "Kate, please believe me. Your freckles and your hair . . . I *like* them."

Kate stared at him. "I don't understand."

"Don't try to understand. Just accept it. Please."

She nodded, dubiously.

A smile cleared the shadows from James' face. He hugged her to him. "Thank you."

She leaned into him and closed her eyes. He was so large and solid, so wonderfully male.

"I'm sorry, Kate, it must be a special license. My birthday is too soon for the banns to be read."

"I know," she said against his shoulder. "It's all right. I don't mind, truly."

He didn't release her, but continued to hold her close. "Kate, I know you heard everything I said to Harry, but . . ."

When he didn't continue, she pushed herself away from him and looked up at his face. "But what?"

James held her eyes. "I love you."

Kate frowned. "James—"

"I beg you to believe me. I wouldn't lie about such a thing!"

She stood motionless, scarcely breathing, hearing the truth in his voice, seeing it in his face. "James—"

He took her in his arms again, roughly, fiercely. "It's true, Kate," he said, into her hair.

She closed her eyes and tried not to cry. Her cheek rested against his riding coat. The heat of his body beat at her. She heard his heart. His breath was in her hair. "You do believe me?" he asked finally.

"Yes."

She felt his tension ease. "Thank you," he said.

They stood like that for long minutes, in warm, close silence. Then James stirred. He loosened his grip and drew her over to a couch. He pulled her down to sit. "Italy first," he said, holding her hands. His eyes smiled at her. "And then Greece. Or would you prefer the other way around?"

Kate laughed. The sound came out rather wobbly. "I don't mind."

James released one of her hands. He touched a light fingertip to her cheek. "Hunt out your maps, Kate. We shall go wherever you want."

"That's a dangerous promise," she said, as names began to flick into her head: Florence and Rome, Athens, Delphi. "There are so many places I'd like to see!"

James laughed. He bent his head and kissed her.

The doorknob rattled. They sprang apart on the couch. Kate rose hastily to her feet. "Good morning, Yule." She smoothed her muslin gown with trembling fingers.

"Miss Kate." The butler bowed. "My lord. I have the *Gazette*."

"Thank you," Kate said. She glanced at James, standing alongside her. His expression was composed. She thought her own cheeks were flushed. Yule was as poker-faced as only a butler could be, but something in his manner told her he'd seen their embrace. There was no censure in him, though. Rather, there was approbation.

The knowledge that Yule had seen—and approved of—James kissing her brought more heat to Kate's cheeks. She walked over to one of the windows and stood so that her face was shadowed. Yule placed the *Gazette* on the desk and bowed again, somehow instilling the movement with a hint of complicity, and left the library.

James crossed the room. He stood behind her and slid his arms around her waist, leaning lightly against her. "Your butler approves," he said, faint laughter in his voice.

"Yes," Kate said, taking pleasure in the warmth and strength of his body. His height, the sheer size of him, made her feel—not dainty, precisely, but . . . perhaps feminine was the word. It was quite marvelous.

Outside, she saw Harry and Lizzie on the lawn. Lizzie was still without a bonnet. They were deep in conversation, their heads bent close together. Cousin Augusta, if she could have seen them, would have—

Kate sighed. "We shall have to have Cousin Augusta live with us."

"No," James said firmly. "I refuse to have that woman in my house."

"She can't stay here. It wouldn't be fair on Lizzie."

"Then she must go somewhere else."

Kate sighed again, resigned to her fate. "We promised Mother to give her houseroom, Harry and I. If he doesn't have her, then I must."

James was silent for a moment. "Was she a favorite of your mother's?"

"Oh, no! Not at all. But . . . Mother felt sorry for her. She's quite alone in the world and has only a few pounds to her name. Her father was a . . . to be perfectly honest, James, he was a wastrel!"

"Is there no one else she can go to?"

"No. At least, there are none who will have her."

"I'm not surprised." His tone was dry. "No, it is clear, Kate, she must live in Bath."

"In Bath?" Kate pulled away and turned to face him. "Are you mad, James?"

"Not at all," he said, smiling. "It's the perfect place for such an invalid, even one who is merely a *malade imaginaire*—or perhaps I should say, especially for one such! I wonder Harry did not think of it himself."

"But we promised—"

James laid a finger on her lips, silencing her protest. "You promised houseroom. Well, I shall give your cousin more than that: I shall give her a house of her own."

Kate's eyes widened at the thought of such expense. "Oh, but—"

His finger silenced her again. "I am plump enough in the pocket to provide for any number of indigent relatives, Kate. Let me do this. Please."

Kate looked at him for a long moment. It was a solution even her mother would have approved of. Her heart lightened at the thought of no more Cousin Augusta. "Thank you."

"Not at all. My motive is entirely selfish." His arms were around her again and he was laughing. He kissed her, and she opened her mouth to him.

Several long, heated minutes later, James released her. "Show me the priest's hole, Kate," he said, his face flushed. The familiar dark glitter was in his eyes.

"Why?"

He stroked down her throat with a light fingertip. "Why do you think?"

Heat scorched Kate's cheeks. "We can't!"

"The attics, then?" James asked, in a hopeful tone.

Kate's laugh was slightly shaky. "Not the attics either, James."

He gave a melancholy sigh. Kate wasn't fooled; his eyes were laughing at her.

"I'll show you the priest's hole if you promise to behave yourself," she said, her tone severe.

James bowed low. "But of course."

Kate took him across the room. She must show Harry, too, just as soon as she'd removed her diaries.

James surveyed the books that were shelved above the priest's hole and laughed. "Mr. Collins," he said, taking down one of the volumes of *Pride and Prejudice* and opening it to the title page.

"They say the writer is a clergyman's daughter," Kate said. "Which is a trifle disappointing."

James grinned. "How so?" He closed the book and returned it to its place on the shelf.

"It's so . . . so *prosaic*. I had hoped for something a little more exciting. A disgraced peer's daughter in a garret perhaps, or—" Kate narrowed her eyes at him. "Are you laughing at me, James?"

"Yes," he said. "I am." He pulled her to him and pressed a kiss into her hair. "I love you."

Kate realized she hadn't told James she loved him. She opened her mouth to rectify the error.

James turned to the wainscoting. "When did you find the priest's hole?" he asked.

"Not long after your first visit. James, I—"

He swung back to look at her. "Eleven years ago. I remember."

Heat flooded Kate's face. It was stupid to feel humiliation after such a length of time, but she did. She'd made such a fool of herself. She looked down at the floor. The border of the carpet was elaborate, with flowers and unfurling leaves in red and green and gold.

James touched her cheek. "You were seventeen," he said softly. "So shy . . ."

Kate fixed her eyes on his top boots. They were very well polished. She could almost see her reflection in them.

"What I said to Harry about you . . . I'm sorry for it, Kate. I should very much like it if you made sheep's eyes at me again!"

This brought a reluctant laugh from her, as must have been his aim, although she was still too embarrassed to look at him.

"Ah, Kate. I said a great many foolish things to Harry. I wish you would forget them." His fingers lightly brushed her cheek, stroking, caressing.

She sought for something to take the sigh from his voice. A fragment of that overheard conversation came to mind: "You fought a duel over a pair of boots?"

James's fingers halted in their movement. "Er . . ." he said.

"A pair of boots," Kate said, raising her head and looking him in the face.

James flushed. "Show me this priest's hole, Kate. How does it open?"

Kate folded her arms. She smiled. "Boots."

James stared at her, tall, strong, handsome. Red-faced.

She waited.

His flush deepened. "They were the most ridiculous boots I'd ever seen," he said defensively. "They had these *huge* tassels and . . . and . . . and it was ten years ago, and . . . dash it, Kate, I was foxed!"

Kate shook her head. "You fought a duel over a pair of boots," she said in mock outrage. "James Hargrave, how *could* you have done such a thing?"

"We both fired into the air," James said, as if this excused his actions.

Kate shook her head again, tutting.

"Dash it, Kate, stop laughing at me and open this wretched priest's hole," James said, looking very hot.

"I love you," Kate said.

James froze. His expression became completely blank. "What?"

"I thought you should know."

"What? . . . You do?" Incredulity spread slowly across his face.

Kate nodded. "Yes. I always have."

"What?"

Kate lowered her eyes from that shocked gaze. She reached out and opened the priest's hole. The oak panel slid aside.

"But . . . but Kate, why did you refuse my offer?"

"I wanted you to be happy," she said, not looking at him. "I didn't think you would be with me."

"Kate—"

She looked at him, then. She saw in his face what she'd heard in his voice: distress. "Kate . . ." James said again. "Oh, God, *Kate*." He was holding her now, quite fiercely, his arms so tight it almost hurt. "You humble me." His voice was low, hoarse.

"No."

"Yes!"

The doorknob rattled. They both stiffened. James eased his grip on her as the door opened the merest crack. Yule's voice came loudly: "I'm certain she's not in the library, Miss Stitchcombe."

"The priest's hole," James whispered, pushing her towards it. "Both of us. Quickly!"

Much as she wished to avoid her cousin, Kate hesitated. James's height was considerably over six feet. "You won't fit."

"I don't care," he said. "In!"

With a glance at the opening door, she obeyed. James crammed in alongside her, ducking his head and crouching on the hard floor. Kate closed the panel hastily. "I have a tinderbox and candle," she whispered, reaching past him in the sudden darkness.

He stopped her with a hand on her arm. "There's no need."

A tiny shaft of light shone through the peephole. Sound came, too. Footsteps, and then: "I thought I saw her enter," Cousin Augusta said. "Not ten minutes ago! Where can she be?"

Yule's voice came loudly: "Perhaps she stepped out on the terrace."

Cousin Augusta clicked her tongue, audibly. "I suppose I must fetch my bonnet and look for her!" Her tone was cross.

The door closed. Kate peeked through the peephole. The library was empty. "They've gone."

"Good." James shifted in the dark. The candleholder fell over with a clang. "Sorry." He shifted again. Something skittered across the floor. Probably the pen-knife she used to trim the goose feather quills. Kate began to laugh.

"What *is* all this stuff?" James said, in a slightly harassed tone.

"I wrote in here."

The diaries slithered over one another as James moved again. "Oh, your diary. I think my foot is on it. Or . . . Kate, how many of the wretched things do you have?"

Kate groped past him and rescued the diaries from beneath his boots. "A few. I've kept them in here for years. I didn't want anyone to . . . to see what I had written."

"Secrets, Kate?" She heard a smile in James's voice. He was teasing her.

"You were the only secret."

There was a moment's silence, and then: "You wrote about me?" The teasing note was gone from his voice.

"I wrote about other things, too. But . . . there's a lot about you. Often it was easier to pretend that I didn't . . . didn't like you so much . . . if I'd written about it."

It sounded dreadfully foolish, said aloud, but there was no laughter in James's voice when he spoke her name. Indeed, he sounded aghast: "Kate . . ."

"I didn't want you to see that I . . ." She fingered the covers of the diaries. The calfskin was soft and fine-grained. "I didn't want anyone to know."

"No," James said flatly. "That is very evident."

Kate waited, clutching the journals, aware that he was angry but not understanding why.

Long, dark seconds passed. When James spoke, his voice was low and rough, little more than a whisper: "I never saw you, Kate. Not properly. To me you were Harry's sister, nothing more. I never . . . I never saw you as someone I could love."

Kate placed the diaries on the floor. "James," she said, reaching out in the darkness and finding the sleeve of his riding coat.

"Can you forgive me for being so blind, Kate?" he whispered. "For being such a fool?"

"Of course." She touched his shoulder, kneeling in the dark. "And you are no fool, James."

"Yes," he said. "I am."

"I would not marry a fool! Enough of this, James." She shook his shoulder gently. "It's unnecessary. Don't do it."

"I love you, Kate," he whispered. "I will always love you."

"And I, you."

His head was bowed. She stroked his hair and then touched his face with gentle fingers, tracing the features that gave him such a misleading appearance of sternness—and such striking good looks. Her fingertips brushed lightly along the slanting eyebrows and down the straight line of his nose, across his strong cheekbones and along the firm jaw. They outlined his wide, well-shaped mouth. She couldn't see the strength and balance of those features, but her fingers felt it and delighted in it.

He was so large and strong and warm, so kind, so generous, so . . . so *James*. There was no one else like him. He was unique, and he was marvelous, and he loved her. Honey-sweet heat began to rise in Kate's body. She longed to have him inside her again.

"James, what I said about behaving yourself if I showed you the priest's hole . . . I wish you wouldn't."

She felt him raise his head. "What?" he said. The bitterness was gone from his tone. He sounded startled.

"I'd like to do it again. What we did last night."

James heard the astonishing words, but could hardly believe they were true. "You do?"

"Yes." Kate touched her mouth to his. "Please."

She kissed him. It was a kiss unlike the others he'd shared with her, in the woods and in her bedchamber, or even in the library earlier. This time she initiated it, kissing him as he'd kissed her. She bit into his lower lip with exquisite gentleness, and then licked where she had bitten.

Heat flared in him. He opened his mouth and kissed Kate back, deeply, hungrily, pulling her close, clutching her as a drowning man would clutch a rescuer, his grip almost fierce. She loved him. Eleven years! He could think of nothing he'd done to deserve such depth of feeling, such constancy. It stunned and humbled him, and he knew it would take a long time to recover from hearing her speak those words.

He kissed Kate and held her, aware of a joy deeper than any he'd known in his life.

"Will you object if I remove your neckcloth?" Kate asked, against his mouth.

"No," James said, with no thought for what his appearance must be afterwards.

He assisted Kate to unbutton his riding coat and waistcoat, to open his shirt as far as was possible and tug it loose from his breeches. Then he stretched out in the cramped space and pulled Kate on top of him. The floor was cold and hard beneath his back, even through the layers of his clothes, but James easily ignored the discomfort. His fingers found the fastenings at the back of her gown, although with her kissing his throat it was almost impossible to concentrate on his task.

He slid the gown and petticoat from her shoulders. The laces of her corset took longer, baffling his fingers in the darkness until he was tempted to rip them free. Finally they loosened. Kate lifted her mouth from his skin and gave a choke of laughter as he removed the stiff garment. "How shall I ever get it on again?"

"I don't care," James said, his voice hoarse with need, breathless. He pushed the thin chemise down, baring her breasts, and groaned with pleasure to feel them in his hands. They were soft and smooth, sweet and round.

He lifted Kate higher on him and licked the curve of one breast. She clenched her fingers in his hair. "Oh . . ."

The door to the library opened. They froze.

"Can you see who it is?" James whispered, against her soft skin.

Kate shifted slightly on top of him. There was a moment's silence, and then: "Cousin Augusta!"

The crinkle of a newspaper came clearly through the wainscoting.

"She's reading the *Gazette*," Kate said. "Oh, Lord, she'll be forever."

"It doesn't matter." James released her and let her inch her way down his body until she lay with her cheek on his shoulder. "We can wait."

They lay in silence. James thought of all the things he wanted to tell Kate. The most important was that he'd never share his body with anyone except her. It shamed him deeply that he'd planned to have lovers if he married her. He needed to tell her he wouldn't, but that had to wait until he could see her face. He wanted to look into Kate's eyes and know that she believed him, to know that she trusted him as completely as he trusted her.

That moment was not now. James held her in the dark and listened as Miss Stitchcombe rustled the pages of the *Gazette*. He stroked Kate's bare back, wholly happy, utterly content. *We can wait, Kate. We have all the time in the world.*

Time had been his enemy the past few months; now it was his friend. The future he'd wanted, that he'd thought he'd never have, was his. It stretched before him, full of laughter and sunshine, companionship and love.

A future with Kate.

There was nothing better in the world.

# $\mathcal{T}$HANK $\mathcal{Y}$OU

Thanks for reading *The Earl's Dilemma*. I hope you enjoyed it!

If you'd like to be notified whenever I release a new book, please join my Readers' Group, which you can find at www.emilylarkin.com/newsletter.

I welcome all honest reviews. Reviews and word of mouth help other readers to find books, so please consider taking a few moments to leave a review on Goodreads or elsewhere.

If you'd like to read the first chapter of *My Lady Thief,* a Regency romance novel featuring an heiress with a dangerous pastime and a bachelor who thinks very highly of himself, please turn the page.

# My Lady THIEF

## CHAPTER ONE

The thief stood in front of Lady Bicknell's dressing table and looked with disapproval at the objects strewn across it: glass vials of perfume, discarded handkerchiefs, a clutter of pots and jars of cosmetics—rouge, maquillage; many gaping open, their contents drying—two silver-backed hair brushes with strands of hair caught among the bristles, a messy pile of earrings, the faceted jewels glinting dully in the candlelight.

The thief stirred the earrings with a fingertip. Gaudy. Tasteless. In need of cleaning.

The dressing table, the mess, offended the thief's tidy soul. She pursed her lips and examined the earrings again, more slowly. The diamonds were paste, the sapphires nothing more than colored glass, the rubies . . . She picked up a ruby earring and looked at it closely. Real, but such a garish, vulgar setting. The thief grimaced and put the earring back, more neatly than its owner had done. There was nothing on the dressing table that interested her.

She turned to the mahogany dresser. It stood in the corner,

crouching on bowed legs like a large toad. Three wide drawers and at the top, three small ones, side by side, beneath a frowning mirror. The thief quietly opened the drawers and let her fingers sift through the contents, stirring the woman's scent from the garments: perspiration, perfume.

The topmost drawer on the left, filled with a tangle of silk stockings and garters, wasn't as deep as the others.

For a moment the thief stood motionless, listening for footsteps in the corridor, listening to the breeze stir the curtains at the open window, then she pulled the drawer out and laid it on the floor.

Behind the drawer of stockings was another drawer, small and discreet, and inside that . . .

The thief grinned as she lifted out the bracelet. Pearls gleamed in the candlelight, exquisite, expensive.

The drawer contained—besides the bracelet—a matching pair of pearl earrings and four letters. The thief took the earrings and replaced the letters. She was easing the drawer back into its slot when a name caught her eye. *St. Just.*

St. Just. The name brought with it memory of a handsome face and gray eyes, memory of humiliation—and a surge of hatred.

She hesitated for a second, and then reached for the letters.

The first one was brief and to the point. *Here, as requested, is my pearl bracelet. In exchange, I must ask for the return of my letter.* It was signed Grace St. Just.

The thief frowned and unfolded the second letter. It was written in the same girlish hand as the first. The date made her pause—November 6th, 1817. The day Princess Charlotte had died, although the letter writer wouldn't have known that at the time.

*Dearest Reginald,* the letter started. The thief skimmed over a passionate declaration of love and slowed to read the final paragraph. *I miss you unbearably. Every minute seems like an hour, every day a year. The thought of being parted from you is unendurable. If it must be elopement, then so be it.* A tearstain marked the ink. *Your loving Grace.*

The thief picked up the third letter. It was a draft, some words crossed out, others scribbled in the margins.

*~~My dear~~ Miss St. Just, ~~I have~~ a letter of yours you wrote to a Mr. Reginald Plunkett of Birmingham has come into my possession. ~~If you want it back. In exchange for its return~~. I should like to return this letter to you. In exchange I ~~want~~ ask nothing more than your pearl bracelet. You may leave ~~it~~ the bracelet ~~for me~~ in the Dutch garden in the Kensington Palace Gardens. ~~Place it~~ Hide it in the urn at the northeastern corner of the pond.*

The thief thinned her lips. She stopped reading and picked up the final letter. Another draft.

*Dear Miss St. Just, thank you for the bracelet. I find, however, that I ~~want~~ require ~~the necklace~~ the earrings as well. You may leave them in the same place. Do not worry about ~~the~~ your letter; ~~I have it~~ it is safe in my keeping.*

The thief slowly refolded the paper. Blackmail. There was a sour taste in her mouth. She looked down at the bracelet and earrings, at the love letter, and bit her lower lip. What to do?

St. Just.

Memory flooded through her: the smothered laughter of the *ton,* the sniggers and the sideways glances, the gleeful whispers.

The thief tightened her lips. Resentment burned in her breast and heated her cheeks. Adam St. Just could rot in hell for all she cared, but Grace St. Just . . . Grace St. Just didn't deserve this.

Her decision made, the thief gathered the contents of the hidden drawer—letters and jewels—and tucked them into the pouch she wore around her waist, hidden beneath shirt and trousers. Swiftly she replaced both drawers. Crossing the room, she plucked the ruby earrings from the objects littering Lady Bicknell's dressing table. The rubies went into the pouch, nestling alongside the pearls. The thief propped an elegant square of card among the remaining earrings. The message inscribed on it was brief: *Should payment be made for a spiteful tongue? Tom thinks so.* There was no signature; a drawing of a lean alley cat adorned the bottom of the note.

The thief gave a satisfied nod. Justice done. She glanced at the mirror. In the candlelight her eyes were black. Her face was soot-smudged and unrecognizable. For a moment she stared at herself, unsettled, then she lifted a finger to touch the faint cleft in her chin. That, at least, was recognizable, whether she wore silk dresses or boys' clothing in rough, dark fabric.

The thief turned away from her image in the mirror. She trod quietly towards the open window.

Adam St. Just found his half-sister in the morning room, reading a letter. Her hair gleamed like spun gold in the sunlight. "Grace?"

His sister gave a convulsive start and clutched the letter to her breast. A bundle of items on her lap slid to the floor. Something landed with a light thud. Adam saw the glimmer of pearls.

"Is that your bracelet? I thought you'd lost—" He focused on her face. "What's wrong?"

"Nothing." Grace hastily wiped her cheeks. "Just something in my eye." She bent and hurriedly gathered several pieces of paper and the bracelet.

A pearl earring lay stranded on the carpet. Adam nudged it with the toe of his boot. "And this?" He picked up the earring and held it out.

Grace flushed. She took the earring

Adam frowned at her. "Grace, what is it?"

"Nothing." Her smile was bright, but her eyes slid away

from his.

Adam sat down on the sofa alongside her. "Grace . . ." he said, and then stopped, at a loss to know how to proceed. The physical distance between them—a few inches of rose-pink damask—may as well have been a chasm. The twelve years that separated them, the difference in their genders, seemed insurmountable barriers. He felt a familiar sense of helplessness, a familiar knowledge that he was failing in his guardianship of her.

He looked at his sister's downcast eyes, the curve of her cheek, the slender fingers clutching the pearl earring. *I love you, Grace.* He cleared his throat and tried to say the words aloud. "Grace, I hope you know that I . . . care about you and that I want you to be happy."

It was apparently the wrong thing to say. Grace began to cry.

Adam hesitated for a moment, dismayed, and then put his arm around her. To his relief, Grace didn't pull away. She turned towards him, burying her face in his shoulder.

It hurt to hear her cry. Adam swallowed and tightened his grip on her. She'd grown thinner since their arrival in London, paler, quieter. *I should take her home. To hell with the Season.*

The storm of tears lessened. Adam stroked his sister's hair. "What is it, Grace?"

"I didn't want to disappoint you again," she sobbed.

"You've never disappointed me."

Grace shook her head against his shoulder. "Last year . . ." She didn't need to say more; they both knew what she was referring to.

"I was angry—but not with you." He'd been more than angry: he'd been furious. Furious at Reginald Plunkett, furious at the school for hiring the man, but mostly furious at himself for not visiting Grace more often, for not realizing how lonely she was, how vulnerable to the smiles and compliments of her music teacher.

The anger stirred again, tightening in his chest as if a fist was clenched there. *I should have horsewhipped him. I should have broken every bone in his body.*

Adam dug in his pocket for a handkerchief. Grace had come perilously close to ruin. Even now, six months later, he woke in a cold sweat from dreams—nightmares—where he'd delayed his journey by one day, where he'd arrived in Bath to find her gone. "Here," he said, handing her the handkerchief.

Grace dried her cheeks.

Adam smiled at her. "Now, tell me what's wrong."

Grace looked down at her lap, at the papers and the pearls. She extracted a sheet of paper and handed it to him.

*~~My dear~~ Miss St. Just, ~~I have~~ a letter ~~of yours~~ you wrote to a Mr. Reginald Plunkett of Birmingham has come into my posses-sion. ~~If you want it back. In exchange for its return.~~ I should like to return this letter to you. In exchange I ~~want~~ ask nothing more than your pearl bracelet.*

"What!" He stared at his sister. "Someone's blackmailing you?"

Grace bit her lip.

Adam's fingers tightened on the sheet of paper. "Why didn't you tell me?"

Her gaze fell.

*Because you were afraid I'd be angry at you, disappointed in you.* Adam swallowed. He looked back at the blackmail letter without seeing it. He rubbed his face with one hand. "Grace . . ."

"Here." She handed him another piece of paper. The writ-ing was the same as the first, the intent as ugly.

"You did what this person asked? You gave them your pearls?" His rage made the sunlight seem as sharp-edged as a sword. The room swung around him for a moment, vivid with anger. He focused on a chair. The rose-pink damask had become the deep crimson of blood, the gilded wood was as bright as flames. *How dared anyone do this to her?* The sheet of paper crumpled in his fist. *I'll kill them—*

"Yes." Grace gathered the bracelet and the earrings within

the curve of her palm.

Adam blinked. His anger fell away, replaced by confusion. "Then why—?"

"Tom returned them to me."

"Tom?"

He blinked again at the elegant piece of paper she handed him, at the brief message, the signature, the cat drawn in black ink at the bottom of the page. His interest sharpened. *That* Tom.

*I believe these belong to you,* Tom had written. *I found them in Lady Bicknell's possession.*

"And the letter to Reginald Plunkett?"

Grace touched a folded piece of paper in her lap.

Adam read the note again. *Tom.* "The devil," he said, under his breath. He fastened his gaze on his sister. "Was there anything else? Anything that might identify him?"

Grace shook her head.

Adam touched the ink-drawn cat with a fingertip. It stared back at him, sitting with its tail curled across its paws, unblinking, calm.

He lifted his eyes to the signature, and above that to the message. "Lady Bicknell," he said aloud, and the rage came back.

"Apparently," Grace said.

The blackmail letters were clearly drafts. "You have the ones she sent you?"

Grace shook her head. "I burned them."

Adam reread Lady Bicknell's letters, letting his eyes rest on each and every word, scored out or not. "She'll pay for this," he said grimly. "By God, if she thinks she can—!" He recollected himself, glanced at his sister's face, and forced himself to sit back on the sofa, to form his mouth into a smile. "Forget this, Grace. It's over."

"Yes," said Grace, but her expression was familiar: pale, miserable. She'd worn it four years ago when her mother died, and she'd worn it last November when she'd learned the truth about Reginald Plunkett.

Adam reached for her hand. "How odd, that we must be grateful to a thief." He laughed, tried to make a joke of it.

Grace smiled dutifully.

Adam looked at her, noting the paleness of her cheeks, the faint shadows beneath the blue eyes. "Grace, would you like to go home?" Away from the press of buildings and people and the sly whispers of gossip.

Her face lit up, as if the sun had come from behind a cloud. "Oh, yes!"

"Then I'll arrange it."

"Thank you!" She pulled her hand free from his grasp and embraced him, swift and wholly unexpected.

Adam experienced a throat-tightening rush of emotion. He folded his sister briefly in his arms and then released her. *How did we become so distant?* He cleared his throat. "Have you any engagements today? Would you like to ride out to Richmond?"

"Oh, yes! I should like that of all things!" She rose, and the pearls tumbled from her lap onto the damask-covered sofa. A much-creased letter fluttered down alongside them. It was addressed to Reginald Plunkett in Grace's handwriting.

The delight faded from his sister's face, leaving it miserable once more.

Adam gestured to the letter. "Do you want to keep it?"

Grace shook her head.

"Shall I burn it for you? Or would you prefer—"

"I don't want to touch it!" Her voice was low and fierce.

Adam nodded. He scooped up the pearls and placed them in Grace's palm, curling her fingers around them, holding her hand, holding her gaze. "Forget about this, Grace. It's over."

Grace nodded, but the happiness that had briefly lit her face was gone.

Adam stood. He kissed her cheek. "Go and change," he said, releasing her hand.

When she'd gone, he picked up the pieces of paper: Grace's

love letter, Tom's note, Lady Bicknell's blackmail drafts. He allowed his rage to flare again. Lady Bicknell would pay for the distress she'd caused Grace. She'd pay deeply.

But some of the blame was his. The distance between himself and Grace was his fault: he'd been his sister's guardian, not her friend. She'd been too afraid of his disappointment, his anger, to ask for help.

Adam strode from the morning room. His shame was a physical thing; he felt it in his chest as if a knife blade was buried there.

He had failed Grace. Somehow, without realizing it, he'd become to her what their father had been to him: disapproving and unapproachable.

*But no more,* he vowed silently as he entered his study. *No more.*

Adam grimly placed the letters in the top drawer of his desk. He put Tom's note in last and let his gaze dwell on the signature. "I would like to know who you are," he said under his breath. And then he locked the drawer and put the key in his pocket.

Arabella Knightley, granddaughter of the fifth Earl of Westwick, paused alongside a potted palm and surveyed the ballroom. Lord and Lady Halliwell were launching their eldest daughter in style: hundreds of candles blazed in the chandeliers, a profusion of flowers scented the air, and yards of shimmering pink silk swathed the walls. An orchestra played on a dais and dancing couples filled the floor, performing the intricate steps of the quadrille. The débutantes were distinguishable by their self-consciousness as much as by their pale gowns.

Grace St. Just wasn't on the dance floor. Arabella looked

at the ladies seated around the perimeter of the ballroom, scanning their faces as she sipped her lemonade. Her lip lifted slightly in contempt as she recognized Lady Bicknell.

The woman's appearance—the tasteless, gaudy trinkets, the heavy application of cosmetics—was reminiscent of her dressing table. Her earrings . . . Arabella narrowed her eyes. Yes, Lady Bicknell was wearing the diamond earrings she herself had discarded as worthless.

If the woman's appearance was in keeping with her dressing table, her figure brought to mind the mahogany dresser: broad and squat. *Like a frog,* Arabella thought, watching as Lady Bicknell's wide, flat mouth opened and shut. She was declaiming forcefully, her heavy face flushed with outrage. One of the ladies seated alongside her hid a smile behind her fan; the other, a dowager wearing a purple turban, listened with round-eyed interest.

*Telling the tale of Tom's thieving,* Arabella thought, with another curl of her lip. The woman certainly wouldn't mention the other items that had gone missing last night: the pearl bracelet and earrings, the blackmail letters.

Arabella dismissed Lady Bicknell from her thoughts. She continued her search of the ballroom, looking for Grace St. Just.

She found her finally, seated alongside a St. Just aunt. The girl wore a white satin gown sewn with seed pearls. More pearls gleamed at her earlobes and around her pale throat. She was astonishingly lovely, and yet she was sitting in a corner as if she didn't want anyone to notice her.

Arabella was reminded, vividly, of her own first Season. It was no easy thing to make one's début surrounded by whispers and conjecture and sidelong glances.

*And I had advantages that Grace does not.* She'd had the armor her childhood had given her; armor a girl as gently reared as Grace St. Just couldn't possibly have. And she'd had advice—advice it appeared no one had given Grace.

Arabella chewed on her lower lip. She glanced at the dance

floor, trying to decide what to do. Her eyes fastened on one of the dancers, a tall man with a patrician cast to his features. Adam St. Just, cousin to the Duke of Frew.

She eyed him with resentment. St. Just's manner was as aloof, as proud, as if it was he who held the dukedom, not his cousin. *How could I have been such a fool as to believe he liked me?* She should be grateful to St. Just; he'd taught her never to trust a member of the *ton*—a valuable lesson. But it was impossible to be grateful while she still had memory of the *beaumonde*'s gleeful delight in her humiliation.

Arabella watched him dance, hoping he'd misstep or trample on his partner's toes. It was a futile hope; St. Just had the natural grace of a sportsman. His partner, a young débutante, lacked that grace. The girl danced stiffly, her manner awkward and admiring.

Arabella's lips tightened. No doubt St. Just accepted the admiration as his due; for years he'd been one of the biggest prizes on the marriage market, courted for his wealth, his bloodline, his handsome face.

She looked again at Grace St. Just. The girl bore little resemblance to her half-brother. Adam St. Just's arrogance was stamped on him—the way he carried himself, the tilt of his chin, the set of his mouth. Everything about him said *I am better than you.* Grace had none of that. She sat looking down at her hands, her shoulders slightly hunched as if she wished to hide.

*I really should help her.*

Arabella looked at St. Just again. As she watched, he cast a swift, frowning glance in the direction of his sister.

*He's worried about her.*

It was disconcerting to find herself in agreement with him.

Arabella swallowed the last of her lemonade, not tasting it, and handed her empty glass to a passing servant. No one snubbed her as she made her way through the crush of guests, her smiles were politely returned, and yet everyone in the ballroom—herself included—knew that she didn't belong.

The satin gown, the fan of pierced ivory, the jeweled combs in her hair, couldn't disguise what she was: an outsider.

Music swirled around her, and beneath that was the rustle of silk and satin and gauze, the hum of voices. Her ears caught snippets of conversation. Much of tonight's gossip seemed to be about Lady Bicknell. Opinion was divided: some sympathized with Lady Bicknell; others thought it served her right.

There was no doubt why Tom had paid her a visit last night.

"That tongue of hers," stated a florid gentleman in a waistcoat that was too tight for him.

"Most likely," his wife said, glancing up and meeting Arabella's eyes. For a brief second the woman's smile stiffened, then she inclined her head in a polite nod.

Seven years ago that momentary hesitation would have hurt; now she no longer cared. Arabella smiled cheerfully back at the woman. *Only four more weeks of this.* Four more weeks of ball gowns and false smiles, of pretending to belong, and then she could turn her back on Society. *But first, I must help Grace St. Just.*

The girl looked up as Arabella approached. She was fairer than her half-brother, her hair golden instead of brown, her eyes a clear shade of blue. She was breathtakingly lovely—and quite clearly miserable.

"Miss St. Just." Arabella smiled and extended her hand. "I don't believe we've met. My name is Arabella Knightley."

Grace St. Just flushed faintly. She hesitated a moment, then held out her hand. *Her brother has warned her about me.*

Arabella sat, ignoring the St. Just aunt who frowned at her, lips pursed in disapproval, from her position alongside Grace. "How are you finding your first Season?"

"Oh," said Grace. She sent a darting glance in the direction of the dance floor. "It's very . . . that is to say—"

"I hated mine," Arabella said frankly. "Everyone staring and whispering behind their hands. It's not pleasant to be gossiped about, is it?"

Grace St. Just stopped searching the dance floor for her

brother. She stared at Arabella. "No. It isn't."

"Someone gave me some advice," Arabella said. "When I was in a similar position to you. If you don't think it impertinent of me, I should like to pass it on."

She had the girl's full attention now. Those sky-blue eyes were focused on her face with an almost painful intensity. "Please," Grace St. Just said. Even the aunt leaned slightly forward in her chair.

"It was given to me by Mr. Brummell," Arabella said. "If he were still in England, I'm certain he'd impart it to you himself."

"The Beau?" Grace breathed. "Truly?"

Arabella nodded. "He said . . ." She paused for a moment, remembering. The Beau's voice had been cool and suave, and oddly kind. "He said I must ignore it, and more than that, I must ignore it *well*."

It was the only time Beau Brummell had spoken to her. But he had always nodded to her most politely after that, his manner one of faint approval.

"And so I did as he suggested," Arabella said. "I gave the appearance of enjoying myself. I smiled at every opportunity, and when I couldn't smile, I laughed." She smoothed a wrinkle in one of her long gloves, remembering. A slight smile tugged at her lips. "I believe some people found it very annoying."

She looked up and held Grace St. Just's eyes. "So that's my advice. However difficult it may seem, you must ignore what people are saying, the way they look at you. And you must ignore it *well*."

"Ignore it?" Tears filled the girl's eyes. "How *can* I?"

"It isn't easy," Arabella said firmly. "But it can be done."

Grace shook her head. She hunted in her reticule for a handkerchief. "I would much rather go home." Her voice wobbled on the last word.

"Certainly you may do that, but if I may be so bold, Miss St. Just . . . the rumors are just rumors. Speculation and conjecture. If you shrug your shoulders, London will find a new target. But if you leave now, the rumors will be confirmed."

Grace looked stricken. She sat with the handkerchief clutched in her hand and tears trembling on her eyelashes.

"It doesn't matter whether you committed whatever indiscretion London thinks you did," Arabella said matter-of-factly. "What matters is whether London *believes* it or not."

Grace St. Just bit her lip. She looked down at the handkerchief and twisted it between her fingers.

"Be bold," Arabella said softly.

"Bold?" The girl's laugh was shaky. "I'm not a bold person, Miss Knightley."

"I think you can be anything you want."

Arabella's voice was quiet, but it made the girl look up. For a moment they matched gazes, and then Grace St. Just gave a little nod. She blew her nose and put the handkerchief away. "Tell me . . . how you did it, Miss Knightley. If you please?"

Arabella was conscious of a sense of relief. She sat back in her chair and glanced at the dance floor. Adam St. Just was watching them. She could see his outrage, even though half a ballroom separated them.

It was tempting to smile at him and give a mocking little wave. Arabella did neither. She turned her attention back to Grace St. Just.

Adam relinquished Miss Hornby to the care of her mother. He turned and grimly surveyed the far corner of the ballroom. His sister sat alongside Arabella Knightley, as she had for the past fifteen minutes.

They made a pleasing tableau, dark and fair, their heads bent together as they talked, Miss Knightley's gown of deep rose-pink perfectly complementing his sister's white satin.

Adam gritted his teeth. He strode around the ballroom, watching as Grace said something and Miss Knightley replied—and his aunt, Seraphina Mexted, sat placidly alongside, nodding and smiling and making no attempt to shoo Miss Knightley away.

Grace lifted her head and laughed.

Adam's stride faltered. Arabella Knightley had made Grace *laugh*. In fact, now that he observed more closely, his sister's face was bright with amusement.

*She looks happy.*

Arabella Knightley had accomplished, in fifteen minutes, what he had been trying—and failing—to do for months. How in Hades had she done it? And far more importantly, *why?*

Miss Knightley looked up as he approached. Her coloring showed her French blood—hair and eyes so dark they were almost black—but the soft dent in her chin, as if someone had laid a fingertip there at her birth, proclaimed her as coming from a long line of Knightleys.

His eyes catalogued her features—the elegant cheekbones, the dark eyes, the soft mouth—and his pulse gave a kick. It was one of the things that annoyed him most about Arabella Knightley: that he was so strongly attracted to her. The second most annoying thing was the stab of guilt—as familiar as the attraction—that always accompanied sight of her.

Adam bowed. "Miss Knightley, what a pleasure to see you here this evening."

Her eyebrows rose. "Truly?" Her voice was light and amused, disbelieving.

Adam clenched his jaw. This was the third thing that annoyed him most about Miss Knightley: her manner.

Arabella Knightley turned to Grace and smiled. "I must go. My grandmother will be wanting supper soon."

Adam stepped back as she took leave of his sister and aunt. The rose-pink gown made her skin appear creamier and the dark ringlets more glossily black. A striking young woman, Miss Knightley, with her high cheekbones and dark eyes.

And an extremely wealthy one, too. But no man of birth and breeding would choose to marry her—unless his need for a fortune outweighed everything else.

She turned to him. "Good evening, Mr. St. Just." Cool amusement still glimmered in her eyes.

Adam gritted his teeth and bowed again. His gaze followed her. Miss Knightley's figure was slender and her height scarcely more than five foot—and yet she had presence. It was in her carriage, in the way she held her head. She was perfectly at home in the crowded ballroom, utterly confident, unconcerned by the glances she drew.

Adam turned to his aunt. "Aunt Seraphina, how could you allow—"

"I like her," Aunt Seraphina said placidly. "Seems a very intelligent girl."

Adam blinked, slightly taken aback.

"I like her, too," Grace said. "Adam, may I invite her—"

"No. Being seen in her company will harm your reputation. Miss Knightley is not good *ton*."

"I know," said Grace. "She spent part of her childhood in the slums. Her mother was a . . . a . . ." She groped for a euphemism, and then gave up. "But I *like* her. I want to be friends with her."

*Over my dead body.*

"Shall we leave?" Adam said, changing the subject. "It's almost midnight and we've a long journey tomorrow." To Sussex, where there'd be no Arabella Knightley.

He began to feel more cheerful.

"I've decided to stay in London," Grace said.

Adam raised his eyebrows. "You have?"

"Yes," Grace said. "This is my first Season, and I'm going to *enjoy* it."


Like to read the rest?
*My Lady Thief* is available now.

# $\mathscr{A}$CKNOWLEDGMENTS

A number of people helped to make this book what it is. I would particularly like to thank my copyeditor, Maria Fairchild, and my proofreader, Martin O'Hearn, for their hard work.

The cover and the formatting are the work of the talented Jane D. Smith. Thank you, Jane!

And last—but definitely not least—my thanks go to my parents, without whose support this book would not have been published.

Emily Larkin grew up in a house full of books. Her mother was a librarian and her father a novelist, so perhaps it's not surprising that she became a writer.

Emily has studied a number of subjects, including geology and geophysics, canine behavior, and ancient Greek. Her varied career includes stints as a field assistant in Antarctica and a waitress on the Isle of Skye, as well as five vintages in New Zealand's wine industry.

She loves to travel and has lived in Sweden, backpacked in Europe and North America, and traveled overland in the Middle East, China, and North Africa.

She enjoys climbing hills, reading, and watching reruns of *Buffy the Vampire Slayer* and *Firefly*.

Emily writes historical romances as Emily Larkin and fantasy novels as Emily Gee. Her websites are www.emilylarkin.com and www.emilygee.com.

Never miss a new Emily Larkin book. Join her Readers' Group at www.emilylarkin.com/newsletter and receive free digital copies of *The Fey Quartet* and *Unmasking Miss Appleby*.

# Other Works

## THE BALEFUL GODMOTHER SERIES

### Prequel
*The Fey Quartet novella collection:*
Maythorn's Wish
Hazel's Promise
Ivy's Choice
Larkspur's Quest

### Original Series
Unmasking Miss Appleby
Resisting Miss Merryweather
Trusting Miss Trentham
Claiming Mister Kemp
Ruining Miss Wrotham
Discovering Miss Dalrymple

### Garland Cousins
Primrose and the Dreadful Duke
Violet and the Bow Street Runner

### Pryor Cousins
Octavius and the Perfect Governess

Printed in Great Britain
by Amazon

66286820R00154